BABY KILLER

Frank Cassese

D1572454

NINE-BANDED BOOKS

Baby Killer
© 2019 Frank Cassese

Published by

Nine-Banded Books
PO Box 1862
Charleston, WV 25327

NineBandedBooks.com

ISBN 978-0-9896972-3-1

Cover design by Kevin I. Slaughter

When you think about names for your baby, you'll find yourself daydreaming about what he or she may look like. And you'll find yourself thinking about your hopes and dreams for the newest member of your family.

—Bruce Lansky, *35,000+ Baby Names*

Nihilism is not only a meditating over the "in vain!" not only the belief that everything deserves to perish; but one actually puts one's shoulder to the plough; *one destroys*.

—Friedrich Nietzsche, *The Will to Power*

Childhood is short and maturity is forever.

—Calvin and Hobbes

BABY KILLER

．　　．　　．

They call me the Baby Killer. Two capitalized words, one space, no hyphen.

At first, it was the Baby Snatcher. I could not abide this. There is something ugly and vaguely indecent in the sonority of it, something that calls to mind a campy horror movie or some odd sort of parenting contraption designed for safety, not to mention its depictive incompleteness; I did not merely snatch babies. I did so much more.

So I had to issue an official corrective, a concerned nudge in the right direction, a suggested alteration that was, to my surprise, taken into account. As a result, they have changed my sobriquet to the Baby Killer. It is, without question, a more fitting signature. But I think there is still room for improvement. Perhaps I am guilty of pedantry, but I do worry that it could potentially be mistaken to mean that I am a baby that kills (evoking a comic image of a demonic infant; Satan in a crib) rather than one who kills babies (much less comical, to most).

Were it not for the preceding definite article, it might also sound like a somewhat silly first/last name combination, a macabre version of those ridiculous New Age hippie handles parents gave their kids in the late sixties, like Moon Rider or Wind Tamer or River Phoenix, maybe even a symbolic Native American name like Wolf Watcher, or a transliterated Asian one (I had a Chinese friend in school who claimed his name meant Immortal Warrior, though we always just called him Hank, and there was nothing remotely warlike about him, much less immortal, though he was practically unbeatable at Mortal Kombat), even though I am neither Indian nor Asian.

What am I? Other than the Baby Killer? To outward appearances, I am just another middling, middle-class thirty-year-old male; a standard-issue suburban Caucasian with a forgettable moniker that doesn't mean or signify anything more than the utilitarian minimum, a way of getting me to turn around when called, of making sure that my mail is delivered correctly, that my taxes are collected, that the proper identifying markers are etched on my tombstone, lest it be suspected that I was never actually here.

$\bullet$ $\bullet$ $\bullet$

Beyond the problem of literal ambiguity, one of the more pressing issues I take with my public alias concerns its perilous imprecision. If you knew nothing of me apart from my stage name, you could conceivably construe the first half—*baby*—metaphorically, perhaps as a diminutive pet name for a lover (which would make me a killer of those with whom I am romantically entwined) or as a nod to some specific way of carrying out the killing (this is a stretch, I know, but such is the nature of metaphor), though there is nothing metaphorical or symbolic or figurative about my brand, no subliminal significance or subtle undertone or euphemistic camouflage. I slaughter infants. I kill babies. My *nom de plume* is as literal as a certificate of birth.

Whatever ambiguity I am prone to belabor with regard to the interpretation of this byname may, of course, derive from the inherent insufficiency of language to accurately represent ideas. Words are a flawed medium through which thought travels, an imperfect vehicle for vague, clandestine passengers who are themselves unsure of their identity and purpose. Think of water flowing through a series of pipes before arriving at its destination; faulty seals and leaks are inevitable, and there will always be some degree of contamination as the liquid comes into play with metal or plastic, particles shedding and sharing with each other as they meet, regardless of how pure the source or how clean the channel. And really, nothing is that pure or clean to begin with. Existence is a dirty, messy business.

Perhaps if I had given some forethought to how much publicity my recent acts would attract, I would have picked a better autograph. This is not to suggest that I could have come up with anything too impressive. Though I would have preferred to define myself in my own terms, the alternatives that come to mind tend to be risible in their alliterative contrivance, or else they lack resonance. The Infanticider? The Newborn Nullifier? The Toddler's Terror? I was never good with names. And for all my obsessive grumbling, I am resigned to accept what I cannot change. I am the Baby Killer. It is not the worst name by which I could be remembered for posterity. Perhaps it is too pedestrian, or too *tabloid*, but it is succinct; notwithstanding such potential ambiguities that I have already articulated, it tells you all you need to know in two quick words and four smooth, even-keeled syllables—emblematic of our hyper-informed, super-fast age of information, where every byte of data is a casual screen-tap away, all the useless information and superficial facts you could want are literally at your fingertips—and it has an unsettling ghoulishness that I find somewhat flattering, if not wholly deserved. Perhaps it is the facile one-dimensionality that sustains my demur, the way this (or perhaps any) nominative reduction functions to box me in, to flatten and label me as this one single thing, how it claims an unearned monopoly on my essence and leaves little room for other facets of my being to share the stage. Yes, I have killed babies. But that is not all I have done. I have given spare change (and once an old pair of mittens) to the homeless, for example. Should this justify calling me a philanthropist? There was also the time when I helped an elderly woman in a bad wig and stained ochre house-dress and battered slippers carry several bags of groceries from the supermarket to her car. As I proceeded to neatly pack said bags into said car, the woman told me that I was "a nice young man." Does this make me "a nice young man"?

I may never get beyond this business of brand. I am acutely aware that my circling ruminations may come off as vain or petty, yet I am constitutionally disposed to follow the churn of thought where it will lead. Sartre said we are defined by our actions—we are what we do. I am, among other things, one who kills—or one who has killed. And I have killed the most helpless beings among us. My reasons, which I will articulate in time, will not matter. By overwhelming consensus, my crimes are too abhorrent to warrant nuanced understanding or to be mitigated by such other deeds that, according to a dead existentialist, must also define me.

Sartre also believed that we have a choice in such matters. I disagree.

There is no death penalty in my state. There is no legal recourse upon which to rest your frankly understandable wish that I should meet a punishment commensurate with the heinous misdeeds that I neither deny nor regret. If it is any consolation, there is always the chance that some righteous convict vigilante will plunge a shiv deep into my back or slit my throat with a homemade razor whittled from a toothbrush. He would be a champion of the cell block, a hero to the world at large. The Baby Killer Killer. But does anyone remember the name of the man who killed Jeffrey Dahmer?

I am the Baby Killer. I am also a creature of ritual, a lover of music, a teetotaler, a fitness enthusiast. I enjoy solitude and browsing in used book shops. I have reasonably informed opinions about many subjects: the novels of William Faulkner, the philosophical implications of quantum theory, dietetics, movies, fashion, etc. I am prone to bouts of insomnia and vertiginous mood swings. It is likely that I have an eidetic memory, though I have not been tested. I am an only child. I am not, by reference to a strict construction of the relevant statutory language, an orphan.

•   •   •

Even if I knew it would have saved me from capture and let me continue to live my life of anodyne reclusion and quiet desperation, I would not have stopped. I could not. And if I could, I would not want to. Maybe I could have stopped for a while, even a long while, but not forever.

There were three. That might not seem like much of a body count for a serial killer, but it is important to note that my crimes were carried out over a relatively short span of time. By any rational account, my rate should matter. This fixation on quantity is a crass distraction. The quality of my work is, I insist, easily distinguished from the wanton mayhem that clots the minds of most true-crime enthusiasts. The most prolific killers are driven by lust, by madness, by unhooked instinct. I was doing philosophy.

My rise to notoriety was meteoric, just the same. My exploits were all over the news, ubiquitous online, rampant on the radio and cable talk shows, pilfering airtime from various international conflicts and territorial spats, stealing the headlines from all the political scandals and other everyday tragedies and celebrity pulp that would ordinarily keep the talking heads bobbing for hours in argument. It was fascinating how they all seemed to agree—conservatives and liberals, right-wing nutbags and far-left dingbats, Republicans and Democrats, black, white, Asian, Hispanic, pro-life, pro-choice, anti-gun, gun-fanatic—about the Baby Killer. The watchword was "justice," as if such a thing exists. They all screamed for justice.

These calls for justice were, needless to add, bullshit. They wanted to see me taken down, or worse. It was a unified chorus of thinly veiled—and sometimes explicit—bloodlust. I might have been nonplussed over the absence of nuance, but I do have a sense of humor, and I still take some measure of pride in this secondary accomplishment, in having engendered such a resounding and unprecedented armistice among disparate tribes and warring factions. I provided a reprieve from the interminable cacophony of partisan argument, a much needed sense of common ground. A *rapprochement*—with better ratings.

There is nothing more evil than a baby killer, after all. There is nothing more abhorrent than one who extinguishes the light of humanity's most precious commodity. People were frantic, up in arms, terrified, disgusted, out for blood—my blood. Public outrage boiled over. The local authorities were at their wits' end. How could the police have no leads? They should drop everything else and dedicate all their resources to catching me, impose a strict curfew, declare martial law, do whatever is necessary to bring the monster to heel. What can be worse than a baby killer? What can be more harmful to society? Baby killer trumps cop killer, rapist, pedophile, maybe even terrorist.

Yes, I was worse than the alpha criminals of our time. They wanted me dead. One imagines the townsfolk of another era preparing their torches, building their gallows in the city centers. That would at least have been more dramatic—and more aesthetically satisfying—than the electronically mediated spectacle that currently prevails. The mob instinct is, to be sure, merely attenuated. Instead of wielding torches, the rabble now clutch their mobile devices and type "monster" into a fleeting comment thread. Or they nod in vicarious agreement as bobble-headed pundits and experts ventilate on the larger screens in their living rooms and bedrooms and kitchens and remodeled basements. Or they gather to discuss the situation, being mindful that their children are distracted by PlayStation or parentally controlled entertainment or, better yet, safely tucked away and out of earshot of such grisly but necessary adult talk.

The neutered mob would look away from their screens long enough to organize neighborhood watches and community outreach programs. They assigned rotating contingents of parents to patrol playgrounds, parks, and schoolyards. There was a spike in gun sales. One man maimed his wife with a shotgun purchased for the defense of their newborn. I wonder if I could somehow be charged with that crime? I bet Sam Waterston could make the case, and I would probably agree with him by the time he wrapped up his closing argument. *Law & Order* is one thing I do miss.

Jake

. . .

My first time? Ah, how can one look back at one's virgin experience with anything but candied, carefree nostalgia, with anything short of a gilded remembrance that only shines brighter with time's passage, where even the pratfalls of inexperience, the minor mistakes of a novice, can be forgiven with a bonhomous smile and wink that make them seem endearingly naive in the light of later refinement?

I am being somewhat facetious—and for reasons that will become clear. Yet the sentiment rings true.

My first time was at the park. I have always hated that trite phrase, *It feels like yesterday*, yet that is exactly how it feels, as though I can still detect the faint breeze wafting in off the man-made lake, still see the swans cutting lazily through the water and smell the swampy pond scum floating on the surface. And yes, it was the sweetest, this first time. Had my project not been curtailed, I imagine that subsequent rites would have come to yield diminishing returns. I would be forever chasing the dragon, trying in vain to recreate the initial thrill, the nervous uncertainty, those taut, tender moments of indecision and deliberation, the rush of spontaneity and finally the orgasmic intensity of releasing my inhibitions and unleashing whatever was there, crouching in the darkened corners of my being, clawing at the strictures of my soul, raging, roaring, begging to be let out.

It was a splendid early fall day, the temperature a degree or two above normal, the open sky as clear and bright as sun-sparkled Caribbean seawater, subtly bejeweled with a few clean, cottony clouds widely spaced and placed with expert decorum and just a hint of autumnal nip announcing itself when the wind picked up. Though I hesitate to use such a clichéd superlative, it was as close to a *perfect day* as can be had. And as fall is my favorite time of year, I decided to make the most of it by spending some time in the park in the next town over from where I live, about a twenty-minute drive away. It is a quaint suburban park, large enough for a little privacy but not vast enough to get lost in, with a smooth, brick-laid path circling a lovely amorphous lake replete with ducks and turtles and fish and frogs and the occasional beaver, and a few tendrillar trails through well-kept lawns and rolling hills and shady dales. Burly oaks and evergreens rule the grassy areas, while red maples guard the lake, neighbored by some ornamental bushes and lively flower patches. There is a playground at one end with swing sets and monkey bars and other childish apparatus. I never sat there for fear of being taken for a pedophile, even though I usually went on off-peak hours when the kids were safely occupied at school.

I would typically situate myself at the other end, the quiet, child-free zone near the parking lot, on an isolated bench just off the lake, overhung by some sad old elms that provide relief from the sun and a sense of seclusion that you can't get out in the open.

So there I was, quietly minding my own business with my head resting on the back of the bench, soaking in the gorgeous solitude of my quiet little corner and watching the fluffy, fair-weather clouds skirt through the blue-gray sky, my eyes shaded safely by my Ray-Ban Wayfarers, my head covered with a lightweight gray newsboy cap to provide a little extra sun shielding. A timeworn Faulkner paperback was place-marked at my side as I listened to Lou Reed plaintively protest his lover's "Pale Blue Eyes" on my iPod. I was breathing in the clear autumn air mixed with the pungency of the fresh fall mulch scattered around the hedges bordering the fence.

As the song strummed its final chord, I heard approaching from my right the squeak of rolling wheels on pavement. I didn't have to look to know what this was. But look I did. I straightened my head to see a man of about thirty-five, in knee-length camouflage shorts, heather NYU T-shirt, gray Saucony Jazz Originals, and a fitted Yankees cap, pushing an oversized black stroller slowly my way. The humongous thing lurched over the pavement like a tired Sherman tank, and I wondered fancifully over what kind of giant mutant child could be swaddled soundly within such a rumbling monstrosity.

The man stopped a few feet away and leaned down to coo or kiss or whistle or whatever at the child, who was much tinier than I had imagined—a baby, lying open-mouthed, moving its little arms and legs up and down like an awkward white dancer. And he (as I would soon learn the child's gender) was, indeed, very white. Almost artificially so: a soft pasty face with patches of pink at the cheeks and sparse strands of bleached wheat falling over a smooth creamy scalp and large, beaming blue eyes, so large they were hypnotic, sparkling like marbled doll eyes. He seemed to be looking at me, analyzing me, judging me, and I found myself staring back through my shades, oddly possessed by shame, embarrassment, guilt.

Luckily, the next song—"Jesus"—started, and I managed to wrench my eyes away from the toddler. I leaned my head back into place and concentrated on zoning out the interlopers before they could pass in front of me and potentially interact. In my limited experience with such types, I have found that people with babies invariably expect some form of acknowledgment—*Aw, isn't he cute?* At the very least a wide, warm smile, an endearing head tilt, an innocuous nod, perhaps an inquiry as to the age of the new being or some token *goo-goo-ga-ga* interplay with the child itself. When they are denied this expected reaction, when in fact their offspring is ignored and passed over, they must assume that the ignorer is an emotional ignoramus, or worse, some kind of hideous reprobate, because everyone simply must find their little clones as precious and irreplaceable as they do. And if someone does not—if, for whatever perverse reason, some aesthetically tone-deaf individual does not see their little one as anything less than perfectly scrumptious and fails to actively express this appreciation, then surely the lack lies with the other.

•   •   •

"Excuse me. Excuse me."

I heard the words, clear as the sky I was ogling, blare into my head through the music. But I pretended not to. Maybe he would think I was asleep. Or maybe he would realize I just didn't want to be bothered and walk away, as any considerate person would have—or should have. Of course, a considerate person would not have disturbed me in the first place, so obviously wrapped up in my own thing as I was.

"Excuse me, sir," he persisted, closer to my ear and louder. I could no longer politely feign not to have heard him. I knew he was not going to stop, so I paused the music, slowly leveled my head, slipped out my earbuds, and looked at him.

"Hey man." He smiled chummily under the bill of his ball cap—perched upon his head at a jaunty, upward, somewhat off-balance angle—quickly switching from the formal *sir* to the male-casual *man*. I suppose he assumed this was an acceptable way to greet a youngish guy in stone-washed jeans and faded black T-shirt and beat-up Chuck Taylors. But then, why even start with *sir*?

"Sorry to bother you."

Was he really sorry? I understand these things people say are social niceties and are not meant to be taken literally, but I find it tiresome. I wish we would just say what we mean without lathering our words in false contrition and paltry periphrasis.

But we are all slaves to civility, myself included. So I responded in kind, and with my own friendly smile.

"No bother," I said.

"I hate to ask you this, but—" another conversation opener that I cannot tolerate; if you really *hated* to ask, then you wouldn't "—you don't happen to have a cigarette on you?" His eyes brightened hopefully as he put two fingers to his lips and mimed a drag.

"Sorry, man. I quit last year." I have never smoked a cigarette in my life.

He dropped his hands in disappointment. "So did I, apparently."

He laughed. I laughed. The baby made a high-pitched cheep that sounded something like a chipmunk. Maybe it was a chipmunk.

"Yeah. Probably better off. My wife can smell the smoke on me a mile away, and she'd give me shit for it all night. Totally not worth it."

He paused before asking the question I had already anticipated. "You married, man?"

A woman would have simply observed that I was not wearing a wedding band, but men are often blind to subtlety, to the myriad social cues and signifiers that lie at the foundation of civilized order. They really should not be entrusted with the care of children.

I understood that the question was meant as an ingratiating gesture. Having importuned me with his initial request, the father-husband hoped, through this ostensibly innocuous conversational move, to affirm a spirit of casual fraternity.

"No," I said. "Not yet, anyway."

His smile widened as he adjusted the brim of his cap like a pitcher setting up between batters, lifting it almost off his head before clamping it back down a little higher than where it had been, so that more of his face came into view as the sun sliced down on it.

"Enjoy it while you can, man. I mean, I love my wife, but sometimes it's like having a second mother."

He was younger than he had seemed at first glance, early-thirties, with a day's stubble and soft, dirty blond hair creeping out from under the hat like some semi-famous indie rocker trying to hide his identity. Flush with sunlight, his face appeared pleasant and comradely, or maybe this was just the expression he chose to reveal in the presence of someone who seemed a social peer, another harmless middle-class white guy in his thirties with the latest iPod and a paperback book on the bench beside him, just an ordinary Joe whiling away this superb day in the park before the harsh Northeast winter blew in.

"That's what I hear," I replied. "Seems like all my friends are getting married."

I was resigned to play out the exchange, the path of least resistance. I did not have friends, married or otherwise.

As the father-husband interjected with increasingly casual niceties, I observed that he was handsome, if not a bit pretty, with a lean angular face and fine strong features, his gym-toned torso and well-defined arms showing under his thin, form-fitting cotton shirt. His eyes were big and blue, but not as bright as his son's, as though the child had stolen something of his father's fire.

"Great day, isn't it?" he said, staring sunward.

"Beautiful."

We took the requisite deep breaths, as though inhaling the beauty I had observed, and we looked around like landscape painters preparing to put it all on canvas. I turned my attention to the infant, whose azure eyes were still locked on me. His mouth was open and two fingers of his right hand probed his lower lip. It was as if he suspected there was something not quite right about me, or so I imagined as thoughts formed.

"Cute kid," I said. "How old?"

"Eight months." He looked down at him with me.

"Cute kid," I repeated, nodding my head for emphasis.

"Yep, that's my Jake. I took a spontaneous day off. Woke up and it was just so amazing out that I said *fuck it*. I decided to call it in and spend the day with my little shit-stainer here."

I took note of the casual profanity, one more indication of presumed familiarity, a subtle rite of male bonding. Another social threshold had been crossed. This seemed potentially significant, or useful somehow.

The baby looked up at his father, nonplussed. The father leaned over and wiped some saliva dripping down his son's chin with the bottom hem of his shirt.

"We love the park, don't we, Jake?" He spoke in a normal adult voice—none of that ridiculous baby talk.

Jake didn't answer. He just gazed silently at his father

with those cold blue eyes of his, then turned them back on me. He seemed on the verge of a sobbing fit but managed to keep composed. He moved his limbs around as though trying to escape.

"Mom took a spa day, so the boys came out to play."

"When the cat's away…"

He clicked his tongue against the roof of his mouth and mimed a finger-pistol at me. "You know it."

I had no familiarity with anything close to the situation, but I went with the momentum. "Off days are always best when they're not planned."

"Yes. Yes they are," he agreed, as though I'd opened his mind to a revelation that had been hidden all these years. "The best things in life are usually unplanned." At this, he raised an eyebrow and dipped his chin toward his son, lowering his voice in a mock suggestion that the little one might be hurt by the insinuation.

"So I've heard." I nodded my in-the-know, and we shared a moment of unspoken masculine communion.

Then his phone rang. The ringtone was the opening riff of Black Sabbath's "N.I.B." Jake stirred in his seat and squeaked at the new sound. I amused myself imagining that the child might be a budding Sabbath fan. I had loved them from an early age myself, being partial to the Ozzy years. Capturing his attention, I couldn't help but rock my head in playful affirmation of his apparent delight.

"Do you like Black Sabbath, Jake?" I asked in my normal adult voice. This prompted another squeal from the child and a nod of acknowledgment from the father-husband, who proceeded to withdraw the phone from his rear pocket.

I find it rather feminine to keep a phone in one's back pocket. It is also dangerous. A seasoned thief could easily slip the exposed device out of one's ass pocket and take off the other way without notice. It amazes me how carelessly people look out for the things that matter most to them, as though they just assume they'll always be there, that no one will try to take them away.

He put the phone to his ear and answered in a very businesslike manner: "Yes. Hold on a minute," then turned to me with an expression of tactful apology and said, "Excuse me."

I declined my head in a by-all-means gesture and he turned his back to me and his son and started speaking in hushed tones. I couldn't make out any distinct sentences, just a few isolated words, until he raised his voice and said clearly: "Yes! Yes! I'm going to tell her. Just give me a little time. I have a fucking baby, for Christ's—"

He yanked the phone away from his head and turned to me with a sheepish grin, then once again put his back to us, stepped a few paces down the path, and resumed the conversation, his voice becalmed, at least for the moment.

It was then just me and the child. I regarded him as he lay there, a confused lump of flesh, waving his limbs as if to signal something he wasn't quite sure of. I leaned over with my elbows on my knees and winked at wee little Jake and made a few funny faces at him. I stuck out my tongue idiotically and I pulled at my ears like a clown. He smiled tentatively, still unsure, and yet I was so playful and friendly and accommodating that for a second I became the person I was pretending to be, a momentary babysitter, intently watching over and entertaining this defenseless newborn until his philandering father returned.

Jake continued to scrutinize me until his wide eyes seemed precociously trained only on my aspect. It was unsettling how he looked at me, and I struggled against an irrational certainty that he was seeing into my soul and detecting something dark therein, something behind my veil of lighthearted silliness. Yet I persisted with my attentive smiles and funny faces.

When I looked up, Jake's father was at the edge of the lake. Though I could no longer make out his words from the gaining distance, I observed a dire intensity in his manner, in the strident tone of his voice. He gesticulated fervently with his free hand as he paced and quarreled. I could still see those Saucony Jazz Originals, my all-time favorite footwear. It made me regret not having worn my own pair. I looked down at my Converse with displeasure; they had suddenly become uncomfortable.

Jake made a curious sound, and his arctic blues were again locked on me as he vocalized. It almost had the cadence of speech, as though he were trying to tell me something in a language I couldn't understand. Something comforting. Something encouraging. Then he went silent. I looked over at the father-husband, who had strayed farther along the water's edge. Now his shoes were indistinct. He seemed ready to fling the phone into the water.

It occurred to me that we had not exchanged names. He would come to know mine in time.

•   •   •

It is crucial to note that I did not plan on any of this. I did not wake up that morning and tell myself that it would be a fine day to go to the park and kidnap a baby. It was like watching some strange facsimile of myself, a simulacrum locked in a behavioral sequence that my original self would never have been capable of. I did not know exactly what I was doing, nor did I know precisely why I was doing it. Yet it was thrilling. I slipped my iPod into my back pocket—my back pocket!—bounced up off the bench, unbuckled little Jake from his seat and lifted him carefully out of his stroller—being sure to cradle his soft, delicate head and neck with one hand and cushion his diapered bottom with the other—stood up straight and bobbed him gently and patted his back tenderly, grabbed his bottle and shoved it into my hoodie's pocket, then calmly but briskly walked toward the nearest exit—only a few feet away—keeping my strides smooth and unrushed and inconspicuously determined as I headed down the battered brick path and off onto the dirt trail through the grassy area and finally out onto the street on the other end of the park. I was mindful not to look around in a manner that might arouse suspicion, which wasn't difficult because there was scarcely anyone there. Odd for such a delightful day, that the park would be so quiet, without old folks dawdling around the oval path in their pastel pants and Florida visors, without jabbering flanks of soccer moms in tank tops and lululemons and designer glasses power-walking their way past me, without other random daytime dads with strollers or young punks playing hooky or families feeding broken crusts of white bread to the ducks. If I entertained thoughts of providence, I reminded myself that it was, after all, late in the season.

It was just me and little Jake, absconding, fleeing, sailing our way sans obstacle. Even the main street was relatively vacant. A few cars passed by, but there was nothing about our innocuous passage to draw attention. To any party who might have seen us, I would appear only as a caring father eager to get his wee one home for a much-needed nap after a tiring day at the park. Perhaps this good father, barely noticed and soon to be forgotten, would look forward to hitting the couch with a cold beer just in time to catch whatever game was being broadcast. There was nothing to see.

Though I had proceeded without circumspection, my shirt was sweat-stuck to my back, and I was winded and trembling slightly as I turned down the first side street and unlocked my gunmetal gray Honda Civic from about halfway down the block and looked around to make sure no one was watching and slid stealthily into the front seat, placing Jake softly on my lap, well below the angle from which anyone could see him from outside.

It was then, as I sat hunched and huffing—the panic I had somehow circumvented during my getaway having pounced upon me all at once—that I realized how strange it was that the baby had not cried. He had not uttered so much as a muffled squeal or a hiccuped whimper, even as I rolled him hurriedly through that unpaved park pathway and over unforgiving asphalt and down a tree-shaded side street and into a strange vehicle. Surely there had been some degree of turbulence, regardless of how I tried to steady him. The short journey could not have been wholly pleasant for little Jake, yet he remained the picture of calmness, quietly cuddled in my lap, secure between my abdomen and the steering wheel, gazing up at me with newly tinted eyes that seemed to have lost all trace of the wary suspicion I had perceived upon our first encounter. Dare I say his eyes were beaming at me with something akin to trust, something similar to love?

Then something astounding happened. As I adjusted myself in preparation to drive away, taking one last glance around to ensure I was neither followed nor spotted, his lips slowly spread and parted and his eyes narrowed, as if in prelude to a long-overdue tantrum, a well-deserved and justified fit of sobbing. I was prepared for the eruption; I had been awaiting it. But instead, to my surprise, it was a smile—a wide, deep, playful, tender, open-mouthed smile that exploded onto his face as he looked up at me.

I slipped my forefinger into the grip of his little fist, provoking a short fit of laughter, and I smiled back down at him.

$\bullet \quad \bullet \quad \bullet$

I could not dwell in the moment. I was certain that the father, irresponsible though he was, had called the police, who would be on their way to put the park on lockdown. They would confront suspicious characters and question every shocked mother in that now-tainted sanctuary. *Did you notice anything that seemed in any way out of the ordinary? Anything at all?*

I removed my sunglasses and cap, wrapped the glasses gently in the cap's crown and placed them in the glove compartment. Then I took a long deep breath and started the car. Resisting the impulse to rush away, I slipped my iPod off my belt and plugged it into the auxiliary port of the stereo. Lou Reed and the Velvet Underground were still playing. I worried that Jake might not appreciate this (it takes time for youth to cultivate certain musical tastes), so I switched it to something more contemporary, Nirvana's *Nevermind*, jumping right to "Drain You," which I considered highly appropriate. The dirty, jangling chords and crunching distortion and hammering drums and Kurt's straining pleading throbbing voice cut through it all as I made sure the road was clear and pulled out smoothly onto the street, one hand on the wheel and the other still captive in Jake's fist:

> One baby to another says
> I'm lucky to have met you
> I don't care what you think
> Unless it is about me
> It is now my duty to completely drain you

Several patrol cars blew by us, lights and sirens screaming, overtaking traffic as they hurried to the scene of the alleged abduction, but there was no hitch in my path as I cruised home. I even sang along as we turned onto the main road heading away from the park, careful to stay a few steady miles per hour above the speed limit—going too slow could rouse as much suspicion as speeding.

By the time I arrived safely in the driveway, "Something in the Way," *Nevermind*'s somber closing track, had a minute and a half to go. I let the garage door close behind me, shut the ignition, and sat there until the final notes faded.

I love when things are timed perfectly.

•   •   •

Jake had let go of my finger and was sound asleep in my lap. With deliberate slowness and precision, I lifted him in my arms, opened and gingerly closed the car door, tiptoed to the entrance of the house, slowly slipped the keys in the lock and opened the door and pressed the alarm code faster than I normally would to ensure that the piercing electronic buzz that precedes the blaring bell would not wake him. Then I quickly reset the alarm, bypassing the interior motion detecting zones so that I could move freely about the house while still having the exterior secured. As soon I entered the house proper, I drew all the blinds in the kitchen and mudroom, a precaution warranted in the exceedingly rare event that someone should trespass into the backyard.

All this I achieved with astonishing success. And only then, when I sat down at the kitchen table to collect myself, did little Jake finally start to cry. Without even seeming to wake up, his face crinkled and his arms curled up and in on themselves as though he were having a seizure, and then the tears and bleating came, like a sudden storm. I gently dandled him, making scrunched faces and high-pitched sounds, even singing a few lines of Leonard Cohen's "If It Be Your Will," which I've always found to be among the most soothing of songs. But nothing worked. His crying persisted, and I realized the honeymoon was over. I also realized, a few seconds later, what the cause of his fit was: Jake clearly needed to be changed.

I had never changed a baby before, but how hard could it be? First, I removed his black down jacket, then took off his tiny red shirt that said *CHAMP* in embroidered yellow lettering with two black boxing gloves on either side of the word, then slid off his clean white sneakers (the soles of which appeared never to have touched the ground) and socks and brown cargo pants, putting all his clothes in a big plastic bag that the county distributes free in bulk every fall for leaf cleanup (as I hire a landscaper for such needs, these bags are free to be used in other ways). Holding my face away from the stench—surprisingly foul for such a tiny creature—I peeled off his soiled diaper and placed it in a separate bag, then placed that bag in another bag and twisted the top and tied it with two heavy-duty plastic twisties and stuffed that inside a triple-layered brown paper shopping bag (my local supermarkets were no longer distributing these freely, so I horded them whenever possible, taking dozens at a time). Holding him softly but firmly with one hand clamped around his torso from behind, I stood him in the sink and sprayed him with the faucet hose as though preparing a Rock Cornish hen for the oven, making sure the water was a comfortable temperature and the stream not too strong for his sensitive skin as I showered the soft, sticky waste from his ashen body, reminding myself to thoroughly disinfect the sink with several doses of Comet and boiling water later on. Indeed, I almost became sick at the sight of that muddy fecal matter splashing around the same basin in which I cleaned dishes and rinsed vegetables.

After thoroughly rinsing the shit away, I sponged my charge down with a brand-new super-soft Ocelo No-Scratch Scrub Sponge and some Dove liquid soap with moisturizer. My instinct was to give him a good scouring with a Dobie and some Dawn antibacterial dishwashing detergent, but I decided not to chance his infant epidermis reacting to it, even though the packaging of the cleaning pad clearly advertises that it "scours without scratching," and the detergent claims to be "safe and nourishing" for hands. Finally, one last thorough rinse, a delicate shake, and a light tap dry with a freshly laundered towel followed by a blow-dry on low/warm (which he seemed to enjoy immensely) and a nice talcking with Johnson's Baby Powder (which I use myself after every shower). I had no diapers, so I wrapped his bottom half in a few sheets of Bounty super-absorbent paper towels—the Select-A-Size variety, which made it easier to adjust and fit around the contours of his body—and then laid him on a raised cushion of soft pillows within a ten-gallon basin that I placed on the sofa, surrounded by a wall of other pillows so he wouldn't slide off if he started squirming. Shaking it first to unsettle the milk, I eased the bottle's nipple between his welcoming little lips, and immediately his eyelids fluttered like tiny butterfly wings as his fingers lightly clenched the plastic, grazing my own.

I was exhausted, as I imagined Jake was as well. It had been a trying day for both of us. But rewarding. I would have liked nothing more than to sit on the sofa next to Jake with a mug of Tazo Emperor's White Tea and a low-fat carob chip cookie and watch whatever I had recorded on my DVR the night before (incidentally, it was the defunct *Law & Order: Criminal Intent*, not my favorite of the franchise, though I stick with it for D'Onofrio's dark and endearing quirkiness), but there was too much to take care of in order to clean the slate for later on. Also, I didn't want to watch television. Surely, it would be all over the news by now: *Baby abducted in local park. Area manhunt. AMBER Alert*. It was best to focus on the task at hand. There were things to do, and I feel agonizingly incomplete if I fail to accomplish even the most minor detail of my daily routine.

Jake was already dozing off, snug and secure in his makeshift couch-crib. I would take advantage of this downtime to check off the items on my to-do list, then devote my full concentration to the night's unplanned special event.

. . .

It was late afternoon, when my energy level was usually at its highest, and though I was abnormally fatigued and mentally stressed, I knew that my daily workout would go far in relieving both symptoms. One might not have been able to tell from a casual glance, but I was a specimen of fitness: 5'9", 150 pounds of hard lean meat and bone. My routine consisted of fifteen minutes of preliminary stretching, followed by half an hour of Dynamic Strength exercises (derived from a martial-arts-based system of self-resistance techniques that pits muscle against muscle, a kind of hardcore isometrics where the body part provides its own tension, something along the lines of a super-intensive Qigong), resulting in an incredibly powerful full-body workout that creates muscles of tempered steel without swelling them like those juiced-up gorillas at the gym. I would finish with six five-minute rounds of boxing the heavy bag (with exactly one minute of rest between rounds), topped off by three sets of fifty fist push-ups and 200 crunches and three sets each of ten pull-ups and chin-ups. Again, though it may not have shown under my clothes, my body was an exceptionally well-toned and efficient machine, with biceps, triceps, laterals, and pectorals chiseled like an ice sculpture, veins pulsing strong and proud under taut, trim skin, tendons like piano wire linking sinewy muscle to solid bone. I am very pleased with how I have developed my physique, and I spent a great deal of time looking at myself (both naked and in varying degrees of dress and undress) in the full-length mirror on the outside of my closet door. On occasion, I even masturbated while gazing at my self-sculpted form, posing and flexing and struggling to find that perfect angle, that elusive money shot. Lest this be grossly misinterpreted, I do not get off on the idea of having sex with myself. Nor do I imagine having inter-course with someone else. In fact, I'm not even sure what arouses me so when I look at my body, though I suppose it could have to do with how someone else might see me and be stimulated by the sight of such perfection. And just for the sake of accuracy, I never (or almost never) masturbated to a climax. I believe it is an essential element of internal strength to keep one's seminal fluids intact, an excellent exercise in self-discipline to bring oneself to the edge of release and then stop cold before discharge. Yes, it is physically frustrating, even excruciat-ing at first, but once sufficiently trained and accustomed to the procedure, I have found it gratifying in ways that far surpass simple corporeal orgasm. Of course, I would sometimes go too far and end up spurting my seed all over the mirror, which always left me feeling empty (physically, emotionally, and spiritually) and full of regret. But this was rare.

The program was set almost to the second, rarely varying more than a minute or two from one day to the next, unless some unforeseen glitch occurred, like a shoelace coming untied while whaling on the bag, or a muscle tweaking a touch too painfully during the strength training portion. I listened to the same three full LPs in the same sequence every day, the Stooges' three studio albums, starting with *Funhouse* (I realize this is out of chronological order of release, and though it does irk me a bit, I had to play them thus for the sake of starting out with "Down on the Street," which never failed to pump me up, no matter how tired or uninspired I might be) and working through *Raw Power* and *The Stooges*. Iggy Pop provides more than musical inspiration for me. It is his physique that I have struggled so diligently to emulate, that slender and unyieldingly firm but flexible rock-and-roll body that looks like molten metal forged in a flawless cast and annealed to an adamantine hardness. I keep a 24" x 36" framed poster of him on the wall in front of my workout space in the basement—a candid shot captured at that famous 1972 Cincinnati show when he walked shirtless into the crowd and was held up by a sea of hands on his feet and legs, his eyes open wide and his features drawn fiercely down in an expression of unabashed bellicosity. Legend has it that he later smeared peanut butter over his bare chest and threw some into the audience, spackling adoring faces and heads with so much sweet stickiness. But this picture was snapped minutes before, as he glared out into the crowd and pointed an angry finger at them, at all of them and none of them at once, as though he were some kind of forgotten field general leading a charge of devoted soldiers in a war only he is fighting. I find the scene unflagging in its inspiration.

My workout was done with religious regularity. I rarely missed a day. I suppose if I were sick, I mean ill to the point of not being able to lift my body from bed, perhaps I would have considered skipping, but I would prefer not to entertain the thought of such an event. The slightest crack in the foundation can bring down the entire structure. Sometimes I would even run through the routine twice in one day, especially on such occasions when I would experience insomnia or find myself in a restless or hyper or otherwise irritated state. A proper workout regimen is more than merely physical; it is meditative. One comes to understand a spiritual calisthenics, something approaching transcendence. Both body and mind are served through training, and it is only by pushing both against their limits that a semblance of wholeness can be achieved. There comes a feeling of completeness, a unity of body and self, a seamless merging of soul and substance, time and place, being and nothingness. It is the only time there is no space between the shadow and the act.

． ． ．

So I finished my workout—not my best, admittedly, as I was distracted by a feeling of mounting anticipation and found myself rushing halfheartedly through the last few sets. I then checked on Jake. To my surprise, he was still sleeping.

I took a peek outside to make sure there were no cops about. I was alone. We were alone. I dumped my shorts in the hamper and ran upstairs naked to shower, indulging a cursory appreciation of my physique in the bathroom mirror before stepping into the stall. I scrubbed myself thoroughly, using hotter water than usual, as a zealot might in preparing to perform some sacred oblatory ceremony.

It was in the shower, while the near scalding, barely tolerable water sluiced over me and the steam clouded the area and fogged up the bathroom mirror, that the thought came to me. Until that moment, I had only vague, inarticulate, and frankly not very good ideas, but as I caught a glimpse of my face, deeply flushed with sodden rosiness, in the small round shaving mirror that was suctioned to the wall opposite the shower head, an image came into my mind of a lobster. A nice plump one. A big ruby-red cockroach of the sea. And I thought of how certain seafood restaurants have those large tanks displayed in the front of their dining rooms, 100-gallon death-row waiting areas stuffed with dozens of these doomed crustaceans crawling miserably about one another with rubber-band-bound claws, in total ignorance of the fate that awaits them on the other side of the glass. I thought of some overeager tyke pointing to one of the lobsters as it lay there, listless and immobile in the center of a stack of its brethren: *Mommy, mommy, can I have that one?*, leaving a greasy print on the face of the tank as he presses his soiled little forefinger against the glass to indicate the animal he would like freshly killed and cooked and placed on his plate, and his mother gently rubbing the top of his head and smiling/ nodding in buoyant approval. *Of course you can, honey*, and then signaling to the black-vested waiter that this is the one they've chosen for execution, with the waiter bowing demurely, *Very good, Madame*, then turning with overwrought formality to the boy and bowing again, *Sir,* eliciting a giggle from the boy and overall merriment from all involved, excepting the lobster, but that doesn't matter because, as Kurt says, "it's okay to eat fish 'cause they don't have any feelings." Plus, a lobster is not even a fish, so there's still less to be concerned about. And then the mother leads the kid back to the table as the sous-chef extracts the condemned from the tank and plops him into a pot of salted boiling water. Most people justify such ostensibly inhumane methods of cooking by declaring that a lobster has a much less complex nervous system and does not feel pain the way humans or, say, dogs, might. Others will tell you that, though a lobster might not express the sensation of pain as illustratively as other creatures, it certainly experiences it, as evinced by its frantic thrashing about when dropped in, so much so that the pot will occasionally joggle on the stove or the cover will rattle and rise as the lobster claws at the top and sides of its prison in a frantic effort to escape (this depends of course on the size and strength and will to live of the lobster in question; surely some lobsters accept their fate quietly while others simply lack the strength to struggle) during the thirty to sixty seconds it takes for it to boil to death. There is even a kind of urban legend wherein the lobster can be heard screaming underwater, a scorching crustacean sibilance that shatters the sangfroid of even the most battle-hardened chefs. This, however, is most likely not the tortured shrieking of a dying animal but the steam piping between skin and shell, which, screaming or not, cannot be comfortable.

But this is all secondary. The point is, I got this picture in my head of a lobster in a pot of boiling water.

As I finished my shower, I took another brief look at my clean wet naked body, then dried off, dressed, and hurried down to Jake. It was perfect timing. He was just waking, stretching his plump miniature sausage arms and yawning widely and blinking out the remnants of his long nap. He seemed a little irritated. Maybe he missed his parents. More likely, I suddenly realized, he was hungry. As was I. But his needs would come first. This is one of the perks of being a baby.

•   •   •

Nature engineered a baby's cry to be inimitably eardrum-piercing, about 115 decibels, louder than a snowmobile, a lawnmower, a hairdryer, a helicopter, a chainsaw, a motorcycle, a snowmobile, a tractor, a car horn, and about five decibels lower than an average rock concert. The maximum unprotected exposure time to such a sound level before damage is done to the ear is about fifteen minutes. What happens is, the 15,000 to 20,000 microscopic hair cells that act as sensory precep-tors for the cochlea—the primary auditory component of the inner ear, whose name is derived from the Latin word for *snail*, which is in turn derived from the Greek word for *snail*, and which does in fact bear a striking resemblance to a snail—become corrupted and can no longer transmit information (sound) to the brain. So if you sat next to a full-on wailing baby for fifteen consec-utive minutes, you would probably incur some degree of hearing loss. The upshot is that the human infant's cry has been perfectly adapted by evolution to be so shrill and annoying and unignorable within any reasonable proximity that the mother simply must attend to its needs or risk detriment to her own physical well-being, and tangentially, detriment to those in the immediate area, which might include movie theaters, restaurants, buses, subways, neighboring apartments, etc.

Jake's inchoate crying was thankfully not near its maximum, perhaps because he was still weary and unable to summon the strength for an all-out aural assault.

In what some have since construed as evidence of premeditation (but certainly was not), I happened to have baby food in my possession. For as long as I can remember, I have suffered from a sensitive stomach. Though never able to isolate a specific food source as the cause of my periodic discomforts, I had discovered one curious salve: banana baby food. In addition to soothing my stomach, it is a tasty and nutritious snack, and it was for these reasons that I always kept several small jars of Gerber banana baby food on hand. I never imagined that my eccentric habit would serve another purpose.

I went to the pantry and grabbed a couple of the little glass bottles, one for Jake, one for me. Snacking so close to dinner was not something I made a habit of, but the occasion merited an exception. His crying was becoming more energetic as I took two spoons and some napkins from the pantry and hurried back into the den, easing him out of the basin and propping him up in a sitting position against the sofa's cushioned back. It was seven p.m., around which time I would usually be settled down on the couch after my grueling workout and long hot shower to relax, shut my eyes for a few minutes, and catch up on some cable news while flipping through the night's programming to make sure my DVR was set correctly. My 55" Mitsubishi widescreen LCD hi-def television stared at me forlornly, awaiting that click of the remote's power button to snap it into life. I resisted. It wasn't easy, but I resisted. I was not yet ready to see whatever coverage would be splattered across the local channels.

I unscrewed the caps of both jars of banana baby food, stuck a spoon in each, placed mine on a coaster on the sofa table, and proceeded to feed Jake. I was worried about how he would take to my feeding him, and I was prepared to start playing airplane with the utensil, but no such gimmick was required; little Jake was more than willing to accept the spoon in his mouth, contently gumming the viscous nutriment, swallowing, and just as soon opening for more until the bottle was scraped clean. I was so pleased by his appetite that I couldn't help but utter, "That's a good boy," while tickling his adipose under-chin. I considered opening another jar for him, but he seemed rather full, burping a few times as he sat back against the couch like a toothless old man, so I let him wash it down with a couple of long suckles from his bottle and left him to relax and digest. Only then did I attend to myself, digging into my own jar and polishing it off in less than a minute. This did nothing to curb my hunger, however, serving as little more than an appetizer, or a complimentary *amuse-bouche*. But it was too early for dinner. As a rule, I would never eat my evening meal before eight p.m. because I am regularly up until four a.m. and prefer to have about eight hours of awake time to digest. I feel this helps to keep one slim. Having just turned thirty the previous month, I had officially entered the decade when a man's metabolism begins its first serious slowdown and the paunch inevitably starts to appear. It is important to be mindful of every morsel.

Rather than give in to my gnawing hunger or my intensifying curiosity about the local news, I laid little Jake back in the basin, hoping he would remain quiet as I closed my eyes for a five- to fifteen-minute power nap. I was surprisingly relaxed, graced with a generalized sense of *eudemonia*, a kind of singular contentment that only occurs after focused activity and accomplishment. For the Greeks, this was the goal of life, to achieve a pervasive feeling of fulfillment, though their major thinkers, all those ancient dead names that today resound through the halls of academia and almost nowhere else, from Plato to Aristotle to Epicurus, could never quite agree on what was necessary to achieve this lasting state of overall moral/physical/intellectual excellence. Yet they all concurred that virtue is inextricably bound to it, that living a life in accordance with virtue and reason—where virtue, or *arête*, which represents the more classical conception of the word, denoting not merely moral but practical excellence in certain qualities or abilities that allow one to realize one's greatest potential—is the ultimate aim of existence, the highest attainable human ambition. Michael Jordan's kinesthetic prowess and Einstein's mathematical genius would be illustrations of great virtue. It's all about *telos*. The great and gloriously rewarding finality. Anything that aids in finding one's personal goal, the gold at the end of our individual rainbows, qualifies as virtue. But what exactly is the right way to go about determining the goal? I sunk into the couch pondering this, thinking I may have inadvertently tripped onto my own path to *eudemonia*. I grasped to find words with which to capture or describe the feeling, soon becoming embarrassed over my ridiculous effort. Shakyamuni Buddha sat under a tree for six years before reaching enlightenment. Bodhidharma sat *zazen*, staring at a wall, for nine. Socrates chose to swallow poison rather than abandon his quest to enlighten the denizens of his native Athens. And there I was on the couch next to a stolen baby, both of us dipping softly into sleep as evening deepened and the house grew darker and quieter, thinking I had somehow stumbled ass-backwards into the meaning of my life. I turned and smiled sleepily at Jake, who was staring up at the ceiling with quarter-closed eyes.

I was feeling well, feeling *the good*, as the Greeks might say; drowsiness was seeping into my head like a slow anesthetic, my limbs and lids growing nicely numb and heavy when, with a stab of horror, an almost physically painful pang in my viscera that stole my breath for an instant and immediately imploded my shell of well-being, I realized I had left my book at the scene, in the park, on the bench, right where I had been sitting.

$\bullet \quad \bullet \quad \bullet$

My adrenal glands kicked into gear. My heart pounded. Sweat beaded about my face. My entire body stiffened and cramped, unslouched itself and sat up, as though this new position would help me work through the chaos that had obliterated the cosmos of my tranquility.

First of all, I absolutely hate losing things. But more frightening was the possibility that the book could be traced back to me. I tried to calmly think through this potentially fatal oversight, putting every risk on the table. My fingerprints were bound to be all over it, yes, but my prints would be nowhere in the system, and neither would my DNA. This realization provided a modicum of relief, even as I pictured Stabler and Benson from *Law & Order: SVU* knocking on my door then tackling me and slapping on the cuffs much tighter than necessary, with Stabler whispering into my ear his minatory musing of what he was going to do unless I told him where the kid was that very second, how official protocol and professional consequences would mean nothing to him if I held out.

But prints would yield nothing. I was safe, at least in that regard. The book was purchased secondhand back in college, and it was highly unlikely that it could be traced to any store. I could breathe again. There was no reasonable fear of being apprehended on account of the book. Still, as panic abated, I became increasingly annoyed with myself over leaving the novel behind. It was one of my favorites, a faded old verdigris volume comprising the Modern Library editions of Faulkner's *The Sound and the Fury* and *As I Lay Dying* (complete with that revelatory appendix to the former that the man himself added years after, which, strangely, doesn't appear in all editions, though it should). But worse than the loss itself, my oversight betrayed a certain carelessness that I would have to avoid in the future, now that I had taken this cardinal step past the point of return. I already knew I had a future in this field, a calling for this specific work, but if I wanted to pursue it successfully, I would have to be much more thoughtful, much more deliberative and conscientious about every tiny, apparently insignificant detail. The slightest misstep could be my undoing. A seemingly immaterial lapse could prove fatal.

My muscles tensed and my fists tightened. I considered going down to hit the bag again to relieve this wave of stress, but I decided the better plan would be to eat, then get to the main business of the night. That would make me feel better.

It was nearly eight, a little early for dinner, but I liked to take my time preparing, and exceptional circumstances called for exceptional scheduling. I consumed one of three meals every night, seldom varying from rotation: (1) canned yellowfin tuna (none of that sub-par supermarket Starkist or Chicken of the Sea for me) with Goya black beans and Nisen sushi rice; (2) 90% lean gruyere-topped hamburgers, a side salad with fat-free ranch dressing, and kettle-cooked chips; (3) a half-pound of DeCecco penne with a half-bottle of Barilla sauce (usually a simple marinara but maybe a pesto or arrabiata if I'm feeling frisky or there's a great sale) and a baguette or peasant loaf (the bread must be freshly made, either from the bakery section of the supermarket or, preferably, direct from the oven of a bakery, though one loaf would usually last three meals; I would crisp it up for five minutes at 400 degrees on the last two nights). With each meal I drink copious amounts of water. No soda, wine, or cocktail. Just plain H20, and lots of it, which keeps me pissing regularly day and night and helps me stay lean.

It was pasta night, which was perfect. I surely needed the carbs, and it would be easy to prepare. I had been eating this way all my adult life, and I did not foresee a change. Regularity bespeaks stability, and what better way to facilitate overall stability than with a firm and constant meal plan? When my parents were around, our meals would vary greatly, since my father was known for his sophisticated palate (long before the emergence of crass "foodie" culture), and my mother was an excellent cook. But they had been gone for over twelve years, so what I ate and how I ate was completely up to me.

•　　　•　　　•

I still lived in their house, my parents' house, as I had since birth. Though the property had legally and officially transferred to my name, I still thought of it as my parents' house. I will always think of it as my parents' house.

I still slept in my bedroom, though nothing would have prevented me from moving into the parental suite, where I would have enjoyed more substantial square footage, a large, southerly exposed double-hung window, a sprawling king-size bed, and a full master bathroom. I don't know why I never made this simple transition. I was the master of the house, after all. Perhaps there was no specific reason, no emotional blockage or psycho-logical prohibition or morbid avoidance that prevented me. Perhaps I was simply comfortable enough in my old room. And it seemed like a great deal of work to move all my carefully laid possessions, even if the destination was just down the hall.

After my parents died, friends and family urged me to sell the house and "move on." The repeated advice was that I should get something new and youthful, more suitable to my unique situation, more age-appropriate, a nice little condo in the city, a newly constructed townhouse in a younger community where I could meet more people in my own age group, maybe even take a roommate so I wouldn't have to be alone. People are so concerned with being alone, living alone, dying alone—as though living by oneself is an embarrassment, a kind of pathetic existential failure that marks you in some ineffable way, as if you had some kind of disease or social disorder. Some people would rather live with someone they don't like than be alone. I could never live with someone else. I could never entertain the thought of having another human being in the house with me. That is, until Jake came along

After all, they used to try to speak some sense into me, those few oh-so-concerned acquaintances who claimed only to have my best interest at heart: *what eighteen-year-old lives alone in a 3,000-plus-square-foot five-bedroom suburban home with a two-car garage and an acre of land*? Such homes were designed for families with frolicking children swinging on backyard jungle gyms, learning to swim with water wings in designer pools, for white-collar fathers who pull in at least a couple of hundred grand a year and for their bejeweled bourgeois wives taking the Jaguar to the supermarket after a mani/pedi or a blowout at the local salon. I was advised of the great expense of maintaining such a property, the landscaping and snow removal and yearly repairs—my parents' financial advisor (now mine) informed me that a typical house requires five percent of its market value to be renovated every year, and that's not taking into account the undermining costs of unforeseen major repairs that inevitably pop up over the lifetime of a house: a new roof, a replacement boiler or hot water heater, black mold in the basement, cracked concrete in the foundation. It was unanimous; everyone involved thought unequivocally that I should sell the house for a decent profit (real estate was pretty good then, and the area had always been desirable to affluent young families) and start afresh, if not simply for financial reasons, then surely for emotional ones. Nobody could imagine why I would want to remain alone in a house where I had lived my entire life with my recently deceased parents. But I was comfortable where I was. So I stayed.

Financially, it proved to be a fine decision. Housing prices soared, almost doubling what I could have sold it for back then. Despite the recent crisis, I would still cash out with a bundle if I put it on the market. Not that I ever had to worry about finances, considering the great sum of money and assets left to me, their sole heir, upon my parents' demise. My father, a successful self-employed attorney, was highly insured (even having the foresight to purchase mortgage insurance, which automatically paid off whatever debt remained on the house), and my mother inherited well when her own parents died within a few years of each other during the early years of her (my mother's) marriage. In short, I stood to take over a fairly substantial estate.

They died on their way back from a week-long trip to Cancun, back before it was an overrun tourist resort and Mecca for hard-partying college kids, before Mexico as a whole became a playground for cartels with military grade weapons kidnapping children of the wealthy and assassinating politicians. We used to go every February, during my school's spring break week. It was a pleasant respite from the brutal northeast winters, a few days of sun, sand, and ocean, tacos and mariachi nestled between months of cold dark days and frigid nights. This was the first—and ultimately only—time I opted not to go with them. As an only child, it had always been only the three of us, mother, father, and me, and whenever they went on trips, I would accompany. We had visited a number of major American cities—Chicago, Philadelphia, New Orleans, Seattle, San Francisco, Los Angeles, Charlotte, Savannah—in addition to some hot spots to the north: Montreal, Toronto, Vancouver. They took me on a month-long excursion across Europe when I was fourteen, and there were frequent weekend road trips to wooded upstate oases and other bucolic getaways. I don't think there was a particular reason why I chose to stay home that last time. I was a senior in high school, on the cusp of adulthood, and I wanted some time alone, wanted to exercise my right to be by myself, to exert my burgeoning sense of identity, my maturing manhood, by staying home, if only for a few days. And I simply did not want to go to Mexico. It was not as if I had plans to transform the house into an adolescent den of iniquity in their absence, throwing nightly keggers and using every room for fantastical sexual purposes. I kept mostly to myself throughout school, with a few quiet male friends who would come over to watch television and play table tennis in the basement. I never had a girlfriend.

My parents called from Mexico several times a day to check on me. They left plenty of food and money and a list of emergency contacts. They ensured that the neighbors would stop by to see if I needed anything. When they called, they told me how much they missed and loved me, that they couldn't wait to get back home. I told them to stop worrying, that I was well past the age of worry, that I would see them before they knew it and then they would wish they had spent more time enjoying their vacation instead of talking to me. My mother told me that parents never stop worrying about their children, no matter what age, and that one day I would understand. Actually, I already understood something of that sentiment, but from a different vantage: growing up as an only child, I harbored an intractable fear of losing my parents at a young age. I thought about this often, imagining what kinds of sinister situations might steal them from me. Maybe fear is not the right word. It was more of a morose curiosity, or an unspoken dare to a fate that had been forever taunting me, holding this cruel contingency over my head, making me constantly aware that it would take little to render me an orphan, to play this kind of pitiless cosmic prank on me and whisk away the only two people on Earth who cared for me. And I kept standing up to it, calling its bluff, defiant, until one day the universe made good on its threat. So while I wouldn't say there was no shock at the news, though I would never deny that the event overturned my young life and radically altered my existence, the thought of losing my parents had never been foreign to me. It had always been hidden somewhere in my head, a sort of subconscious aware-ness that I could at any moment find myself completely alone in the world, an impendent potentiality curled up like a scheming homunculus, biding its time, waiting for the opportune moment to birth itself. It's not that I was afraid of being alone. As I said, I like being alone. And like it or not, everyone is always and ineluctably alone. As an only child, I believe I came to that visceral realization earlier than others. And it's not as though other people haven't experienced devastation; it's just that, being such a small contingent to begin with, it always seemed more likely that my family would find itself diminished sooner, statistically speaking.

The interesting part of the story is that, as they made that last call to me from the airport in Mexico City, the conscious thought that they might perish in a plane crash came hurtling into my mind like the kind of clairvoyant premonition that I never believed in, and I couldn't get it out until they called me from Kennedy well after midnight, aggravated and weary from the delayed departure and tardy arrival due to inclement atmospheric conditions (which included, in my mother's words, "some seriously scary turbulence... I had visions of you getting a call from American Airlines with their condolences.") but otherwise safe and anxious to claim their luggage and get home, while I waited on the couch in the den, watching MTV. At that time of night the ride should have only taken about half an hour, plus whatever time spent in customs and luggage claim and whatnot. I had offered to pick them up—with a newly minted driver's license, I would jump at any excuse to get behind the wheel—but as it was a school night and a late flight, they insisted on taking a car, one of those shiny Lincoln limos from the same company we had been using for years, with tinted windows and a small-screen television and a minibar in the back. I always thought it wasteful to pay for such luxury on so short a trip, but I still got a kick out of taking a Coke from the bar and watching that pint-sized TV, despite the fact that the reception was invariably awful.

When an hour passed I became a little worried, but I told myself that they probably got hung up at customs, my mom having bought bags of presents for me, little onyx replicas of the pyramids of Teotihuacan, and iconic, vibrantly colored tapestries depicting Quetzalcoatl, the feathered serpent deity of ancient Mesoamerica, in addition to the well-priced, high-quality Mexican silver jewelry they never failed to splurge on, despite promising themselves each time not to. I still have several sterling silver bracelets and a large crucifix with a thick rope necklace that I wore for my confirmation, along with all my parents' jewels, gathered together in a large box under their bed. I never went in much for jewelry; never saw the attraction of adorning one's person with sparkling metal and shaped stones. I would wear a wristwatch, but that was a practical matter.

Shortly after the hour passed, I fell asleep. I didn't wake until two hours later when the phone rang, which was strange because I can rarely do more than lightly doze with the television on. Yet there I was, out for hours with *120 Minutes* blasting, Matt Pinfield's froggy monotone punctuating the expositional segments. Surely it was my parents calling with some sadistic travel horror story to explain the delay: customs confusion, lost baggage, terminal lockdown, passport problem, construction closing the highway, a flat tire, an overheated engine. It turned out to be a wrong number. Some girl looking for a guy named Chuck. I thought it might have been a prank, but there was no sign of mischief in her register, just a pleading voice asking for Chuck with the cheerless urgency of one who has just learned of a tragedy and has been burdened with the unasked-for task of transmitting this news to another. I told her there was no Chuck at this residence, that she had the wrong number. She apologized profusely for having awoken me. I assured her I was already up, even though I wasn't. The call was unnerving. I convinced myself it was nothing more than a heartbroken young woman's tearful middle-of-the-night call to her lying cheating boyfriend that she nonetheless wanted back. Chuck must have been a real prick.

I checked the time—2:09. I stretched, turned off the television, peed, got a drink of pink lemonade, and sat down at the kitchen table to think of other scenarios that could account for the holdup, now moving from the airport to the car: flat tire, fender-bender, the driver was having chest pains and my dad had to take the wheel and get him to the ER, they forgot a piece of luggage and had to return to pick it up. This was just before the ubiquity of cell phones, so I couldn't call to see what the deal was.

At 2:21, the doorbell rang. I didn't move. I considered that it might be my parents, having somehow lost their keys. It rang again, a longer, sibilant chime, accompanied by three harsh knocks. My heart beat faster. I shook off the remaining creeks of sleep, grabbed the large Santoku from the knife block, and tiptoed to the door, peeking out of the picture window at its side. It was the police.

I rushed back into the kitchen and slipped the knife into the block. The doorbell rang again. More impatient knocking. I hurried back toward the door yelling, *Just a second*, like a harried housewife. Then I thought, *What if they're not real cops but crooks disguised as cops*? I ran back to the kitchen to fetch the knife again—this time opting for the serrated meat slicer—and made it to the door just as a third and extended round of knocking/ringing began. I laid the knife on the landing of the stairs to the left of the front door, with its handle facing me so I could make a quick lunge for it in the event that these so-called peace officers proved to be malevolent brigands in masquerade. Quickly composing myself and taking an extended deep breath, I unlocked the door and opened it a crack, just enough to peek out and make eye contact.

There were two of them. Tall, well-built men with glossy dark hair and scrubbed, fine-featured faces, white faces with a tinge of something innocuously ethnic, a splash of the Mediterranean, a smattering of Latin, a soupçon of the Dark Continent, just enough to add a touch of non-threatening interest as you wondered over their ancestry. For a second, I imagined they were models dressed as cops, perhaps from one of those strip-tease services that women book for bachelorette parties.

"Good evening, officers." This sounded so artificial and ridiculous. *Good evening*?

One of them stated my name.

"Yes, that's me."

"We're here about your parents," said the other.

"Oh. They should be back any minute. Should've been here hours ago, actually." I knew they knew this.

"We need you to come with us."

"It's about your parents."

"There's been an accident."

・　　・　　・

This is really what they say when they make that home visit to inform you of a tragedy: *There's been an accident.* It must be in the training manual at the academy, this brief declarative phrase that suffers no objection, that can be used and recycled without ever losing its mysterious potency. It conveys just enough information to snare one's attention without spoiling the climax.

"Are they okay?"

"There's been an accident."

That four-word wall again, impossible to breach.

"We need you to come with us, please."

"Let me… get…" Get what? A change of clothes? An overnight bag? Some money? "…my shoes." I turned to go in, then swung back. "And a jacket. And my keys." I stood there, staring stupidly at the modelesque policemen who looked back at me with a mixture of pity and a kind of glad-we're-not-you superiority.

It was the first time I had been in a squad car. It felt a bit strange back there, facing the partition of chunky bulletproof Plexiglas with a small centered circle of perforations in case the perp had to communicate with the cops. Or vice versa, I suppose. For some reason, I wanted to speak through it but could find nothing to say. I knew where we were going and why, and that was all I needed to know. I remember being impressed by the upright shotgun next to the passenger seat. I remember the officers driving in stony silence. Whether this was out of some kind of respect for the situation or because they simply had nothing to say, I would never know. I kept wondering if they would go lights and sirens, but there was no need. I remember zooming through dark, empty suburban streets, and how they swung into priority parking at the entrance of the hospital. It was a cold mid-winter overnight, a clear frosty darkness. There were patches of soiled ice hardened like bedrock at various spots in the parking lot, and invisible glazes coated the sidewalk, just waiting for some poor soul to slip and fall. In one lonely corner, snow left over from the last storm had been plowed to an uneven mound at least ten feet in height. It would refuse to melt until April's final thaw.

They accompanied me in and checked in with the nurse at the front desk.

"We're sorry, son," one of the cops said.

He spoke the words quietly. I think it was the first time anyone besides my parents had called me *son*.

"Good luck," the other offered, just as quietly.

They turned and strode silently back toward the exit, hands on their utility belts, and then disappeared through the automatic doors. *Son?* They couldn't have been more than ten years older than I. Maybe that's another one of those drilled-in training manual words: *Son. Ma'am. Sir.* Politely neutral yet authoritatively distant.

The nurse checked my name against the admission screen, and I noticed a scarcely perceptible facial twitch as she scanned the information and looked up at me with a besieged smile that was so forced she shouldn't have bothered, because it did nothing to reassure me. Then she paged Dr. Smith, looked up at me with another sad smile, and told me softly that he would be there momentarily to fill me in.

"Are they okay, my parents?"

I think I asked just to see her squirm, which she did.

"There's been an accident." *My God, was it in the nurses' manual, too?* "The doctor will fill you in on everything."

She craned her neck over the desk and peered down the hallway. To her noticeable relief, a doctor was swiftly approaching. He was a short man in a roomy white lab coat that reached past his ankles and whooshed up behind him like a cape as he walked toward me, with thin wisps of light brown hair framing his head like a poorly placed toupee, rimless glasses, and pink-hued, fatigue-stained eyes that radiated a certain avuncular gentleness, a kind of individuated warmth, despite the overwhelming business he was obviously plagued with.

"I'm Dr. Smith." He shook my hand. "I'm afraid there's been an accident."

"Yes. I've been told."

He laid a palm on my shoulder and squeezed gently. "Would you come with me, please?"

We walked down the eldritch nocturnal corridors, past orderlies rolling trays of overnight meds and clean bed sheets, paired nurses talking quietly, weary doctors making their way from room to room with eyes fixed on charts. After what seemed a good quarter of a mile—which we walked in awkward silence—we arrived at his office, a small room with walls covered in diplomas and various honors and a desk full of papers, folders, and framed family photos. Dr. Smith sat in the large leather chair behind his desk and I in one of the two smaller seats on the other side. For the first few seconds, he looked at me with a pained expression, as though struggling to find the right opening, but then he cut right to the chase, leaning over on his elbows with his hands pressed together and his fingers tightly interlocked.

Yes. There had been an accident. A bad one. My father was dead. Died at the scene. Instantly. Probably painlessly, although that's something we can never know. My mother was in critical condition in the ICU. They were waiting to determine which course of action to take, if any.

It happened on the highway, a few exits from the house, in the left lane, on a clear and calm and low-trafficked night, an ideal time to be on the road. They should have made it home in half an hour, tops, and they most likely would have, had not the driver of an eighteen-wheeler fallen asleep at the wheel and crossed over the median, hitting them head-on, smashing the front of their town car into the back like a Slinky crushing in on itself and forcing it to flip several times before sliding thirty yards to an inverted halt in the center lane. There were no other vehicles involved. The driver of the truck suffered some minor scrapes and bruises but nothing serious. He had apparently been driving for close to twenty-four hours. The police suspected that he had only dozed for a few crucial seconds. His spilled load was toys bound for various area stores, so the road became littered with crippled action figures and mottled teddy bears, dented dolls and mashed board games and, in a dry twist, some smashed-up toy cars and trucks. There was no trace of alcohol in his system. The limo driver also died instantly, making my mother the only survivor. They had to use the Jaws of Life to pull her out.

We sat there for a few moments after he finished delivering the news. He seemed unburdened but also somewhat embarrassed to be there with me, anxious to go about his duties but not wanting to rush me out. I wasn't sure how I felt. I suppose I was too traumatized for the sadness to set in, too overwhelmed by the fact that my worst childhood fear was becoming a reality. There was no room for grief.

"Do you want to see her?"

"Who?"

"Your mother."

"Oh." I looked down at the marbled linoleum, then back up at the doctor. "Should I?"

Dr. Smith scratched his chin with a thumbnail. I could hear it scraping his stubble.

"I'm going to be honest here."

What choice was there?

He trained his eyes on mine. "It doesn't look good. This might be your last chance to say goodbye."

I nodded and turned my eyes back down to the linoleum. Dr. Smith gave me a few more seconds, then he got up and came around to my side of the desk and put his hand on my shoulder again. He led me on another silent, quarter-mile stroll to my mother's room in the ICU.

Indeed, it didn't look good. I didn't need medical training to know that. My mother was broken. I knew as soon as I saw her that she wasn't going to make it. She was comatose, her face a canvas of cuts and swelling bruises, tubes everywhere, machines flashing and beeping and monitoring ceaselessly. She was deathly still. I knew she would never move again, yet I instinctively reached for any scrap of irrational hope, telling myself that miracles happen, that medical science is now so advanced it's amazing anyone dies at all, that fate could not possibly be so cruel. But I knew I was deluding myself. Human life is so fragile and the world so precarious that it's amazing we live as long as we do. And I never believed in fate. There was no way that battered shell in there, which was once my mother, would ever be my mother again. I sat in silence in the chair next to her bed until dawn broke and the room filled with unwelcome light, harsh, unfiltered early morning sun that made everything in that dismal little room look even more dismal.

I was just shy of eighteen. It was a matter of days until my birthday. But in the eyes of the state, a minor is a minor, and I was not allowed by law to go home by myself. So my closest relative, my only living relative, Aunt Anna, my mother's sister, a bitter, ragefully jealous and borderline psychotic spinster, was charged temporarily with my care. She had never gotten along with my mother. She hated my father, and she barely tolerated me, but she was happy to take me in, most certainly in the hope of securing some kind of financial boon for her efforts. I also suspect that she was more than a little satisfied with my parents' untimely end. Since my father died first, his estate and all joint marital assets went to my mother, and if she had died while I was still a minor (as my aunt was do doubt praying for), even by a few days, all that would have gone to me in trust, with my aunt as the trustee, and who knows what kind of mayhem she could have wrought on my inheritance? But this soon proved irrelevant. My mother went into acute cardiac arrest and died six days after the accident, one hour into my eighteenth year, making me an official, state-certified adult, legal and autonomous, full and sole inheritor of everything that belonged to my parents. My aunt wanted nothing more to do with me, and the feeling was mutual. I had been staying at the hospital most of the time, anyway.

I went home to my parents' house, to *my house*, and to a new reality. I was alone. I was also *free*.

. . .

And I was very comfortable, as I soon discovered. Even wealthy. In addition to the two-million dollar life insurance payout that passed directly from my father to my mother to me, there was the handsome stock portfolio, the hefty bank account, assets from a couple of investment properties my father had shares in, and a decent return on the trust fund that my mother had inherited from her paternal grandmother, which was now mine as well. I had no idea we were this flush.

There would also be liability settlements from the accident, which made front page headlines in the local newspapers the day after it happened. My father's best friend and law school buddy swooped in to guide me in all matters litigious, wasting no time in bringing suit against everyone involved and setting things into motion days after the funerals. Complaints were filed against the truck driver, the truck company, the limo company, the insurance companies, even the Department of Highways for not having sturdy enough median dividers. Anyone who could be sued was sued, and as my parents were the only truly blameless parties, hapless victims of circumstance and grave negligence, I, as their only living representative, was in a practically invulnerable legal position. No one wanted to see things go to court. It was a messy enough situation, and there was no way the defense attorneys were going to get a jury to rule against a newly minted orphan (though, having reached the age of majority prior to my mother's death, I was not an "orphan" in the strict legal sense), an only child whose parents had been forever whisked away because some overtired truck driver dozed on the job. Everyone paid up handsomely. I'm talking millions. Enough for several lifetimes. Literally more money than I knew how to squander. And money loves to reproduce. My parents' financial advisor set me up with a conservative risk portfolio that, considering the huge sums involved, delivered regular dividends that were enough to support several extended families in significant luxury, and since I am no spendthrift, my lifestyle not demanding much more than the modest minimum required to survive without working, the compounding principal continued to grow exponentially. Material comfort was never something I would have to be concerned with. Ever.

So I remained in the house. I once believed I would die there.

Continuity of place pleases me. People are always extolling the pleasures and benefits of travel, moving from place to place like restless insects, in search of new experiences and interesting times, exotic overseas adventures and domestic discoveries. They love to talk about relocating and starting fresh, reinventing themselves and broadening their horizons. They brag about how lightly they can pick up and create new beginnings, a new life for themselves, a new self for their lives. It's nonsense, all this wanderlust, a terrific waste of time, energy, and resources. Socrates hardly ever left Athens. Moses only left Egypt because he had to. Jesus never traveled more than thirty miles from his birthplace. "Traveling is a fool's paradise," Emerson said. "The soul is no traveler, the wise man stays at home." You can flee to the farthest, remotest nooks on the planet, hide yourself from civilization and everyone in it, or you can insert yourself into the thickest, most bustling cities on Earth, surrounding yourself with pullulating crowds and swarming masses, drop right into the center of the bubbling corpus of humanity or do your best to flee from it, but you cannot escape your own sad, solitary self; you cannot outstrip the confines of your own life. The past follows. It hunts relentlessly. It never tires. "The past is never dead," my favorite Mississippi man says. "It's not even past." It reaches into the present and stretches toward the future until it all becomes one jumbled, indistinguishable bulk of cancerous being. There is no refashioning the self, no remaking of one's essence. You can circle the surface of the Earth until your dying day, walk the land until there is no more land to walk, but you will never be other than what you were when you started. You are who you are, regardless of where you are.

And I was where I had always been. I lacked nothing. If I'd had my druthers, I would never have ventured out. The world is where I lay my head. It always has been.

$\bullet \quad \bullet \quad \bullet$

I tried not to scarf down my dinner, but the excitement was such that I couldn't help rushing through it. There are so few pleasures in life, but there were pressing matters on my mind. I didn't want to watch the news, which I usually do while eating, and the silence unnerved me, so I put on some Charlie Parker. A shot of old-school bebop to go with my meal.

By the time I finished rinsing the dishes and loading them into the dishwasher, it was nearly eight. Prime time. Perfect. I was buoyed with eagerness and light-footed anticipation. I had only to brush and floss, as I always do after a meal. Then … showtime.

Making a mental inventory of what I would need to actualize the bold vision that had come to me in the shower, I went to the basement and retrieved from the storage room an old twenty-gallon Farberware stockpot that my mother used the day after every Thanksgiving when she made her family-famous turkey soup with the left-over bird, letting the carcass soak for hours as the broth thickened and absorbed the flavor, yielding enough for several post-holiday meals. I hadn't thought of this pot in years, and yet when the need arose, the image of it appeared in my mind as though I had just used it yesterday. I could even recall the scent of my mother's soup, the warm aroma of boiling vegetables and poultry wafting through the house as fall morphed into winter and the last clinging leaves lost their purchase. And I remembered the flavor of that smoking liquid, plentiful and savory, the hot spoon on my tongue as my mouth closed around it, full of carrots and celery, parsley and leeks and plump strips of turkey meat. I was never one for soup, at least not as a meal in itself, but this was different. I looked forward to it every year.

I fetched the pot, which was enclosed in a taped-up cardboard box and lovingly wrapped in tissue paper with the cover securely fastened. Apart from a little dust, it was in fine condition. I removed it from the box, uncovered it and peered inside the clean, shiny interior, which showed nary a scratch or nick, nor any sign that anything had ever been cooked in it. My mother was fanatically protective of her possessions, a trait which she passed on to me, either genetically or through careful instruction, or perhaps a bit of both. Curiously, the pot seemed even larger than I remembered it. I wondered how my mother, a petite woman, maneuvered it with such agility; it was a minor struggle to lug it up through the narrow basement staircase, hugging it in font of me like a giant strapless steel drum.

By the time I hefted it onto the countertop next to the sink and began to hose in hot tap water, I had begun to sweat. I considered taking another quick shower. Instead, I lowered the thermostat (65°) and dabbed at my skin with a damp paper towel. While the pot was filling, I triple-checked the locks on the doors, made sure all the blinds were tightly drawn, and reset the alarm. I turned the burner on high, positioned the pot over the flame (the full pot was very heavy, and I made a mental note that if I were ever going to use it again I should fill it while it was already on the stove, though I wasn't sure if the sink hose would reach that far, in which case I would have to manually pour the water in, perhaps using a pitcher, which would seem to take more effort than carrying the dead weight a few feet), and fastened the lid.

With faultless timing, Jake was just waking when I eased on the lights, keeping them half dim so as not to strain his sleep-sensitized eyes. I slowly lifted him out of the basin. His bottom was warm and wet, the paper-towel diapers soaked. I wondered how such a tiny creature could produce so much waste, especially considering how little he ate and drank. With a flush of guilt, I was in turn reminded that I hadn't given him much to drink. A baby is all but inseparable from his bottle, and Jake had only enjoyed a few suckles before and after dinner. I genuinely regretted this, but he seemed fine. Except for the wetness. His expression seemed merely to convey slight inconvenience, as though the novelty of this change in routine were wearing thin. I imagined that he was now regretting his involvement in this strange fiasco—though it might have seemed fun at first. I imagined Jake wishing himself back home, to the security of his crib, to the warmth and safety of his familiar enclosure—mother and father gazing down lovingly over him after his evening bottle, watching the mobile spin slowly above him as he drowsed and dreamed his infant dreams.

"Dreams are a waste of time," I said to him.

He turned his head a tick, as though struggling to understand.

"Don't worry," I continued, softly tapping his little button nose in rhythm with the words. "They don't mean a thing."

I rocked him.

When we started for the kitchen, our eyes remained locked. It was important to me that I not look away, that I allow him to sense, in whatever shapeless and instinctual way, that I had nothing to hide from him, that I was being completely honest with him. My intentions had nothing to do with him personally, after all. I liked the little bugger. As far as babies were concerned, he was all right; he didn't cry too much, he stayed put, he wasn't overly clingy, and he had a pleasant demeanor.

Yet I would not be distracted or deterred. The deed would be done. The symbolic and philosophical imperative was greater than Jake, greater than myself. I wished I could explain this to him—that the fate of the individual accounts for so little. Yet humanity is nothing but a collection of individuals, and the world itself is nothing but an assemblage of atomized worlds, inextricably linked like the multitude of tiny dots in a pointillist painting, each lost to view in the distance but playing its own part in the grand form. The elimination of one of these dots, even to the trained eye, will almost certainly go unnoticed. What matters is the idea that it's missing, that the whole has been diminished by a part. If one of these points can be erased, so can the rest. The entire picture can be nullified, point by point. The virgin purity of the untouched canvas can be restored, returned to its beautiful bursting blankness, so much fuller than a congested accumulation of specks. This is the concept. It makes me smile. I know I can never ablate them all, never succeed in ridding the world of infestation, but it is my moral imperative to do my share. However futile and frustrating, it is my ethical duty to play my paltry part in saving the human race from itself. If I should remove even a few points from the painting, then at least I have acted. At least I have tested the strength of my convictions.

It had to be done.

First, I had to clean him.

I peeled off the jaundice-colored paper towels and sprayed him down again in the sink, soaping and rinsing him until there was no sign of urine, until he smelled as fresh as he looked. I turned up the cabinet-inset CD player. It was Leonard Cohen's masterpiece, *Various Positions*. As I sat at the kitchen table swinging a squeaky clean and naked Jake in my arms, I heard the steam rattling the pot's cover. Oddly but not unpleasantly, the sound complemented Cohen's coarse-grained vocals:

> *Dance me to the children who are asking to be born*
> *Dance me through the curtains that our kisses have outworn*
> *Raise a tent of shelter now, though every thread is torn*
> *Dance me to the end of love*

"It's about that time."

I spoke plainly to Jake, giving him the respect of an adult voice, undisguised by baby blathering. He replied with an open mouth and scrunched eyebrows, but no sound came forth.

Cradling the baby in the crook of one arm, I went over to the stove and slid the lid back a crack to reveal a rapid boil, its potent puff of steam wafting over my face like a superheated cloud rushing out into the atmosphere. I instinctively turned away to shield Jake from this blast, grabbed a potholder to grip the lid, and dropped it in the sink. I then turned on the vent fan above the stove.

I remember a trance-like surreality, where you feel your body act on its own as you observe, as though I were a captain relaxing at the helm as the autopilot carried out programmed orders. My senses blurred, or amalgamated, into a kind of supersense—a heightened synesthesia, with everything around me melding into one distinct feeling that was at once terribly strange and intimately familiar, like a recurring dream I had as child, a dream of a warm and easy place where I had always wanted to be but could never quite locate, someplace that only existed in that particular dream. In the moment, I felt I was close to the place that my dream had promised. Eyes closed, I stood still and soaked in this rare sensation, this keen awareness of self and selflessness. For the briefest speck of an instant, I let go; I let Being *be*.

And yet I was somehow even more invested in myself and my actions than I ever had been. I knew exactly what I was doing and why I had to do it. There was not the slimmest shadow of doubt about the absolute necessity of my actions.

I opened my eyes. I skipped forward to "If It Be Your

Will." The music invaded my senses and I felt myself merge with my surroundings, no distance between mind and body, thought and movement. I smiled down at Jake, my little unwitting conspirator, and he smiled back. I wished so badly that he could sense the urgent beauty of what we were doing. Did he feel as one with me as I did with him?

I lifted him from under his armpits, holding him high above the steaming pot. His legs darted and kicked a little as though trying to run, and I could swear a precocious little smile crossed his lips. Then I lowered him into the bubbling broth, not too fast lest his body should plop and splash water all over, nor too slow lest I should recoil from the task. He slid in. His face curled into a strained rictus.

It wasn't pain. It was something beyond pain, something that registered beyond sensation. His arms and legs spasmed, but not that much. Not much at all, really. There was no thrashing and clanging of the pot such as would be expected with a lobster. There was just a bit of quiet twitching.

The churning water turned his body over on itself, twirling it like a capon as it reddened and swelled and bobbed just above the surface. I grabbed a heat-proof plastic spoon from the drawer and plunged it in, prodding at the boiling meat and fully submerging the body, which, only seconds in, had already stopped moving. No sounds, no struggle, no drama. He went like a martyred saint who knew his end would serve a greater good, a valiant front-line soldier accepting his role in battle, willing to sacrifice himself in a war declared against being, against life, against everything.

I watched as the roiling bubbles grew in ferocity, the splashing turbulence taking Jake under and throwing him up like a baby seal tossed by shoreline waves. Though I suppose it wasn't Jake anymore. Just a hardened fleshy shell.

• • •

I am not a religious man. I do not believe in God. I do not believe in an afterlife. I do not believe in good and evil, reward and retribution. I believe life is an exceedingly rare cosmic event that just happened to happen, and shouldn't have. In its chaotic sprawl, the universe stumbled upon the recipe for the formation of organic matter—the right materials at the right temperature for the right amount of time. Set the timer for few billion years, and here we are, surfing the Internet for porn and watching celebrity chefs on TV. There are billions of stars and planets in the observable universe, so the chances of life bubbling up from time to time are fairly good, but this does not mean it is supposed to happen. This does not mean there is any meaning behind it. If I were to blindfold myself and throw a billion darts at a dartboard twenty feet in front of me, I would probably hit the bullseye a good number of times.

No, I do not believe life is anything special. There is no soul or spirit. There is only meat and gristle and bone and the chemical reactions necessary to make them move.

Yet I couldn't help but wonder what happened to the essence of that baby when his life was boiled away. The first law of thermodynamics states that there is a fixed amount of energy in a closed system, and that energy cannot be created or destroyed; it can only change form. If our consciousness, our *élan vital*, our essence, or whatever it is that so many made-up religions take for the immortal part of our human being, is a form of energy, as everything is, then where does it go when the organic shell can no longer support it? When you turn off a light, that energy goes somewhere. Did Jake, or the energy that constituted baby Jake, simply wash into the water and evaporate into the air as steam, somehow sifting into me as I inhaled? Was I unknowingly absorbing his soul? Or did it dissolve into the boiling liquid like so much bouillon, to be sucked down the drain and drawn into the sewer system, to wherever that waste ends up?

Again I stuck the spoon in and prodded the body, watching the lifeless husk slowly sink and rise. I stared hard at the scene. There was no soul escaping. No journey up and out and onward to another plateau. There was just this dead red flesh, the spark of life extinguished forever. He had been alive. Now he was dead. And his death—as any death—offered no more meaning than his short life had.

The magic of the moment had passed. My sense of oneness had proven illusory. I turned off the burner and replaced the lid, letting the boil reduce to a simmer, then to nothing. As I looked at my distorted reflection in the shiny metal cover, I was seized by a violent blitz of adrenaline that flowed from my core outward like voltage. My fists clenched, and I was urged by an internal command to throw or break something, to grab whatever was nearest to hand and hurl it hard against the wall. I resisted. I calmly removed the oven mitt, shut off the CD player, and headed down to the basement, my pace hurried but collected, even as I felt this inexplicable rage building on itself with each step. In one rough upward motion I ripped the shirt from my body. I blasted The Stooges' *Funhouse* and tore into the heavy bag with unprecedented ferocity. The bag is exactly half my weight, seventy-five pounds, and I made that hunk of sand-filled leather dance around its chain as though it were possessed, swinging so fast and hard I could hardly feel my fists make contact. It felt as if I were punching through it, as though the bag were a flimsy children's piñata that would burst open at any second and shower prizes on the basement floor. By the end of the first song I was well soaked in sweat and heavily winded. I dropped to the floor and did 200 push-ups and sit-ups in alternating sets of 50, then shut off the stereo, jogged up to the ground floor, jogged up another flight to the second level, ran to my room, scanned my iPod for something aggressive, decided on Nine Inch Nails' "Broken" (which I probably hadn't listened to in years), stood in front of the mirror and flexed and posed and strained my muscles for show. Then I dropped and did another couple of sets of sit-ups and push-ups, flexed again, brusquely unbuttoned and unzipped my pants and kicked out of them and mas-turbated in front of the mirror, letting myself go to a rare climax.

Once finished, I ran to the bathroom with a handful of cum and showered in water as hot as I could stand, scrubbing my body hard with a freshly laundered, heavily lathered pouf. By the time I got out I was both physically and mentally spent. I returned to my room, put on a clean pair of boxer briefs, shut off the light, put on Chopin's *Nocturnes*, and collapsed on my bed. I was asleep in seconds.

Minutes later, it seemed, I was awake. Only it was hours later, not minutes. There was no music. No sound anywhere. Every light in the house was off, even the dual floods above the kitchen sink, which are set on a timer to go off at one a.m. It was 1:26. I sat up, took in some air, and let my eyes gather the darkness around me, making out the recognizable shapes and objects that greet them every day upon waking. From the depths of the full-length mirror hanging on the closet door directly across the room from the bed I saw my adumbrated shadow self, sitting up shirtless in the glass, looking cruel and clueless. I watched myself for a long time, stone-still and propped up against the headboard. For a few seconds, I almost didn't remember what had happened, what I had done, what was waiting for me downstairs. Was there really a boiled baby in a pot on my stove? I thought of the lobster scene at the restaurant again. The kid, the mother, the waiter. This time it is a baby they pick out of the tank, a nice plump infant, and the waiter asks: *And what would you like with your baby, sir? Baked, mashed, or fries?*

Of course, I would have never even considered eating Jake. I am not a savage.

I broke away from my reflection and turned on my Toshiba 46" ultra hi-def television. The local eleven o'clock news reruns at 1:30. There it was, among the top stories: cop injured in downtown shootout, one suspect killed, one on the run; fire in a ghetto tenement, no one dead but some suffered smoke inhalation and one person broke both ankles jumping to safety from a second-story window; armed home invasion in upscale suburban neighborhood, husband pistol-whipped but otherwise no one hurt, perpetrators apprehended a few hours later with van full of loot; eight-month-old baby abducted from suburban park, AMBER Alert in tri-state area, description and sketch of kidnapper released, male Caucasian, 25–30 years old, 5'8"–5'10", 150 lbs., wearing baseball cap, hooded sweat jacket, black T-shirt and jeans.

First they showed the picture of Jake, a recent photo, judging from his size. He was staring confusedly into the camera. Then came the sketch of me, or what I guess was supposed to be me. I laughed out loud, which I seldom do. Did the father-husband even *look* at me? I have never worn a baseball cap in my life. Granted, I had kept my sunglasses on throughout the brief time we talked, and my newsboy cap was pulled down a bit over my forehead, but the drawing looked nothing like me in terms of facial structure or features. Other than the general description, which would fit thousands of men in the area, there was nothing that could have positively identified me—no distinguishing characteristics, nothing that would make anyone who knew me suspicious. Not that anyone who knew me could possibly imagine me capable of such a thing. Not that there was anyone who knew me in the first place.

I waited through the first two reports, and then it came on. The story was reported by an attractive light-skinned black correspondent who was on scene at the park, still cordoned off with police tape and crawling with uniforms. I imagined them combing for clues with flashlights and surgical gloves, bagging potential evidence and talking to possible eyewitnesses. She interviewed several people who lived in the vicinity, including a woman rolling her twin babies in a double-wide stroller. Everyone expressed horror and shock that something like this could occur at *their* park. And in broad daylight, no less. "If it could happen here, it could happen anywhere," said the mother. She was shaking her head and staring down sorrowfully at her kids, as though fearful for the world they would inherit.

That was it. A three-minute segment followed by a hotline number flashed across the screen, and then on to a movie review, weather, sports, and coverage of a celebrity AIDS benefit. I turned off the TV. I felt relieved, yet strangely disappointed. I did not want to get caught. I did not do this for attention or out of some masochistic need for punishment, but it was as though I was being ignored, as though they were purposely denying me credit. I got up and put on a fresh pair of jeans and a clean T-shirt and headed through the dark hallways and down the stairs and into the kitchen, where, immediately upon switching on the lights, I stopped and peered over at the pot as if half-expecting it to have magically disappeared. Its sides were smooth and cool to the touch. I stood in front of it for a few seconds, then lifted the lid.

Baby Jake was still inside, his body a bloated purple bulk, swollen larger than he had been a few hours before. Skin blistered and coriaceous, he floated facedown with the back of his head and his scalded buttocks just above the surface, perfectly static and centered, like a still life. *Still Life in Stockpot.* There were darkened particles of flesh floating next to him, brining the water. I stuck my spoon in and turned him over. He looked like a dinged-up vintage doll that had been rescued from a fire, intact but severely damaged, arms and legs curled up tightly, face covered with blains. Most of all, however, he seemed so deeply at peace, so blissfully removed from every worldly woe. I envied him. I envied him so much that I felt like whacking him with the spoon, smashing the rounded end of its plastic bowl against his body as though he'd misbehaved.

I realized that I had missed my nightly café latte, which I would normally enjoy while watching the news. I debated whether or not to prepare it, as it was now much later than usual and the caffeine could keep me up until dawn. I usually didn't go to sleep before 3:30 or 4:00, but 4:00 was my absolute limit; if I were to miss that deadline, even by a few minutes, I would feel ruined the next day. Regardless, I had to have my coffee. There was still much to do, and I couldn't risk dozing on the job. I filled the teapot with hot tap water and placed it on the burner next to Jake's pot, prepared the French press, preheated (*à la française*) one cup of skim milk in the microwave, frothed it up with my rechargeable frother, scooped in two heaping tablespoons of Chock Full O'Nuts French Roast Blend, poured in the boiling water, stirred, waited, and poured the coffee into the milk-filled glass.

It was then time to turn my attention to Jake. This was turning out to be quite a bit of work, I thought, sipping my coffee (which was hitting the spot harder than usual, due to the delay). I put on Sonic Youth's *Daydream Nation* and got down to it. I fetched a couple of Hefty Extra Strong Lawn and Leaf bags from the garage and doubled them up. My initial impulse was to simply tip the pot and empty the water out into the sink, but that clichéd phrase *don't throw the baby out with the bathwater* came to mind, so I decided instead to scoop him out with two large slotted spoons. It wasn't easy, and I didn't want to drop him, so I took some time to position the spoons underneath and gently lifted his heavily bloated body up and out, holding him above the water for a while to let the excess drip off, tilting him one way and the other. Then I slowly placed him into the open mouth of the layered bags, pushing as much air out as possible before twisting and tying the tapered ends into a sturdy knot. This seemed preferable to using a twisty.

Here is where I hesitated. Disposal. The biweekly garbage pickup was in a few hours. This probably wouldn't have been the wisest way to eliminate the evidence, though it would have been the most convenient (I had a weekend's worth of trash to lug out to the curb, anyway). There was a sump at the end of the block, but I really didn't feel like walking down the street with several bags of garbage *and* a dead baby in tow. Jake would have to remain on the property; a backyard burial seemed the best solution.

I shut off the motion-activated outdoor lights, took a shovel from the garage, and headed out the back door over the brick patio where we used to have our summer Sunday barbecues and where I would ride my Big Wheel around in tight speeding circles (the barbecue is still there, draped in a sweeping black canvas and unused since the summer before my parents' death), down into the wild, wooded area of the yard, where the healthy, well-maintained rye, fescue, and Kentucky bluegrass gives way to a shadowed jumble of undomesticated weeds and moss, bordered by a line of fairly dense underbrush and burly oaks and years of outdoor midden that the landscapers dumped back there after collecting it from the pristine front lawn. There are houses on either side, but nothing in back—only another fifty yards or so of unkempt, undeveloped forest and finally a chunky, fifty-foot wooden wall that was built as a sound barrier against the service road of the highway just on the other side. The neighboring houses were far enough away and blocked by enough trees that I wouldn't have to worry about snooping eyes. The beauty of this kind of suburb is privacy, anonymity. Don't ask, don't tell. This is the social contract one makes when moving to such a place, acceding to the terms of this tacit agreement with one's neighbors that anyone can do whatever one pleases, provided such conduct doesn't infringe upon another's right to the same private liberty. It is all very democratic. So if anyone happened to be out this late—highly unlikely, as people in the neighborhood were generally in bed by 10:00 on weeknights, with lights out by 11:30 at the latest—and happened to see me digging in the dirt, he might wonder why, he might mention it to the wife, perhaps with a passing comment on the innocuous eccentricity of that guy next door, but he would never be so presumptuous as to ask what I was doing, lest the same audacity be visited upon him at a later date. There is a reason serial killers seldom live in crowded cities.

The night was as beautiful as the day had been. The air was clear and cool, without a hint of humidity. I clicked to the Ramones' first album on my iPod, and as "Blitzkrieg Bop" blasted into my ears, I started digging into the damp earth, swaying and bobbing my head to the music and tossing back shovelful after shovelful of soil like a chain-gang prisoner. It was hard work, but I liked it. It was satisfying. It made me feel masculine. I have never done much in the way of manual labor. When something went wrong with the house, I called a guy—the plumber or the electrician or the air conditioner repairman, the mechanic or boiler man or landscaper or roofer. As long as I could pay, they could fix it. I have never done any kind of labor, physical or otherwise. I never had to work a day in my life, and I probably never will. A pleasant thought. I sung along with Joey, performing little skips and jumps to the refrain: *Hey ho, let's go, Hey ho, let's go!*

By the time the second Ramones album was done, I had worked myself into a healthy sweat and my muscles burned with strain. Though I had ambitiously set out to burrow to the cemetery standard depth of six feet, my efforts were impeded as the shovel repeatedly struck thick gnarls of root and sedimentary rock (at a depth of little more than two feet). Lacking tools sufficient to complete the task I had envisioned, I concluded that a shallow grave would have to suffice. I expended strenuous effort to dislodge the first layer of obstruction, boring the pit to a depth of approximately three feet, squared in width. I returned to the house to collect the doubled bags with Jake and his clothes (one containing Jake, the other his clothes and his soiled diaper). While there, I grabbed a quick glass of water and a protein bar.

I set the bags beside the hole and leaned with an arched elbow on the handle of the shovel, looking down into the pit. My eyes had adjusted to the darkness and I saw with clarity. There, enveloped by layers of thick-ply plastic, was Jake. And there was his grave. I was struck by a strange sadness, an awkward hesitation. It seemed somehow like a premature parting. But relationships only sour with time. It is better to end on the upswing, before tedium and pettiness and peccadilloes muddy the water. Things only get worse. Time does not heal; it only deepens the wounds. Best to leave on a positive note. Best to cut the cord and try to remember the good times.

I edged the bag with his diapers and clothes in first. Then I lifted Jake—careful as always to support him from the bottom—held him aloft above the hole, and laid him softly on top of the other bags. There was an urge to say something, a few words, neither prayer nor remembrance, but simply words.

I couldn't think of anything.

I filled in the hole, tamping down the surface so that the ground hardly seemed disturbed. Before going inside, I spotted a smooth, slate-gray stone a few feet away. It was about the size of both my fists, with a luminous composite surface that sparkled like a dim star cluster. I placed it on top of the spot where little Jake lay, and I stood before it for a few moments. Then I scattered some leaves and twigs over the surface of the freshly dug grave and headed back toward the house.

•   •   •

It was three a.m. I hosed down the shovel and put it back in the garage, then locked up and reset the alarm, only to realize I had forgotten to take out the garbage. I might have let this go, but cans of tuna and other organic refuse could attract insects and vermin. So I dragged the heavy plastic can out to the curb, and just as I got there, an SUV sped in my direction with the bass vibrating at such volume that whatever music was playing could not be discerned above the thudding low frequency, which seemed to shake the ground. The vehicle slowed to a near halt as it approached, and the front passenger side window lowered to reveal a thick-necked fratboy type in a Colorado Rockies cap. I couldn't make out the other occupants. The fratboy bulged his eyes at me and said, *Dick*, in a cartoonish, upswelling voice, the music killed just long enough for him to get the extended syllable out. I heard the other occupants laugh as the bass rebooted and the SUV sped off.

I stood there next to the trash, a bit unnerved but mostly disgusted. What possible pleasure could a person derive from such a display? Could they not have found a better way to alleviate their boredom? It seemed so senseless, so lacking in reward. People were getting stupider. The further civilization advanced, the stupider they became.

I started back up the driveway toward the house, contemplating what had just happened as I looked up between the softly swaying treetops. Clouds crept slowly over a milky moon. The star-speckled sky hung low overhead like a canopy dotted with cheap rhinestones. When I reached the house, I sat on the bench beside the front door that overlooked the lawn and the street, and I watched the trees and listened to night birds twitter as the occasional acorn fell to the pavement, a sure sign of fall's imminence. And still my thoughts returned to those idiotic kids who had disturbed my peace, kids who would soon be idiotic adults—selfish, moronic, ignorant suburban Americans. Worse, they would reproduce. There would be more like them; a self-perpetuating process with no end in sight. How wonderful it would be if there were indeed an end in sight. How much more wonderful it would be if they had never be born in the first place; how even more wonderful it would be if none of us had ever been at all.

Juanita

. . .

I have always hated children. I probably hated myself as a child. Curiously, I don't detest babies with the same intensity that I reserve for young kids—between, say, six and eleven. They are the absolute worst: not old enough to realize the world doesn't revolve around them but not young enough to slide by on doe-eyed innocence.

When it comes down to it, though, I hate them all. I hate the little pissed-pants toddlers and I hate the acne-riddled wise-ass college-bound teenagers, like the ones who had intruded upon my trance. And I hate the grown-up kids, too—the so-called adults, who are just as bad, if not worse. A whole word of despicable kids, all of whom I loathe. Including myself.

But there is something particularly odious about children that gets deep under my skin like a vicious subcutaneous rash. The way they run around with such unconstrained rambunctiousness, their screeching little voices that assail my ears like fingernails on a chalkboard, the way they pick their dirty little noses and stick their filthy little fingers deep in their mouths and other orifices, how they resort to fits and tears when their demands are refused. And heaven forbid you should look at someone's newborn—be it in a photo or in writhing proximity—and refrain from effusing, along with everyone present, over how utterly precious and edibly adorable the child is. You are expected—all but required—to smile and make ridiculous faces at the tiny creature. You are compelled to touch its plump red cheeks or stroke its sparse downy hair or slip your forefinger into the curl of its tiny knuckles and grin at its developing compassion.

I have always found infants repulsive and frightening. They are like geriatrics in miniature, bald and frail and lost and unable to effectively communicate. Little aliens struggling to find a suitable earthly form. Infants are humanity at its purest: unadulterated selfishness. Feed me, change me, wash me, protect me, take care of me. *My* existence is all that matters. *I* am the future, *you* are the past. *I* mean more. Despite the extravagant display of worship people feel the necessity to make in their presence, there is nothing innately cute or appealing about them; they are shriveled little creatures who cry at whim and can't control their bodily impulses. Yet we are genetically engineered to find them adorable and appealing, in order that we will do anything to protect them, anything to ensure the survival of the species. Evolution has arranged it thus—so that we care for our young, rather than leave them out for stray dogs and exposure to the elements.

But if we saw what they really represented, if we took a sober moment to apprehend their actions and instinctive motives, we would realize that they are self-interest personified—tiny, compact versions of our basest selves, before we develop the means and faculties to disguise these desires with ersatz altruism and fatuous concern for others. The truth is, the only time we find occasion to have any concern for others is when the performative gesture redounds to ourselves, even if the benefits are not immediately clear. Peel back the artifice, and you will see that every moment of every life is wholly dedicated to self-preservation, to the protection of a fleshy husk. We like to pretend that it is more complicated. It isn't. Babies are an untainted manifestation of the inherent egocentricity of existence.

•   •   •

I found myself leaning forward and rubbing my hands together, an agitated caballer dreaming up the plot of his next scheme. I wondered if this was how great people—artists, scientists, generals, inventors—felt when they stumbled upon discovery, the moment of kismet. I rocked back and forth with a swelling sense of triumph. I had found my calling. I knew what I had to do, what I had been born to do. My mission had been hidden all this time. I had been groping around in the dark until that chance encounter with a father and his baby boy. It had taken thirty years to find, but now the seal was broken, and there was no stopping, no turning back. I had taken that first dip into the dark waters of my supreme longing, immersed myself in the baptismal font of a desire so strong that there was simply no thought of resistance, nor want. It was religious. Revelatory. I had found my ecstatic love, my raison d'être. There was no unbiting the apple. I knew how good it tasted, and I wanted more.

· · ·

The air had chilled. My body began to feel the afteref-
fects of unusual exertion. Though I exercised regularly,
I was unaccustomed to the labor that circumstances
had demanded; my muscles were not used to working a
shovel. After a good half an hour, I went inside, put on
Radiohead's *Amnesiac,* and began the cleanup. I lifted the
dead weight of the pot off the stove and slowly poured
the water out into the sink, letting it course out at little
more than a trickle to prevent any detritus from splatter-
ing onto the countertop. This took several long minutes,
and my arms tightened and trembled from the strain.
Once empty, I squeezed out a quarter of a bottle of antibacterial detergent and ran the hottest tap water possible
into the pot. I stuck my hands into a pair of pink rubber
dishwashing gloves—the kind that bourgeois housewives
use to protect their freshly manicured nails—removed
a brand-new Brillo Pad from the box, and scrubbed as
though trying to take off a layer of metal, scouring top,
bottom, sides, and handles with equal attention as the

steam curled up into my face. Once done with the pot, I set it on the table, cushioned by some paper towels, then sprayed down the sink, went over it with detergent, sprinkled it with a generous layer of Comet, let it sit for a minute or two, then scrubbed and scrubbed; bottom, sides, faucets, hose, the works.

I was ready to drop, but the end was in sight, so I bore down and did what needed doing. I rinsed the sink, took off the gloves and tossed them in the trash, lathered my hands past my wrist with the remaining detergent and rubbed them together hard under the hottest water I could tolerate, which was more than mildly painful. After double-checking the locks on all the doors, I went upstairs and set the alarm with all zones activated, including the downstairs motion detectors, so that even if someone did manage to penetrate the outer shell, they would have trouble moving through the house and up to me. I showered again, brushed and mouthwashed, and went to bed with a Beethoven sonata playing me off to a sound and dreamless sleep. It had been a good day.

I awoke later than usual the next morning. I never used an alarm clock, but I rarely got up more than a few minutes past ten. On this day, however, my eyes opened to 10:51, the digits staring mockingly at me from the stereo's display, threatening to turn to 10:52 at any second. I shot up too fast, and a disorienting lightheadedness forced me to lie back down for a couple of minutes, further delaying the start of my day. At 10:55, I willed myself up, knowing that if I weren't out of bed by eleven the day would be spoiled. This is how it was with me. Although I never had a job and rarely had anywhere to be at any specific time, I felt it necessary to observe a strict self-imposed schedule—up by ten a.m., showered by 10:30, and ready for my breakfast by 10:50, eleven at the latest. On such occasions when I would fail to observe this schedule, a depressive pall would be cast over the entire morning and afternoon, and rarely would I be able to salvage the evening. So already my day was off kilter, and after such an auspicious start to the week.

Foggy and heavy with inertia, I dragged myself to the bathroom, brushed my teeth, and shuffled lethargically into the shower. Usually, a good hot hose-down would wash off whatever dust of sleepiness remained, but it wasn't doing the trick this time. I found myself sitting, my back against the tile, and letting warm streams of water beat down upon my face and head and body. I closed my eyes and felt as though I could slip away into a dreamscape. It was completely relaxing, but I needed to shake the drowsiness, not drop back into somnolence. I wondered if I should just give up, dry off and head back to bed, chalk up the lost day to laziness and start fresh tomorrow. *No*, I protested, forcing my weary legs to push up the rest of me as I proceeded with the business of washing. I would not let torpor impede the progress I had made.

Feeling not much improved, I dragged myself downstairs, waddled around the kitchen and prepared one of my two standard breakfast meals, which I alternated from day to day: oatmeal or farina, both made with skim milk and brown sugar. Fresh blueberries and walnuts are a must. Blueberries are the ultimate antioxidant, and no breakfast would be complete without the nut that is so good for the brain that it actually resembles one. Both foods are proven boosters of long-term memory and general mental acuity. What is existence but a memory in progress? What is a lifetime but a collection of these memories? Nothing in this lived experience is unworthy of remembrance; every single unenduring moment merits memorialization. No single second is weightier in import than any other, because they are all equally meaningless, identically ephemeral, exactly alike in their makeup of space and time. Life is just a collection of moments, and death is nothing but the annihilation of memory, the breaking off of the chain of moments. This is why I cherish my brain food. This morning was oatmeal.

There were only a few minutes of the morning left, and I hated to breakfast in the p.m., so I scurried around collecting the ingredients and mixing them up. I also made my French press *café au lait* and poured a half-glass of grapefruit juice while still managing to sit down just before the noon bell tolled. After several sips of coffee while letting my oatmeal cool—the jolt of caffeine was invigorating—I turned on the midday news and dug in, hoping some nourishment would succeed where the shower had failed.

Ten minutes into the newscast, after the first commercial break, there was a report on Missing Baby Jake, who was abducted less than a day ago, though it already seemed like anguished ages to the distraught parents (statistically speaking, after the initial 24-hour period, the chances of recovering a kidnapped child drop dramatically), who made a public plea on camera to whoever took their baby to please, please bring back their precious, irreplaceable son, the jewel of their heart, their basis for being, their very lives. They promised that all would be forgotten and forgiven, if only little Jake would be returned, safe and sound, to where he belonged.

I sipped my coffee and scooped my oatmeal and finally began to come to life as the mother spoke weepily on screen—an attractive woman in her late twenties, her wavy, shoulder-length dirty blonde hair tinged with the slightest orange (or was the hue on my 27" hi-def kitchen LCD in need of adjustment?) and her chestnut eyes crystallized with tears and reddened with worry (or maybe, again, this was the hue), while the father-husband held her in stoic silence, glaring out as though he knew I was watching, his own eyes blackened from lack of sleep but showing more anger than sadness, letting me know what he would do to me if we ever met again, what kind of medieval savagery he would wreak upon me for abusing his man-trust when he allowed himself to turn his back and inadvertently left me to watch over his son, for abducting his boy, the bloom of his seed, the future of his name. Each moment I watched further enlivened me. By the time the reporter tossed it back to the anchor, who repeated the hotline and urged anyone with information on the kidnapping to contact the police without hesitation, I was fully awake.

    •   •   •

After watching the weather (another beautiful day ahead) and finishing my breakfast just in time to avoid sports (I hate sports), I washed the dishes.

I was so intoxicated with intensity that I decided to go for a nice long promenade around the neighborhood. Walking is one of my great pleasures. I would often stroll for hours though residential developments and neighboring towns, varying my pace from a casual saunter to a commanding strut, depending on my mood and what music was in my head. There was no route for the day, which is always how I preferred it. I would let the road take me where it may, on a sort of itinerant ramble through the environs of suburbia. I put on my newsboy cap and Ray-Bans and hoodie, selected Radiohead's *Kid A,* and bounded off down the driveway into the street with the alacritous jaunt of a recently recovered cancer patient suffused with a new appreciation for the littler joys of life. Thom Yorke chanted *Everything in its right place,* and the words rang in my ears with no tinge of irony. Clear, contented sunshine. Luscious, limpid air. The scent of crisp cut grass and lawnmower exhaust carried on the breeze of a leaf blower. Clean, paved suburban streets. It was one of those days when I almost felt glad to be alive. Almost.

For the most part, my walks were solitary, contemplative. I would rarely cross paths with or speak to anybody, save to issue a cursory salutation to a fellow pedestrian or a neighborly nod to one of our community's elderly couples out for their afternoon constitutional. If I perceived that someone might be inclined to make a closer connection, I would extricate myself from the situation as hastily as possible. In terms of societal relations, what I value above all is privacy and anonymity. Again, this unspoken devotion to the suburban creed of live and let live and pay no attention to how others live as long as they pay no attention to you, tended to work in my favor. So few people walk in the suburbs, anyway.

But on this afternoon, perhaps on account of the ideal weather, there were a number of human beings on the street. I was barely halfway down the block when I saw the first power-walking housewife strutting toward me in tight, fluorescent pink Speedos and a loose-fitting yellow halter, mid-size breasts jouncing nicely as her arms and elbows rocked back and forth with each stride. She smiled and tipped her head. I did the same, then turned around to check out her ass. I appreciate the efforts these past-their-prime women make to retain whatever sex appeal they can as the irreversible ravages of age and marriage and motherhood whittle away at them.

It was a bit odd to see someone so soon after leaving the house. With any luck, that would have been the first and last encounter of my stroll. But on the very next block, there were two more women, mothers, walking side by side with nearly identical strollers, ambling at a glacially slow pace as they chatted and gesticulated and laughed and complained and gossiped. Their offspring gazed wild-eyed about the surroundings, pacifiers plugging mouths, arms grabbing at the open air, feet flapping wildly, like bound captives struggling to escape. Speeding up, I increased my iPod's volume and tried to keep my head down as I approached the small group, but their screeching, almost cackling voices carried over into my auditory realm, polluting the music and compelling me to look up. My reaction was returned by two non-committal stares as the women continued their peripatetic conversation, noticing me as one would a squirrel hopping into one's path. They couldn't make out my eyes under the deep gray-green shade of my G-14 lenses, so there was no way for them to know that I was glaring down at their two sweet little lambs as I hustled past without a word, not bothering to grace their asses with a backward glance.

I was flustered. It had only been a few minutes, and my solitary walk had already been less than solitary. It seemed like a bad omen, but I may have been making too much of it. It is an unfortunate but necessary truth that occasional contact—direct and indirect—with other people is sometimes unavoidable, and though it felt foreboding, I tried to bury the feeling and keep my stride. My pace picked up in velocity. When I observed my arms flapping at my sides like those of a palsied power-walker, I stuck them in my pockets and hunched forward, drew myself in and concentrated on my breathing. I focused on the music and the empty street ahead, staring fixedly at the ground in front of me. Then I considered that the way I was walking might appear a little sketchy. Though I wasn't overly worried about arousing suspicion, I slowed down and loosened up, trying hard to recoup my equanimity; anything to save this pristine day.

Two more blocks, no people. Few cars, one whose stereo blasted Emimen, which I could easily detect over my own music, another playing Beethoven's Fifth louder than I had ever heard it before. I removed my earbuds. There was the dim twitter of a phone from within a nearby house, a distant lawnmower revving, the faint backfiring of an engine somewhere far off. Otherwise quiet. Pacific. Bright and still. The calming call of a chirping bird. A distant dog's bark. I put my earbuds pack into place. Tension eased its grip. I was finally settling down and easing into my zone as "How to Disappear Completely" came on, blending me into my surroundings as though I were a vital part of it all, as though I were just as necessary as the looming trees and gravelly sidewalks and regal homes that monitored my progress. I breathed deeply and began to relax. Perhaps the day would work out well after all.

And just as this foolish thought flitted across my consciousness, I turned the corner and saw a perfect storm brewing ahead: a tall, thin man in a skin-tight full-body multi-colored marathon tracksuit jogging down the road while pushing a baby-filled stroller with a leashed golden retriever attached to the handle, leading the run. Everything else was instantly tuned out. I paused the music and stood still as the trio headed toward me, not bothering to disguise my stare. The man was moving at an impressive speed. Absurdly, he wore a cyclist's helmet that matched his tracksuit, as though he were the one most likely to be injured, even as the stroller sped over pebbles and uneven pavement, the dog loping ahead of them with his tongue lolling and flapping about. I was certain the stroller was going to tip over and spill out the precious cargo at any moment, but it just kept right on course, rolling smoothly ahead. It must have been specially designed for such activity, with super-tread heavy-duty tires and reinforced axles and ball-bearing wheelbases and a suspension system comparable to that of a small sports car. The kid was well secured to the thickly cushioned housing with a seatbelt and criss-crossed shoulder straps. Is it truly necessary, wise, or in any way practical to be jogging with a baby, not to mention the dog pulling the sled? I was only thinking of the safety of the child. Could this man have possibly imagined that this was somehow beneficial for his small passenger, to be jumbling about and fighting that onrush of air against his little face, to risk flipping out into the middle of the road with the slightest misstep? It was de-cidedly not smart. He was clearly unfit for fatherhood.

Pausing my iPod, I stood dumbly as they advanced. The father's rubber-soled steps provided a drumbeat to the drone of the swooshing wheels and the clicking of the dog's paws. He was wiry and well-defined, with slight but sturdy forearms and nicely rounded biceps bulging under the clinging spandex-blended suit, and he was so gaily colorful, like a plumed peacock. Even his ridiculous helmet sported several bright rainbow tints, drawing a sharp contrast with his extra dark wraparound sports sunglasses. I couldn't move, couldn't stop myself from staring. My eyes roved from man to boy to dog, and again I made no attempt to conceal my contemptuous gawking. It was so blatant that the man stopped short just in front of me, jogging in place to keep his momentum, the dog following suit (in terms of stopping, not trotting in place). He met my sunglassed gaze with his own variation, one that suggested a spark of aggression and a kind of moral superiority, as though he understood why I was looking (though he surely had no idea where my thoughts were headed as I looked at his baby) but felt I was not worthy of a response.

After a few seconds of mute staring—I, plunked into place like a man turned to stone; he, moving his legs over the same patch of pavement; the dog scratching under its chin with a hind leg; the kid watching it all in a semi-interested, semi-lost daze, as if it were a scene from some complicated foreign film that he was trying to follow from context since he was already there but really didn't care too much either way and could have just as happily napped through it all—the man jutted his chin forward confrontationally, spread out his hands, and in a mid-pitched, mildly nasal tone, said, "Got a problem?"

My instinct was to reply, *Fuck yes, I have a whole host of problems,* and to tear off his helmet without bothering to undo the chin strap and pummel his head to putty with it before ripping his son out of the racing stroller and taking him straight home. But of course, there were practical considerations. First, the dog was large enough to pose a threat, and probably protective of both his senior and junior masters. Second, I would surely be brought in for such an assault if I couldn't flee the scene in time, which was the last thing I needed. Still, the impulse was there, clawing at my surface, and while I silently struggled to tamp it down, the guy held his accusatory pose. Then he stopped moving his legs, slanted his body to the left, dipped his glasses so his eyes peeked out over the rims (though I couldn't make out much because I was mostly looking at the child from behind my own glasses), and said, "What?" My jaw dropped but my tongue stuck to the roof of my mouth. "What?" he repeated, yelling this time. The dog echoed with a bark and a lunge, rattling the stroller and provoking a little cough/cry from the infant.

"Calm down, Jake," he reprimanded.

For an instant, my breath caught, and I looked at the child and thought with a burst of excitement: *Another baby Jake!* Until I realized he was addressing the dog.

"What is your major malfunction?"

I paused, looked down, and mumbled, "Numbnuts." As a Kubrick fan, I was conflicted as to whether I should point out that the omission of that final word leaves the line hanging, impotent, but I could not resist.

"What? What the fuck did you call me?" He jutted his upper torso toward me aggressively, and then the dog lurched forward, as though the insult had been directed at him. The man had to hold the leash with two hands and dig into a deep, bent-knee stance to restrain the animal.

"No. I wasn't—that's the line. 'What is your major malfunction, *numbnuts*?' It's just—it feels somewhat incomplete without…*numbnuts*."

"I said, what is your major malfunction?"

I saw this was going nowhere. My father always said there was no trumping stupidity, so I acquiesced to his ignorance and dropped my charges.

"Nothing, nothing." I raised my open hands deferentially.

"Then why the *fuck*"—he paused for emphasis here—"are you staring at me?"

"Sorry. I thought you were someone else. I thought I knew you."

"Well, I'm glad you don't." He prolonged his pissy stare another few seconds before reprising his in-place trot, then said, "Come on, guys," spurring his company into action.

They were already fifty feet past me by the time I regained enough self-possession to move. I turned and called out, "Nice dog." There was no response.

The day was shattered. I watched the party responsible for this ruination recede out of sight and put Radiohead back on, skipping ahead to "Idioteque."

> *Who's in a bunker?*
> *Who's in a bunker?*
> *Women and children first*
> *And the children first*
> *And the children*
> *I'll laugh until my head comes off*
> *I'll swallow till I burst*

My unfrozen body felt like breaking into a run to shake off the remnants of the encounter, but I held back and walked as fast as possible without slipping into a jog, moving straight and with the fettered focus of a Clydesdale. I arrived back at the house in amazing time, sweat tickling my temples and dripping into one eye. Frazzled and not wanting to break my momentum lest my aggravation get the best of me, I stripped to my underwear, letting my clothes drop to the kitchen floor, went downstairs and hit the bag until my fists throbbed. This was followed by a long, slow dynamic-strength set. Then I ran upstairs to pose in the mirror before my sweat dried, masturbated a little (halting successfully before climax), and stepped into the shower, hoping the warm, sultry water would charm the venomous snake inside me.

Or maybe not. Maybe I didn't want the rage to go away. Because once I stopped resisting and just accepted it, embraced it, absorbed it and became one with it, once I let the rage take over and channel itself, it would allow me to function. If the rage was driving the ship now, perhaps it would let me along for the ride; perhaps it would let me be *me*.

I finished my shower and put on some clean underwear but the same clothes. Then I had a quick peanut butter and jelly sandwich, and I thought on what to do with the rest of the day.

•   •   •

Spending my time had always been an enigmatic issue for me, more so than for most people with regular jobs and familial commitments who come home from a taxing day at the office and a grueling commute to see the welcoming faces of wives and children and talk about their day over warm domestic meals and sneak in an hour or so of television before putting the kids to bed and perhaps getting a little midweek nookie, or the un-married ones who head for happy hour when the work bell rings, maybe share a cab with a coworker and have some dinner or catch a movie, or the ones who sit home alone every night wishing they had somewhere to go, something to do, someone to do it with. I was unlike any of these classes of contemporary humans. I stood alone. I had no work obligations, no friends, and no family (except my insane aunt who I suspect wants as much to be in contact with me as I do with her, which is to say not at all). I rarely had anywhere to be. My days conformed to no formal schedule apart from such that I arbitrarily devised. There were no external time constraints or agendas to be observed. I reveled in the wide-open nothingness of my life, luxuriated in the radically free nature of my hours. The thought of having to be somewhere at a certain time still evokes a kind of mental nausea in me. I would rather do nothing than have any sort of stricture imposed on my time, and most days I did quite a bit of nothing.

After my parents died, the only period of my life that involved any kind of outside influence was during my college years. Though there was absolutely no financial need, I received a full academic scholarship to a local university known dichotomously for its top-notch professors and bottom-notch students, usually spoiled suburban kids with doting wealthy parents. The university was offering full rides to superior high school seniors in order to raise the bar for their own student body, hoping to enhance its reputation and perhaps even bump up a notch or two on the accreditation and rankings scale. This never happened. The scholarship students took their honors courses and mingled almost exclusively with their own, while the moneyed moronic majority continued to doze through classes and congregate loudly in the hallways and commons, talking about football and pussy and the latest online games while the girls flipped their hair and chatted about makeup. Yet many of them managed to matriculate and eventually graduate with a largely symbolic bachelor's degree. As long as their parents still had their wealth, the world was their oyster.

But the brutish masses never bothered me. I enjoyed college. As a commuter, I didn't make any deep or lasting friendships, only the occasional acquaintance of the person sitting next to me in class, with whom I would chat now and then while waiting for the professor to begin. Once in a while we might have coffee in the cafeteria, maybe sit on the bench outside the humanities building on sunny days and discuss a certain book or lecture. I did not socialize off campus. I would drive to school, sit in class, and go home.

I had always been a good student. Though I studied little, I graduated from high school with a weighted average of 95.6. I was in the National Honor Society and on the "High Achiever" list every quarter since tenth grade. This is how I qualified for my scholarship. But regardless of my honors, I gleaned virtually nothing of intellectual substance from my high school years. My experience in higher education was a different matter. By the end of my sophomore year, I had declared a major in philosophy with a minor in comparative literature, two disciplines that have little practical use in the "real world." As I had little practical use for the real world, this was a perfect match. With my material needs well satisfied, I wished only to consume the greatest abundance of my time with reading and thinking. I had my rock to sit on. Why not enrich the mind?

After graduation—*summa cum laude*—the preponderance of my honors classmates went off to find high-profile jobs in the city. Some sought to add more letters to their names in grad school. Some got pregnant and took their posts as housewives. Others went off to Europe or Asia or Africa or some other exotic outpost to suck a bit more marrow out of life before settling down to the drudgery of middle-class American existence. For me, the end of college was concomitant with the conclusion of any kind of external structure to my days, and it represented the de facto terminus of my engagement with the world. Hours after the graduation ceremony—which I attended alone (though a few fellow graduates took pity on my solitude and pulled me into family pictures)—I took off my collegiate cap and gown and began the life I expected would continue until life itself ceased to continue.

Whatever superficial college relationships I cultivated ended abruptly with graduation, despite the customary exchanges of numbers and tepid promises of getting together. My peers from earlier days had mostly gone off to faraway colleges, starting new lives in new cities. Some would call me from time to time, or stop by on those requisite visits to the folks for the holidays. Initially, I indulged them. I would agree to go for a drink or to shoot some pool and talk about the old days that I had absolutely no interest in reliving. Then I shut it all down. I ignored their calls and didn't respond to their messages, left their emails unanswered and their Christmas cards unreciprocated. (It is surprising how many people still send greeting cards.) Eventually, they stopped calling, and I was left alone for good.

In solitude, my life assumed an almost militant uniformity: eating, sleeping, reading, working out, a little TV, walks around the neighborhood, visits to the park now and then—such were the activities that I indulged to pass the time. Some might say that, with all my financial resources, I was wasting my life, that I could have had so much more, that I could have used the financial freedom bequeathed to me through tragedy to transcend that tragedy and make something more of my existence. But really, what more could I want? A penthouse in the city and a young trophy wife to take around to chichi restaurants and tony nightclubs? Lavish overseas voyages? An even larger suburban house, maybe a new construction in a gated community, with a well-paying corporate job to keep my fortune growing and my mind and body busy? A nice plump woman and a couple of adoring (and adorable) children? A family van for the weekends, a sedan for the wife and a flashy sports car to satisfy my own wild side? What is more? More money? More things? More travel? Sex?

No. I was fine as I was. I wouldn't have had it any other way. Whatever benefit a more involved life might offer is easily outweighed by the complications and inconveniences that necessarily attend. Life is a series of inconveniences, one long drawn-out hassle. To paraphrase Cioran: The inconvenience starts with being born and continues until death. Though there is no way to completely circumvent the countless practical mundanities that mire us like quicksand, no way to truly leave behind the *ten thousand things of this world*, as the Asian sages would put it, I believe one would be hard-pressed to find someone who lived less encumbered by the traditional trappings of a bourgeois American life than I. A prisoner in solitary confinement would come close, but he still has to see the guards, to hear the other inmates chatter, to visit the clinic, etc. I, however, could go for weeks or even months without seeing, hearing, or talking to another human being, provided a stocked pantry and other essentials remained at my disposal. I thought about trying this, as a sort of social sensory deprivation experiment to see how long I could thrive in complete and unadulterated seclusion. Society would miss me as little as I missed it.

I could drop out of public sight and nobody would notice. No one would bat an eyelash at my disappearance. If I died in the house, my corpse would lie *in situ* reeking of putrefaction until the authorities showed up to confront me for unpaid property taxes.

I don't care if I'm remembered after I'm gone, or who remembers me. From the viewpoint of eternity—*sub specie aeternitatis*—human existence, collectively or individually, is of no lasting value; it has not the slightest effect on the universe in which we are contained. People like to believe their existence counts for something. They love others, or hate others, or hurt or help others, all under a false conviction that their deeds contribute in some appreciable way to the commonweal. They want to believe that their existence amounts to something more meaningful than a mere concatenation of moments, something more substantial than an inconsequential blip in space and time. Worse, they need to believe that the entire course of human history has a sort of metaphysical trajectory, a greater goal toward which we, as a race, are inevitably moving. Closer with every generation. This is pure illusion. Zero plus zero will always be zero. No single human life counts for anything but a few nugatory years of struggle and suffering, soon to be forgotten forever. And if no individual life has any lasting universal meaning, then neither do a few billion individual lives, nor as many untold billions who have lived throughout history.

Most people are content to lurch forth through this fantasy, building fragile, fatuous bubbles of import around themselves and their connections—empty shells of made-up meaning in which they writhe. They lull themselves into believing they are here for some transcendental reason, that their actions make a difference, that their little lives, their handful of futile years, count for something. It would almost be cute, were it not so sad.

. . .

I was still restless. I would have gone for another walk on such a splendid afternoon, but that option had been blackened by my earlier encounter.

I decided to go to the bookstore. I love the stubborn audacity of books—physical books with deadwood pages. I love that books continue to exist in spite of a seemingly boundless cultural drift toward sterile touch-screen digitization. This fills me with something that dimly resembles joy. Perhaps I would even treat myself to a skim latte and a low-fat raspberry crème fraiche scone while I browsed through fitness magazines and punk rock rags.

The trauma of my earlier confrontation was gradually subsiding. As I started the car, my halo of pique gave way to a feeling of mild optimism at the thought of spending unaccounted hours among books, quietly ambling up and down uncrowded rows of novels and essays, philosophical treatises and reams of unread poetry. The day was still bright and beautiful, though the lowered sun angled its waves a bit more gently, and the air had cooled.

There was a feeling of placid unconcern, as though the entire physical world was done for the day.

I put on the Strokes' *Is This It* and drummed the steering wheel with both forefingers, whining along with Julian Casablanca's lackadaisical vocals and bobbing my head to the school-band beat. It wasn't yet rush hour, so the roads were relatively quiet, apart from some school buses congesting the side streets. The long dirty-yellow beasts ground to slow halts every few blocks, unlatching their big red flashing stop sign appendages to ensure the safe egress of the restive children within. And of course there were the soccer moms in their SUVs, hauling their sons and daughters to various after-school appointments and activities—hockey practice and tae kwon do, piano lessons and foreign language instruction. Mandarin is all the rage in the affluent suburbs.

As I waited behind a school bus, keeping the legally prescribed twenty feet of distance, I noticed a silver Chrysler Pacifica hybrid minivan pull up to the curb on the opposite side of the street. A woman with dark curly hair got out of the driver's side. She was a short Hispanic with wide flat features that reminded me of a young Rosario Dawson, dumpy around the midsection (perhaps owing to some lingering post-pregnancy weight) and big in the breasts. She wore bland gray sweatpants and a matching sweatshirt and new white sneakers. Even from this distance she exuded a bedraggled, too-busy-for-makeup look that women often assume when learning to live with their first babies. I watched as she circled around the vehicle to open the rear passenger side door, as she began to unstrap a child from the car seat. Halfway through the procedure, she stopped and hurried back around to her side, opened the door and leaned down to look for something. The back of her shirt lifted to reveal a roll of side-fat and a solid inch of ass cleavage. As I watched her searching under the floor mat and around the pedals, a sequence of disjointed beeps jolted me from my idling surveillance. I looked into the rear-view mirror to see another woman in the car behind me, and another child in the car seat behind her. She lifted a hand off the wheel in frustration, mouthing some apparent invective into the dash. I waved apologetically and gently accelerated, though I would have preferred to jam into reverse and smash into her with as much momentum as I could have gathered at such short distance, repeatedly ramming her grill until it smoked and leaked mysterious automotive fluids. I would have preferred to then get out and calmly remove the tire iron from my trunk. I would have preferred to then smash her window in and pull her out by her hair and finally shove the business end of the iron down her throat as far as the thing would go.

I made a sleek and careful U-turn, nimbly whirling around into the other lane like a shark bending its body to swim back toward unsuspecting prey. I eased up behind mother and child.

The bus had continued on its route. There was no one else. It was a quiet side street overhung with large leafy trees and well-spaced plots of land. My Civic is an ultra-low-emission vehicle and is extremely quiet when running at low speeds or idling, so even though I was no more than a few feet from the woman, she was none the wiser, squatting now, still rummaging around the floor in search of—what? Money? Keys? Pacifier? Glasses?

I turned off the ignition but left the battery running

so I could continue listening to my iPod on low through the stereo as I watched her frustrated attempts to find whatever. Still no cars. No more buses. No other people. I killed the battery, powered down the iPod, opened the door and stepped out. I flipped my hood up over my head and zipped the front of my hoodie, making sure the Ray-Bans remained secured to my face. I left the door partially open and walked stealthily toward the crouching woman. *Like a ninja*, I thought. I arrived before her and looked around to be sure there were no conspicuous onlookers. It was a residential area, so I couldn't account for meddlesome neighbors peeking out their front windows or suddenly emerging from garages and front doors, but it was a chance I was willing to take. The risk added to the excitement. My heart rate quickened. My palms moistened.

"Can I help you or something?" I said.

She turned and jumped and shrieked all at once, jerking herself out of the car's cavernous bottom and banging her head against the underside of the dash. When she saw me standing there with my hands held up inoffensively, trying to look just as startled, she exhaled nervously and put one hand to her chest and the other to the back of her struck head and looked up and smiled and said, "You scared me." She had just the kind of accent I expected.

"Sorry." I smiled back. "Didn't mean to."

"It's okay," she said, laughing in spite of herself, moving from a squat to a kneel, reaching back into the car with a searching hand.

I inched forward until I was positioned just behind her, blocking any possible route of escape, then I peered over her shoulder at the sleeping child in the car seat.

"Got it!" Drawing herself back out but remaining on her knees, the woman looked up and smiled, flushed with success. Then she held up the object of her efforts: a smart phone in a cyan shell. Tightly clutching the recovered item, she huffed in exasperated relief. "Can't live without these things," she announced, and looked at me expecting casual affirmation, which I offered.

She had a broad face with small dark eyes and a large mouth. Her features were framed by an overflowing crop of ringlets that bounced down her back. I smiled demurely with closed lips, nodded once again as though in goodbye, casually tapped the upper edge of the car door, checked around one last time for witnesses. Then the opening riff of the Stooges' "Down on the Street" discharged in my brain, and I lunged violently forward, laying into her with a vicious right to the chin.

I felt nothing upon impact, as though I had punched through a paper target or a giant soap bubble. An instant KO. She never saw it coming. Her body crumpled like sodden cardboard, slumping back against the car, arms limp at her sides, head dangling over the space where a minute before her hands were searching. My chest heaved and my teeth and fists were still tightly clenched, but there was no panic, no nerves. Just a feeling of urgency, of intently focused awareness. I had a task to complete and I would proceed with expedience and efficiency. I was in full control. A professional at the top of his game.

Prepared to follow up with more blows if necessary (hoping, in a way, that I would have to), I bent down to make sure the woman was out. Then I shifted her around and encircled her torso with my arms, lifted her into the car and positioned her behind the wheel as though she had passed out drunk. She was as heavy as she looked, maybe heavier, a dense little flabby person who smelled of liquid sanitizer.

There were still no cars, still no people. If I were a different sort of man, a believer in anything, any kind of providence or higher power, I would have said it was fate, or the hands of the Gods reaching down to aid me in carrying out such sacred work. But no. I just got lucky. And that's just as good as divine intervention. Probably better, as there is no expectation of gratitude, no debt to pay back in the form of prayer or deed or donation or whatnot.

I closed her door and hustled around to the rear passenger side, where there slept a beautiful little girl in a zipper-front pink onesie with sewn-in rubber-bottom feet and a hood and a big plum heart across the chest in which was embroidered DADDY'S GIRL, in deep purple. It was quite adorable, albeit in a cloying, bourgeois way. I leaned in close. She had the softest-looking olive skin I'd ever seen, and even at this early stage of development she promised to be prettier than her mother. She was about the same size as Jake, maybe a bit smaller.

"Hello there," I cooed, as I carefully unbuckled her straps, shaking my head over the negligence of the poorly fastened car seat.

She awakened with a grunt when I lifted her into my arms, hurrying the process while trying to remain gentle in my handling of her. Just as I secured her and closed the door, a car approached from behind. I slid to the ground and leaned close to the door as it glided past, probably without a second look at us. There was nothing to see. Just a couple of cars parked curbside.

The child was almost fully awake now, and none too pleased to find herself pressed against the shoulder of a stranger. She seemed on the verge of a real hard cry as soon as her faculties were fully regained, so I straightened up and dashed back to my own car, slipping in just as two SUVs rolled slowly by.

"Whew," I whistled at the kid in my lap. "That was too close." It probably wasn't close at all, but it felt like something I should say. And I needed something to say, for her sake.

I also needed a name for the child, but that could wait. My first imperative was to get safely away from the scene. I turned the ignition key and the Strokes' "Barely Legal" swelled to mid-volume, scoring the moments that followed as I checked the rear-view and eased back onto the road toward home.

There would be no book browsing on this day. Greater things awaited.

   •   •   •

I called her Juanita.

She wailed the whole short trip home. The first few seconds didn't bother me. After a minute or so it started to grate. Then it became almost painful, as though the sound were searing my eardrums, boring straight into my brain. I blasted the music to drown her out, but her volume was formidable. Juanita was a good-looking child, but she was clearly no Jake. While Jake had been well-mannered and agreeable from the start, this one hadn't offered me so much as a smile. She just squirmed and tossed and fidgeted on my lap as though it were the last place she wanted to be. Her humorless black eyes glared grimly at me with unmistakable resentment, and her flailing hands made no effort to clutch my fingers; they simply grabbed at the empty space above her as though there were some invisible escape latch she could pull to land herself back with her mother.

Which made me wonder how long the woman would remain unconscious. I had never knocked anyone out before. In fact, I had never even punched a person before. Only a stuffed leather bag. I was impressed with myself. Yes, she was a defenseless and unsuspecting target, and yes, she was smaller than I, but still, a one-punch knockout is nothing to sneeze at. Reflecting on my accomplishment, I looked at my knuckles, curled white around the wheel, and noticed redness and already a little bruising, along with some noticeable swelling around the tops of the first two. There was also some minor throbbing, or so I imagined. It seemed a bit early to feel it. I considered that it might be psychosomatic, a sensory delusion triggered by the sight of damage to my hand and compounded through my recollection of the moment of impact, mental facts translated into physical sensation.

By the time we arrived safely in the garage with the door lowered behind us, Juanita was hysterical. She bawled uncontrollably. I was almost afraid she would choke on her own gasping. I resolved to quiet her.

"There, there now."

This sounded trite. The words felt funny issuing from my mouth, but it was the only script that came to mind.

"Shhhh. Shhhh. It's okay. It's okay."

I patted her soft little head, rubbed the sparse silky hair atop it, bobbed her body rhythmically in my arms.

"Come on, let's go inside. You'll feel better there."

This assurance was mainly for me. Juanita's incessant crying left me feeling unsafe and exposed, anxious to get into the house. Was she, in her own galling, infantile way, trying to upset me? Already I could tell there would be no bond between us, as there had been with Jake. In the moment, I partly regretted the effort I had expended to bring us together, but with or without her cooperation, my work would proceed.

She cried as I brought her inside, cried harder when I sat with her at the kitchen table and tried to rock her into sedation, and cried harder still—which I wouldn't have thought possible—when I laid her in the basin (which I had forgotten to wash the night before and had to thoroughly scrub and dry while baby Juanita lay squirming on the table, almost rolling off at one point) on a nice clean towel.

She was relentless, inconsolable. The effect her unremitting tantrum exacted on my constitution was so utterly exhausting that I considered making a quick end of it and writing the whole fiasco off as a loss; the cost of doing business. But first, I would try reasoning with her. I was fully aware that she wouldn't understand my words, but I hoped her bantling sensibilities would somehow be receptive to their import. I needed her to recognize the stress her ceaseless squawking was levying on me.

"Please, Juanita. You're making this very, very difficult for the both of us," tenderly pleading, imploring her to meet me halfway. "Please, now. Be a good girl."

But no. She refused to give an inch. She was not a likable baby, and I felt certain she would have grown into an even less likable adult, and the thought of this made me angry. The rage I had stifled earlier in the day rose back up like a fever that worsens at night. I banged the kitchen table with the bottom of my fist, vibrating her basin. No change. Covering my ears and closing my eyes, I yelled STOP, holding the word long and loud so it temporarily hushed her howling. But as soon as I finished, there it was again. Clearly, she wasn't going to stop.

Clearly, I had to stop her.

This was unfortunate. I would have preferred to unwind a bit, to get to know the child and have her know me, to let my anticipation grow to its natural peak and allow events to unfold at a comfortable, unhurried pace. As it was, the entire procedure felt rushed and perfunctory, lacking ritual and ceremony. My heart wasn't in it. I wasn't savoring the experience. I felt harried and disorganized, and moreover, I realized that I had no idea how I was going to take care of her. I only knew that it had to be different than it had been with Jake. I did not want to sully his memory by re-enacting the same sacred liturgy with this undeserving infant, with this unpleasant child who just *would not stop crying*.

•   •   •

An idea came to me. I had recently seen a documentary on the Nanking Massacre, when the Japanese invaded China at the start of the Second World War. The atrocities of Nanking are singular in the annals of modern history, rivaling even Auschwitz in their enormity, if not their magnitude. The Japanese soldiers derived sublime pleasure through the infliction of unimaginable pain on the civilian Chinese. It was more like torture porn than a war story. They would bayonet a pregnant Chinese woman, slice her belly open vertically and extract the fetus on the blade's tip as though they were removing an olive from a martini with a toothpick, then stick the butt of the rifle in the ground and let the baby slowly slide down the blade before finishing off the mother, if she survived the initial trauma. They would gang rape pubescent girls and then fillet them, cutting up from the vagina straight through the torso and sometimes right through the head so the body was vertically bisected. Their purpose wasn't extermination as such, but degradation and torment.

They sought to mete out as much pain and suffering as possible.

What struck me most was the primary role the Japanese sword—the katana, the ancient weapon of the samurai that soldiers still carried and used during the war—played in this sickening drama. A well-crafted katana, traditionally made from specialized Japanese steel that has been aged to perfection, hand-forged and polished for weeks with increasingly fine-grained polishing stones until the surface shines like a streakless mirror, can cut through flesh and bone with relative ease. It is said that a skilled samurai could slice off a head in a single fluid arc. There is a Japanese phrase that roughly translates as, "One cut, one kill." This is why.

One of these swords was in my possession. It was purchased for me by my father on one of our weekend trips to Chinatown when I was in my early teens. We would go there one Sunday a month for dim sum. We would stroll the crowded streets that stunk of fish and incense, browsing sidewalk stands full of imitation designer handbags and knockoff high-end shoes. We would stop in the little tchotchke shops full of Buddhist statuettes and good-fortune trinkets and tourist T-shirts with iron-on Chinese characters saying things like LOVE, PEACE, LUCK, WEALTH. Then we would end the evening with espresso and pastry in neighboring Little Italy before trekking back to the suburbs. On one of these monthly day trips, I was seduced into a store by its window display of armed mannequins in ninja outfits and ancient Asian warrior garb wielding short swords and nunchaku, throwing stars and bo staffs. I never imagined I could convince my parents to let me come home with one of these armaments, but my father, perhaps moved by my uncharacteristic enthusiasm, relented. "Choose wisely," he said. I exited the store with an authentic, imported Tamahagane steel Japanese katana, a 40" razor-sharp *daitō*, or long sword, with an elegantly textured black-on-black scabbard, a woven cord handle, and a convenient waist cord to strap around my jeans.

I was ecstatic. And even though I had to promise never to play with it or even touch it without strict parental supervision, I can still summon the residue of the euphoria that flooded through me as I held the sheathed sword on my lap the entire hour-long ride home, caressing it like a beloved new pet while imagining all the backyard adventures I would have with it. No such adventures came to pass. In fact, I hardly ever touched the thing after the first week. What could I have done with it? Chop off my own finger? Break the blade against a tree? I wasn't a martial artist, and I would soon outgrow the fascinations of my childhood.

So it sat on the top shelf of my father's closet, untouched for years, and it was there on that day, as Juanita lay squealing at full volume in the basin in front of me.

Dusk was fast settling, but there was still light in the sky, and though I hated to act prematurely, Juanita left me no choice. I set the basin on the floor—for fear that her tireless thrashing would eventually spill her over the side of the table—took the stairs two at a time, and stopped in front of the closed door to my parents' bedroom.

Rarely did I enter this room. There was always an odd, unfixed sensation when I crossed the threshold. It was neither sadness nor a longing for the past. There was no flood of images of yesteryear, no Proustian flurry of archaic memories, which might or might not be genuine. No pangs of loss, no spasms of loneliness, no rivers of regret. It was just the peculiar impression of being someplace that has no relevance to the present, as though I were watching an old movie that I remembered vaguely from childhood; as though I had entered a wax museum marked by the conspicuous absence of human figures. I would turn the knob and feel the resistance of the warped wooden frame and the click of the metal tongue slipping out of the latch, and a kind of quivering would run through me. With each step deeper into the white carpet, I felt less a part of my life. Yet this was in no way depleting. I was calmly aware, intensely focused.

The room was unchanged from the morning they left for the airport, the bed as my mother made it, the items on the bathroom counter lying where they were—a brand-new lavender-scented hand soap, my mother's brush with strands of her hair coiled in it, my father's razor and aftershave, their electric toothbrushes with individualized heads, a small towel draped neatly over the wall rack, a few random lipstick tubes, a jar of cotton balls and swabs, bottles of body wash and shampoo in the shower—a half-read book on my father's nightstand next to his clock radio (which I adjusted from time to time after blackouts and such), a pump-action jar of moisturizer and a box of tissues and a small framed portrait of my mother and her father (whom I never met) at her wedding, the jewelry boxes and decorative candles and bottles of perfume and cologne on their large shared bureau, my mother's worn white leather slippers beside the door, a fake potted plant in the corner next to the television, atop which rested the remote.

Thom Yorke was in my head again: *Everything in its right place.*

I have a cleaning person who comes every other week, a quiet little old Chilean named Mathilde, and though I do ask her to freshen up the room, it is with strict instructions not to move anything, simply to dust and spruce up the surface of things, leaving the arrangement of objects exactly as it has been all these years. The first few times, I stayed there to watch her work. I'm sure this made her uneasy, but it was important that she understood precisely what was expected. After a few sessions she was well used to it.

Absorbed in my cocoon of awareness and insentience, with even Juanita's tireless yelping drowned out by the nullifying power of this space, I stood in the center of the room, between the bed and the large shared dresser running nearly the full length of the wall. I stood there and looked at myself in the expansive tripartite mirror hanging over the dresser. Seeing one's reflection can be a profoundly uncanny experience, and yet we do it every single day, multiple times a day, usually without a moment's consideration of how bizarre it is to apprehend a detached likeness of oneself. There is always a disturbing sense of distance between me and the image, and this forces me to face the uncrossable gulf between my self—my psyche, soul, intellect, or whatever incorporeal thing makes me who I am or who I think I am—and my body. And this, in turn, compels me to contemplate the mysterious link between my mind and the thoughts that inhabit it—thoughts that come and go, second by second, nesting and plotting and competing for position. There is a part unknown that bridges these thoughts and obscures their wellspring, that conceals what may lie at the lowest level of being, if there is a lowest level. It might just as well be an endless series of images reflecting back on each other, a Cartesian hall of mirrors with no firm center anywhere. Maybe there is nothing solid at the core. Maybe it is all just mirrors.

There was a sword to retrieve. I had to pry away from rumination. I opened my father's walk-in closet and reached back behind rows of hanging dress shirts and shelves of old sweaters and travel pouches for toiletries and a waist-high stack of shoeboxes and a strange white Panama hat that I had never seen him wear, and there it was, wedged against the wall, shoved into the corner with a white sheet draped halfway over it like an ill-fitting burial shroud: my cherished and long-neglected katana.

I brought it out slowly, holding it with both hands so the blade wouldn't slip out. The scabbard was covered in dust, and a strand of spider web hung from its handle. I left the room and crept all the way downstairs while holding it perfectly horizontal like a full platter of dishes. It was only when I got to the kitchen that I proceeded to wipe it down over the sink with a clean damp cloth and some Murphy's Oil Soap, working through the ornamentally cut grooves and surface patterns until they rose from under the accumulation of the years. When it seemed as new as the day I first held it, I gripped the handle just below the guard and firmly but slowly pulled back, snapping the bronze collar free to release a few inches of blade. The white-blue metal glinted in the high hats as I rotated it like a roasting spit. The cutting edge blurred down to a razor-fine sharpness upon whose upper border ran a wavering temper pattern that seemed to absorb rather than deflect light, and an undulated ridge line ran parallel to both cutting and non-cutting edges. It was beautiful.

I drew the rest of the blade out to freedom and held the braided hilt with the dual-handed grip of a warrior, waving it with slow gracefulness as though it were a lightsaber (even hearing that distinctive whirring sound in my head as I cut sharply through the air). Wielding this awesome weapon made me feel larger than life.

I re-sheathed it, held the scabbard to the left of my waist, dropped into an attack stance, reached back with my right hand and yanked the sword out across my body, thrusting it down and forward so it whipped through the air with an authoritative sibilance. I then reinforced my grip with the other hand and swung it back horizontally at neck level, as though to decapitate an adversary, finally bringing it up over and behind my head and pulling it down while dropping to one knee in a powerful *coup de grâce*, whereupon I remained kneeling with the weapon extended before me in both hands, fingers wrapped firmly around the handle, upper arms and forearms taut and hard, shoulders straight and locked, eyes focused down on the unsharpened back of the blade.

$\cdot$ $\cdot$ $\cdot$

Juanita was still crying. It seemed a feat beyond human endurance to cry for such duration and at such volume. I considered that she might be hungry, or thirsty, or that she needed to be changed, but in my haste, I had forgotten to grab her bottle. I didn't want to waste another jar of banana baby food on her. Nor did I feel like washing her if she had wet herself or worse. It was best just to be done with it.

I had to test the blade first. More specifically, I had to test my ability to strike with it. It may have been perfectly honed and balanced, but I was no swordsman, and as a result I could have ended up cutting myself or unintentionally damaging something other than the target. There would have to be some kind of dry run. A rehearsal, of sorts.

I slipped the sword back into its scabbard and placed it on the countertop. As I regarded my surroundings, I remembered that I had purchased a watermelon the previous Sunday when I stocked up on oatmeal, milk, and tuna. I also came home with a few apples, oranges, and pears. This was unusual for me, since I have never cared for fruit of any species. Indeed, it is a small labor to get even a tiny grape down my throat. Just the same, I would from time to time find myself purchasing a variety of fruit in the hope that I should develop a taste for it, in the interest of bettering my health. I never acquired a taste for any of it. It was never more than repugnant medicine. In fact, I find fruit to be so unappetizing that I have cultivated a suspicious regard for people who insist that they enjoy it. I don't believe this is possible—I think anyone who claims to actually like eating fruit is lying to himself, or to others, or both.

I had purchased these fruits for their touted health benefits, dimly imagining I might have a slice of apple or a few balls of melon instead of a Twinkie while watching reruns of *Family Guy* late at night. Even as I was filling my carriage at the supermarket, however, I knew it was more likely that the items would be left to rot in the little ceramic bowl (which my parents, who also were not fruit eaters, used in the same way) until I would accept the loss and toss the remains. Now it seemed the neglected produce would serve a purpose after all. It was most serendipitous.

I removed a large bamboo cutting board from the cabinet, placed it atop the counter, and positioned a plump ripe Granny Smith at its center. It seemed best to practice with a small target rather than risk making a mess of the watermelon—there would be enough of a mess later. Standing with my legs planted shoulder-length apart, knees slightly bent, I removed the sword once again from its holder, fixed my eyes on the blade, and steadily lowered it until it hovered a few inches above the apple. In full focus, I slowly raised the blade back over my head, held it there for a few seconds, and brought it down hard on the exhale, slicing through the target and thwacking the wood with a loud crack. I froze, keeping the blade down against the board. It wasn't a perfectly equal bisection, but the apple was cleanly split in two, with each side toppled so the fleshy, seeded meat of its interior lay exposed. As I slid the blade back, I noticed a groove of about a quarter of an inch in the wood of the cutting board. The board was designed to withstand culinary knifework, but perhaps the warranty did not cover samurai usage.

Juanita finally stopped crying. Her silence seemed to coincide with the sound of the sword striking the board, as though it were a teacher smacking a ruler across her desk to end all the student chatter taking over the room. I tiptoed over to see if she had fallen asleep. She hadn't. She was just lying there, looking up quizzically.

"There now. Not so bad here, is it?"

She turned her head and reached up, her hands grasping out as though trying to get hold of some invisible bar. I bent over and inspected the basin. It didn't smell or look wet.

"Good girl." I attempted to cheer her, smiling widely. This provoked no response apart from the same cagey stare.

"Just relax now," I said. "I'll be with you in a few minutes."

I could have probably gone right to it, but diligence advised another test run. There was nothing worse than a flubbed execution; I had seen enough botched beheadings on the Internet to know what an ugly business it could be. The watermelon closely approximated Juanita's weight and density, so it was in my best interest to see how well I could slice it with one strike. But the bare truth was that I was having fun—I very much wanted to hack into that big burly mound of green rind just to prolong the festivities. I hoisted the massive fruit onto to the cutting board and angled it to receive the blade across its length. Dispensing with elaborate preparations, I lifted the sword over my head and swung it down with a severe grunt. To my profound disappointment, the blade lodged halfway into the melon, stuck like an absurd parody of Excalibur. I jiggled it, yanked it back, thrust it forward, but it was firmly wedged in place, so I had to slide it slowly out backwards. Once dislodged, I brought the sword to the sink and wiped it clean with a damp paper towel. Flustered, but determined not to be bested by this melon, I balanced it again and prepared for a widthwise strike. I gnarled like a beast as the blade whisked and once again became cemented in its center. This was so very disheartening. The only consolation was that Juanita did not witness my sorry performance. It would not inspire confidence.

"Fuck me," I exclaimed in exasperation. Then I froze in fear of rekindling Juanita's hysteria. To my relief, she remained silent.

Fired up with a frustration that verged on rage, I stared down the melon as though it were a recalcitrant enemy combatant. Without bothering to wipe the blade, I began to chop frantically into it, slashing from all angles. Chunks of rind and interior viscera were shaved and lopped off in random, uneven patterns, yet despite doing my worst, the fruit's overall form remained intact. Slivered as it was, the deepest wounds were still from the first two cuts.

I was close to tears.

I paused and took a sharp breath. Summoning my last reserve of strength, I arched the sword as far back over my head as my arms and shoulders would allow, bent low, and then shot straight up, gathering my knees in around my chest and getting a good foot of air as I opened my mouth and let out a bestial war cry and swung down with all my kinetic energy. I shut my eyes at the last second, the moment of impact. Then I felt nothing but the unyielding crunch of metal against wood.

It was a trifling victory, but I was satisfied. Life is such an unrewarding endeavor. It is well that we should graciously accept and cherish these little gifts, especially during the long, lean seasons.

·   ·   ·

Juanita started to cry again. I would not let it get to me. I would not let her ruin this.

I grabbed my iPod and clamped it to my belt and stuck the earbuds in nice and deep to drown out as much of the child's blubbering as possible. Ordinarily, I would listen to the CD player in the kitchen because it is preferable not to have the music tunneled directly into my ears, but I felt like hearing Sinatra's "I've Got the World on a String," and I didn't want to break the momentum by traipsing all the way upstairs to get the album when it was at my fingertips in digital format. Within seconds, Frank's crooning overpowered the baby's sorrowful sobs, and I sung along cheerfully as I cleaned and sheathed the blade, as I scooped and dumped the watermelon's mutilated carcass into the trash, as I scrubbed the cutting board and left it to dry on the rack, as I wiped down the counter and floor, where watermelon innards had sploshed and quickly congealed to a sweet, sticky residue.

Normally, even the slightest untidiness would cause

me conniptions, but on this night, nothing would stand in my way. Frank sang. I sang with him:

I've got the world on a string
sittin' on a rainbow
got that string around my finger
Lucky me, can't you see I'm in love

And I *was* in love—with the moment, with myself in the moment, with life as it was in the moment. Who cared what the next day would bring? I was precisely where I wanted to be, doing exactly what I wanted to be doing, and I wasn't about to let some stupid watermelon or cranky baby muddy the clear waters of my temporal bliss.

I did a little Rat Pack sway and shuffle as I went to the garage to get a piece of heavy-duty tarpaulin that my father used to drape over the outdoor furniture in the winter before we had a shed built in the backyard. He kept the tarp in case a reason for its use ever arose. I smiled, thinking my father could never have imagined what kind of use his son would find for it. I took pride in my resourcefulness.

As I unpacked the tarp from a masking-taped cardboard box, I wondered what other forgotten items I might have to unearth, and I was overcome with childlike hopefulness and optimism. I chose the medium-sized tarp, a shiny dark brown 10' x 10' canvas sheet that was used for the glass-top patio table that we would sit around during summer barbecues. I selected this one as opposed to the smaller ones, which were used for sealing up individual chairs, or the extra-large one that we used to drape over the whole ensemble as a secondary shield against especially harsh winters. They were stacked snuggly on top of each other, folded with military precision into small dense squares arranged by size with the largest on the bottom. My parents were always meticulous in their housekeeping, and I have inherited—perhaps exaggerated—this tendency. As a result, the house might have seemed *unlived in*. To the undiscerning eye, it might have seemed cold and uninviting. This was fine with me. I had no desire to entertain guests.

Juanita was howling at full strength when I returned from the garage, her bawls slicing through Sinatra. "Hang in there, little one," I reassured her, trying hard not to let her get to me. "It's almost time."

I grabbed the sword and cutting board and headed downstairs to make the final preparations, setting up an old 4' x 4' cushioned vinyl soft-top bridge table with folding legs that had been languishing in the storage room for years, even before my parents' disappearance. One more old thing reclaimed from the dust of the past. The basement was large—nearly the full length and width of the house—and nicely finished in cedar paneling running in diagonal slants from floor to ceiling. The panels were interspersed with slats of mirror. The wall-to-wall medium-gray carpet was tightly woven. Aside from my punching bag, which hung from a chain attached to a joist behind a ceiling panel, there was a couch and an ancient TV from the seventies that my parents brought from their first apartment (the thing hadn't worked in years, but I refused to get rid of it) and a ping-pong table that I received for my fifteenth birthday (sagging noticeably in the middle but still playable). I would sometimes flip half of it up to form a wall and challenge myself to a little one-on-one.

I spread the tarp over the carpet and placed the bridge table at its center. Then I placed the cutting board squarely in the middle of the table so that it resembled a ritualistic alter, constructed ad hoc.

I felt I was forgetting something. It had all come together too easily. As Sinatra sang "Fly Me to the Moon," I pranced back upstairs to retrieve the final and most important piece of the puzzle, little Juanita. Having finally tired herself out from another extended bout of crying, she was weakly squirming but otherwise compliant as I lifted her up and out of the basin, held her airborne above my face, and stared at her seriously. She looked around, making the most of this chance to take in her surroundings. Then she focused on me, her black eyes exploring my face as though searching for signs of what I had planned.

"Better not to know," I whispered. "Surprises are fun."

It was then that I noticed her darkened lower half, soiled and wet. Fortunately, I was able to avoid touching that portion of her. Keeping my grip under her arms and holding her out so as not to contaminate myself, we started downstairs. Juanita scanned the strange scenery curiously. She still looked grouchy, but she did not cry. I am very grateful that she refrained from crying during those final minutes. Maybe she wasn't such a bad little girl after all.

Softly, very softly, I laid her faceup on the cutting board on the tarp-covered table, and I thought through the logistical details of what would follow, recalling the trouble with the watermelon. Though I felt certain that she would not present the same degree of difficulty—no baby's body could be as tough as a watermelon rind—I wanted to be sure. I wanted to avoid even a fraction of that mess. Looking up to find my thoughts, I noticed that there were some uncovered quarter-windows at the top of the walls, one opposite and two to the side. These were small windows, not easily accessible from the outside, but eyeballs into the interior nonetheless. A shudder passed through me. I thought of crime documentaries and procedural melodramas where there was always some detail that passed unnoticed, something seemingly inconsequential that would break the case. I ran upstairs to fetch some tin foil and proceeded to block out the windows with reinforced sheets of the stuff. It might have looked a bit suspicious from the outside, but the safety gains made the tradeoff worth it.

The baby on the chopping block was not crying for a change but uttering shallow, breathy noises that seemed to lodge in its throat. It moved its limbs as though swimming in place, reminding me of a fleshy turtle rolled over on its shell.

I looked around to make sure there wasn't anything else I had neglected. Everything seemed to be in place. Everything was secure. The windows were covered, all doors were double locked, and the perimeter was alarmed. The entire house was hermetically sealed, yet something was wrong. I didn't feel *ready*. Was it the music?

I love Sinatra, but the situation called for a different soundtrack. Something with more of a drive. I switched over to the Velvet Underground—"Waiting for the Man." The bursting chords and pounding piano pulsed through me, followed by Lou's implacable monotone:

> *Up to Lexington, one two five*
> *feel sick and dirty, more dead than alive*

I was ready.

I pulled the sword out of its scabbard and took a few practice swipes in the air, and I was even tempted to take a hack at the heavy bag, just to watch the sand spill out. But I loved my bag. I needed it.

Meanwhile, Juanita had somehow managed to turn herself over and was worming toward the edge of the table. I made haste to intervene, laughing lovingly at her mischief.

"Silly goose. You're going to hurt yourself that way."

I placed her back on the block and she began crying again. She really was a bratty little thing, resorting to tantrums whenever she couldn't get her way. I would be glad to be done with her.

"Okay, no more dillydallying," I announced. My voice was authoritative, as though I were spurring myself into action, even if I could barely hear myself over the music.

I raised the volume higher.

I wondered if I should remove her outfit but decided it didn't really matter.

With my free left hand I seized her by the torso. The vehemence of her crying vibrated through my palm and fingers as they touched her chest and swung her sideways so that her body was perpendicular to mine.

> *Baby don't you holler, darlin' don't you bawl and shout*

She squirmed fiercely, as though she knew what was about to happen and lamented the cruel randomness that had brought us together.

"I'm sorry," I said sweetly. I raised the sword, relaxed and ready. "It's nothing personal."

One cut, one kill. One cut, one kill. The words ricocheted in my skull like the whispered advice of a dying parent.

Flexing my fingers around the handle before gradually tensing my grip, I arched back for that last bit of extra strength, feeling the concerted effort of all the muscles of my upper body as I breathed in and out and closed my eyes and opened them and fixed them wholly on the target and whipped the sword down past my face and chopped clean through the baby, slicing her body perfectly in half. The blade made its most penetrating slash yet into the board, a groove almost deep enough for it to rest in, as though it belonged there. I held it in place between a halved Juanita. My body remained rigid, as if I and everything around me were all part of the same still life.

Nico was now singing, that sultry cabaret bass of hers backed up by Lou's off-key whining:

> *Cause everybody knows*
> *(she's a femme fatale)*
> *The things she does to please*
> *(she's a femme fatale)*
> *She's just a little tease*
> *(she's a femme fatale)*

There was less blood than I would have thought.

. . .

The crying was over. So smoothly and evenly cleaved in two, Juanita now resembled an anatomically correct model that medical students use to study the human interior. I guess the innards hadn't had enough time to slacken and hang out, because each half was perfectly flat, with only the blood draining so far. It reminded me of a sushi roll.

I approached and inspected the fascinating specimen. Her eyes and mouth were open, and she looked little different than she had less than a minute before, apart from the fact that she was halved. Whatever was animating her was no longer active. The quiet stillness made her lovelier than she had been, as though the transformation had brought a certain fullness to her being; a body finally at rest after all that maddening motion. This is the ultimate goal of all bodies: to attain rest, to break off this crazed, constant need to stir and wander, to put an end to the fruitless urge to always be seeking, continuously searching. I looked at her in bitter envy. She had found it. She was at rest.

But not me. I was breathing yet and still moving, plasma pumping through veins and engorged arteries, greedily swapping carbon dioxide for more oxygen, cells continually dying and regenerating. All kinds of microscopic bugs and bacteria were crawling over every millimeter of my interior and exterior, feasting on me like carrion while I carried on in less-than-blissful ignorance. Every atom in my body was in perpetual motion. It was much unwanted toil. Condemned to consciousness. Sentenced to sentience.

And then it returned with a vengeance, the unbounded, voiceless, unquellable ire that knows nothing but the need to lash out, to inflict pain and to destroy in the name of its own grasping impotence. I squeezed the handle until my knuckles blanched and the raised edges of the design pattern dug into my palms. I pulled the sword back off the board and arched it up and back over my shoulder like a batter waiting on a high fastball and struck down at Juanita's lower half, hitting her legs mid-thigh and chopping them into quarters. This only fed the flames of rage, so I pulled back and struck again, and again, and again, until it was beyond my count and I just kept hacking at random chunks of meat and bone, dicing the body into indistinguishable pieces, howling out with each blow, screaming above the music as I brought the blade up and down with such ferocity I almost cut my face, nearly poked my own eye out—maybe I wanted to hurt myself. Nothing could stop me. It wasn't enough that she was dead; I wanted to eliminate all physical evidence of her having existed; I needed to keep slicing until nothing was left, and though I knew it was impossible to mince the remains into complete nonexistence, I continued nonetheless, until she was reduced to a mess of unrecognizable lumps and pulp and jelly.

The careful preparations I had taken to ensure neatness and containment had been for naught. Blood spurted and spattered all about. Flecks of skin and viscera skidded off the table onto the floor beyond the tarp's edge. My face was sprinkled with red—a drop getting into my eye—and my cheek was struck with something that might have been a bone fragment. The nearest wall was awash with gore. Beyond the edge of the tarpaulin, the carpet was stained and strewn with fine remnants of body parts. And still I chopped, hysterically, desperately, incompressible animal sounds coming out of my mouth in faltering manic bursts.

My headphones must have been yanked out of the jack, because there was no more music. There was only the sound of the blade striking wood, and my own inhuman noises, which seemed so foreign.

I chopped and chopped until I could barely lift my arms. I fell to my knees, dropping the sword at my side, hunched over, totally winded, covered in sweat and spackled with blood. I let myself fall onto my back and I stared at the black-bordered squares of white ceiling board. It resembled marshmallows, a low sky of fluffy white marshmallows. I smiled at this thought and tried to allow it to push through everything. My body went slack. I was bereft. I looked at the candy ceiling and started to sob.

． ． ．

I thought I heard a baby crying.

My eyes popped open. It was completely silent, the silence of a locked suburban basement. My body ached, so I lay there, reluctant to move, and looked again at the ceiling. The marshmallows were gone. I saw only the distant white of foaming waves.

I raised a heavy hand and squinted up at my watch: 8:51. I had been asleep for a couple of hours and had missed dinner, but I'm rarely hungry upon waking.

After a few more minutes of recumbence, I pushed myself up to a sitting position and surveyed the carnage, mentally preparing for the dreaded cleanup. I feared that the blood would not come off the rug, regardless of how long and hard I scrubbed. If the cops ever came down with one of those hand-held ultraviolet light sensors, they would find no shortage of DNA evidence.

The earbuds were somehow back in my ears—I'm not quite sure how they got there—and the iPod was still clipped safely to my belt. I clicked on the device and scrolled around, settling on Tom Waits: "The Earth Died Screaming." I stood up and shook my arms out, wiggling them into life, craning my stiff neck and jutting my chest forward to work the sore back.

> And the great day of wrath has come
> And here's mud in your big red eye
> The poker's in the fire
> And the locusts take the sky
> And the earth died screaming
> While I lay dreaming

I had assumed that Juanita would go next to Jake in the backyard, but the very thought of digging another hole was unconscionable. I did not have the energy. As I looked at the mess before me, I realized that the tarp would serve as a large, all-inclusive garbage bag in which I could collect the disparate pieces. Once it was tied, there would be no need to bury it; I could simply squeeze it into the fireplace, sit back with a cup of cocoa and a cookie, and watch it burn up into the flue. It was a bit early in the season for a fire, but a nice warm hearth is always a treat. I was starting to feel good again.

I went upstairs, compiling my list as I ascended: dish-washing gloves, a broom, old towels, detergent, and a bottle of Carbona 2-in-1 Oxy-Powered Carpet Cleaner (with pet-stain remover).

It turned out to be less toilsome than I had imagined. Most of Juanita was either on the table or the tarp, and such remnants that had scattered past the perimeter were easy enough to pick up (I tried to think of these as chicken meat) and drop into a heap on the table. The table itself was beyond salvage; its padded surface was scarred all over from my indiscriminate slashing, and fluffy yellow foam tufted out of the lacerated vinyl in a way that made me imagine buried Twinkies struggling to surface. It occurred to me that I was in the mood for a Twinkie. (Along with its cousin, the Hostess Iced Cream-Filled Chocolate Cupcake, the Twinkie is one of my strongest temptations, which I do allow myself to indulge in from time to time, usually atoning with an extra workout.)

When all of Juanita's remains were collected and put in place at the center of the tarp, I collapsed the table and set it aside. Then I carefully lifted each corner of the canvas and pulled all four edges to the center—just as my father and I would when covering the furniture— tucking the edges underneath so that any openings were reinforced until it was a nicely compacted package, like a big brown dumpling ready for the oven. I remembered that there was a large spool of twine in the storage room (yet another abandoned object resurrected), which we used for tying up boxes of Christmas decorations and retired coats, in addition to using it to secure the tarp around the furniture. I retrieved it and unspooled several feet of the strong white fiber, which I wound around my parcel in overlapping crisscrossed patterns, knotting it in several places—not the prettiest picture, but it would hold. Once the package was condensed, I turned my attention to the table, which would have to be disposed of as well. Though I hadn't thought of this table in years, I was saddened over its loss. Life is a minefield of losses.

The carpet wasn't that bad. I crouched to my hands and knees and scrubbed hard with the built-in brush on the bottle of carpet cleaner. At some point I switched to soap and warm water, and after a solid half-hour of determined labor, it seemed that the stains had been erased, though I wouldn't be sure until the foaming cleanser dried.

I wiped the wooden walls with a Mr. Clean Magic Eraser and some Murphy Oil Soap Wood Cleaner. Some of the blood was soaked in like a new layer of paint, so I had to lightly sand it out, gently buffing when done to ensure the grain of the paneling was not too obviously disturbed. Interestingly, only a few tiny drops found their way onto the mirrored slices, and they shined up with nothing more than some Windex and a little elbow grease. This reminded me that the rest of them could use a good cleaning.

I was about to carry the package up to the living room fireplace when I noticed a piece of flesh under the table. This was annoying, as I didn't feel like untying and retying. What I did instead was run up to the kitchen and get a Ziplock Freezer Gallon Bag, into which I dropped the errant chunk before zip-sealing it nice and tight. Problem solved. I was feeling very positive, very proud of how I was rolling with the vagaries of the situation. I put Sinatra back on—"The Sunny Side of the Street"—and jolted up the stairs to the fireplace.

Though anxious to be done with the disposal, hunger was starting to get the better of me. I get migraines when I don't eat for long periods—or when I don't get enough sleep, or when something particularly stressful is on my mind, or when the dew point or humidity is unreasonably high—so I thought it best to fortify myself before proceeding. I left the bagged baby flesh on the marble ledge in front of the fireplace and went to the kitchen to prepare my meal—tuna with black beans and brown rice. The rice takes about forty-five minutes to steam in my Chef Yan professional steamer. After opening the cans of tuna and beans and setting out my plate and utensils, I was still left with a solid forty minutes of downtime before the rice would be ready. I had no intention of rushing the incineration, so I sat at the kitchen table and—stupidly—turned on the news.

I was everywhere. Well, not me, per se, but this guy who was running around stealing babies. There was another sketch. It didn't look like me. It was just a generic rendering of "a Caucasian male between 22 and 27" in a hood and dark glasses. The glasses in no way resembled my Wayfarers.

They talked about the brazen abduction of a seven-month-old baby girl from her aunt's car while she was bringing her niece back to her parents (so it wasn't Mommy), how the perp crept up from behind (probably in a car but there were no witnesses to confirm it, not even the bitchy beeper who glared at me as she sped past) and savagely beat Aunt Josephina into unconsciousness (breaking her jaw in the process) before absconding with the child. As it was the second abduction in as many days, the community was in a tizzy, screaming for the blood of this depraved offender, lambasting the police for not devoting more manpower toward preventing this after the first kidnapping. The parents—a large-breasted Latina with long curly blonde hair (undoubtedly dyed, most likely extensions) and a tall nerdy white man with glasses that kept sliding down his nose—made their obligatory plea to the kidnapper, attempting to appeal to whatever sliver of humanity might have remained in this villain.

"Please, please bring back my perfect little girl," the woman beseeched, sniffling into a torn and crumpled tissue. "She is our perfect little angel. Please, we beg you, please."

How degrading. And why didn't they give the poor woman a new tissue? Snot was running out of both nostrils and seeping through the saturated material onto her hand. It was disgusting.

"Please. We'll do anything."

And what exactly was she proposing? What was she willing to do? I needed nothing from her. There was nothing this woman could do to coax me to bring back her baby. Even if she could have done something, that ship had sailed.

"Please…" she yowled, breaking down in her husband's arms. "Our perfect baby girl. Please… please."

Did she think that if she repeated the word *please* some magic number of times that I would relent and hand her child over? And *perfect*. They are always so perfect, these children. Splendid little cherubs. Faultless microcosms of humanity. Heaven's illusory gift of perfection to an imperfect world.

•   •   •

It irks me to no end, how these mothers speak of their children, as though nothing less than perfection could possibly squeeze out their wombs. They're all little bundles of pulchritude in development, always so cute and smart and precocious, so uniquely wonderful. Behold the toddler who can recite the alphabet backwards, the five-year-old who can write advanced code, the second-grader who's reading on a fifth grade level, the sixth-grader who's doing college calculus! All little Einsteins. This one's going to be the next Tolstoy, that one the future Bill Gates. He's so adorable, he's going to have to beat them back with a stick when he's older. She's such a pretty little thing, she's going to break hearts by the dozen. Mommy #1 whips out her touch-screen photos and her one-minute videos and she smiles so proudly as Mommy #2 effuses appropriately, itching for her turn to show off images of her own litter.

Just one time, I would like to hear a Mommy admit that her child is of average intelligence with middling looks and no extraordinary talents—nothing more than an ordinary member of our species struggling to make do with whatever ordinary species-bound capacities were fixed in the DNA. I'd love to hear a Daddy say that he doesn't like his kid all that much. Just because you made something doesn't mean you have to like how it turned out. Just because something came out of your uterus doesn't make it special. Just because your sperm managed to penetrate and fertilize an ovum doesn't mean that you have accomplished anything exceptional.

Yet parents will protest that they *are* all so special, these wee priceless wonders, these little miracles of nature, each making its own indispensable contribution to civilization. What kind of world would this be without the patter of bantam feet rumbling along its pitted surface? What would the world be without the laughter of children ringing out from schoolyards and neighborhood playgrounds?

A much quieter world, if nothing else.

$\bullet \quad \bullet \quad \bullet$

By the time the clip finished, I was irate. But there was more. After a commercial break—during which I found myself pleasantly seduced by a nonstick silicone spatula/ pancake turner that guaranteed perfectly shaped cakes every time (as though this were possible)—the Chief of Police, Marcus Michaelson, appeared on the screen. Michaelson was a short, broad-shouldered man who held his chest proudly puffed out like a blowfish—he most certainly focused on pecs and lats at the expense of the lower body during his no-doubt daily workouts. The occasion was a prime-time news conference consisting of the usual trite and formulaic assurances. In his address to a frightened and fuming populace, Chief Michaelson promised that he would spare no expense and stop at nothing to track down this heartless fiend and bring him to justice. He pledged to apportion the full resources of his department to this task, bringing his rousing monologue to its maudlin finale with a raised finger (Bin Ladenesque, I thought) and a solemn vow not to rest until this cowardly monster, this *evil, evil, evil beast who preys on the innocent and defenseless*, was dealt with in the harshest possible way under the law.

This blustery, bald little mustachioed man in his tailored blue uniform, festooned with flashing medals and badges, brought me to seething. Who was he to call me *evil, evil, evil*? Did repeating the same adjective three times make me that much *more* evil? Then there was his ludicrous declaration that he *would not rest* until I was caught and duly punished. My work was its own reward, but I wanted desperately to remain at large, if only to spite this officious officer of the law, to taunt and beleaguer him with my exploits, to blacken his name until the public lost all confidence in his ability to restore order. He would be compelled to resign in disgrace. No, even that would not be enough; I wanted to pound his head into gruel. How I loathed his round, well-fed face, his small vulpine features, his red-tinged cheeks and the long flat slope of his nose. His physiognomy alone inflamed me, made me want to take my samurai sword to the top of his porcine pate, which was surrounded, monk-like, by a perfectly coiffed donut of dyed-brown hair. I found my hands sternly locked around the fork and knife, teeth pressed hard against each other. The equanimity that I had struggled so hard for—and had finally achieved— had been hopelessly degraded.

My impulse was to throw something at the television, but this would have only exacerbated my frustration (I adored my screens), so I let the rice steam and headed back to the basement, where I shed my clothes without bothering to change into my workout shorts and hammered the heavy bag with an unfettered reserve of odious energy that blunted any feeling of pain that visited my unprotected knuckles. I tried to see Michaelson's flustered face on the bag as I welted it over and over and over and over. After about ten minutes of nonstop punching, I was struggling so to catch my breath that I felt on the verge of hyperventilation. I could no longer keep my arms up, and my legs were fast losing their ability to hold me vertical. I sank to my knees and closed my eyes and tried to steady my breathing, thinking that this might minimally approximate what a heart attack feels like.

I was naked down to my socks. I was soaked with sweat. Liquid dripped down my body, but on my face the rills of perspiration were joined by two streams from a different source: I was crying again. And again I didn't realize it until I sat up and the tears were in mid-flow. Why was this happening? I considered that it might be some kind of medical condition and made a mental note to do some Internet research on this—involuntary crying—because I didn't think I felt sad, and I didn't think these were tears of rage (certainly not happiness). Yet the tears continued to run, even as I contemplated their source, and this confusion rekindled the anger in me. I almost surged up to take a few more swings at the bag, but my physical exhaustion was too great a barrier. Then came pangs of hunger.

I couldn't sit down to dinner in such a state, naked, drenched and reeking, so I pulled myself up the two flights of stairs and staggered into the shower. As I held the hose handle and maneuvered it around my body, feeling the clean hot water rinse away the rank stickiness, I imagined using it to smash in the face of Chief Michaelson. This calmed me, despite the unremitting hunger.

•   •   •

The rice was ready and waiting. I lifted the cover and sucked in that first fresh exhaust of fibery steam, and I almost couldn't control the primal craving to scoop it up with my hands and shove it into my mouth. But I am no beast. I patiently spooned the rice into a large bowl and dumped in a full can of tuna (including the oil it was packed in) and a half-can of black beans, stirring vigorously until all the juices intermingled and the contents were well distributed. I realized that I had forgotten to toast my bread, which was already on its third and final day, but there was no way I was going to wait for the oven to preheat, so I unwrapped the foil and sliced it up as is—it was still relatively fresh. I filled a tall glass with ice water and sat down at the kitchen table. It was not easy, but I managed to refrain from turning on the television as I scarfed down my entire meal, leaving nary a grain of rice or a crust of bread. It was a fine feeding, but I felt instantly drowsy and heavy with the sudden stomachful of food I had ingested, so I pushed back from the table to lounge in my chair, like a decadent Roman emperor waiting to purge before returning to binge.

Given a few minutes of digestion, I would be ready to put the last part of my plan regarding Juanita into play. But not just yet. I was so comfortable, just sitting there with the weighty eyes of a narcoleptic, my aching body already fatigued from its efforts to repair itself, so *just right* as I let my lids hover down to a close and then lifted them back up in a flirtatious *pas de deux* with sleep. Pushing the dishes out of the way, I leaned forward to sink my head in the pillow of crossed arms, blocking out all light as I drifted into what felt like a long, deep slumber.

It wasn't, really. It was no more than a few minutes, but long enough to feel refreshed, a little less full, and ready to go. I rubbed the remaining drowsiness out of my face, bulged my eyes, and rolled my eyeballs around to stir them back into focus. I brought the dishes to the sink and washed them well before neatly arranging them in the dishwasher—I had to use a fresh pair of gloves, as the previous ones, though relatively new, had to be disposed of after cleaning the basement. The urge to turn on the news, which I always watched while eating and washing, pestered me like an invasive erotic fantasy, but I would not indulge it. Not until the day's work was done.

I prepared my nighttime latte and brought it into the den with two Golden Oreo cookies on a small plate. I placed them on the sofa table and opened the tinted glass doors to the fireplace. The first fire of the season is always a treat. I so enjoy the sight of the blackened bricks, the residual scent of ash and cinders that inhabit the small space. It brings to mind the soon-to-return winter. I am invigorated by winter. I like the cold. I look forward to the early twilight and the whipping winds, that first delicate snowfall and the bracing December chill that seems to set into your bones and spread out to the tips of your extremities. And I remember those long lost pre-Christmas weeks when we would gather *en famille* with mugs of eggnog and platters of holiday cookies, watching *It's a Wonderful Life* or *A Christmas Carol* while my father dozed and I would sneakily toss things into the crisping flames—a tissue, a plastic cup, a paper dish, a half-eaten cookie—just for the thrill of seeing it burn, and my mother would grimace in mock accusation, shaking her head and smiling at my harmless antics. Sometimes she would hand me another sacrifice to offer the blaze. I have always enjoyed a good fire.

I lined the grated iron basket with old newspaper for kindling and opened the flue. Then I placed on top a few dried-out logs that I had collected from the yard over the summer, lit the edges of the paper, and watched the flickering yellow eat its way in toward the wood. It would take a while to get going. Even though I had my latte, the fire and its nostalgic evocations had me in a yuletide mood, so I went back to the kitchen and prepared myself a Godiva Milk Chocolate Hot Cocoa and topped it with a swirled peak of Ready Whip Extra Creamy. For music, I selected *A Jolly Christmas from Frank Sinatra*, plugging my iPod into the Dolby 5.1 stereo surround system and cranking the volume knob healthily. I dimmed the lights and sat back, taking alternating sips of coffee and cocoa between nibbles of Oreo, humming along with Frank. The fire sizzled. I imagined snow falling faintly against the window, and faintly falling upon all the living and the dead.

About twenty minutes later, as Frank began his plaintive rendition of "Have Yourself a Merry Little Christmas," I finished my cookies. The fire was going strong. I stabbed the log a few times with a long iron poker, mostly for the pleasure of hearing it hiss like a molested cobra and seeing the embers dart up the chimney, but also to get the burning surface as flat as possible.

I checked to ensure the package containing Juanita was secure, then I squeezed it tight between the wide grasping clasps of the heavy metal fire tongs and slowly introduced it into the hearth as a pizza man would his pie. No sooner had I laid it on the flaming log than the canvas began to bubble and sputter and melt around the wood like syrup, the twine snapping and curling back its smoldering edges and exposing the chopped-up baby remnant to cook directly over the open flame. If I observed that it smelled rather appetizing, I quickly chastised myself for the thought. Then again, how much different could it be from a nice little milk-fed veal or a tiny, tender squab? Meat is meat.

Leaning back into the couch with my feet propped on the table, I drank my coffee and nursed my cocoa and finished eating my cookies and calmly watched Juanita return to ash, marveling over how quickly and permanently her existence had been erased from the Earth. Such an unbearably light and tenuous life.

I had forgotten the simple joy of a good fire.

•   •   •

It is hard to imagine how we can take anything seriously, how we can waste even a passing second of our lives doing anything but exactly what we want when we know that the guillotine is always ready to drop. This is why I do my best to not let anything bother me much. And yet, as free-wheeling as my existence then was, being completely unregulated and unrestrained by any kind of externally imposed routine or necessity, I never felt more than a few consecutive minutes of contentment before something would inevitably rise up to disturb my peace, spoiling whatever sense of fleeting gratification had come. And the pleasure itself was painful in its evanescence, so insultingly short-lived that I would wonder if it was even worth the comedown.

I had been enjoying my new project, probably more than I had enjoyed anything in years, but what would come next? I feared I would eventually tire of this, as I had tired of so many other things, and that I would have to find something new, and something after that, etc. Self-narration as *mise en abyme*, cascading in perpetuum.

And what about the purgatorial zone, all those moments between the moments? Most of life is spent in limbo.

I swallowed the distastefully cold remainder of my coffee and watched the fire devour Juanita's remains until only stumps of bone and a few metal grommets from the tarp remained. There was plenty of wood left to burn, however, so I turned on the television—carefully avoiding the news—and flipped through cable movie channels until I arrived at *The Breakfast Club*, only a few minutes in. What a wonderfully serendipitous find! I spread myself lengthwise across the couch and settled in for the rest of the film. And if that were not enough, it turned out to be a late-night John Hughes marathon, with *Pretty in Pink* and *Ferris Beuler's Day Off* following.

By 5:30 a.m., the credits on the final film were rolling, the fire was just about dead, and I was far from sleepy. I went to the fireplace to see the results of the cremation. It was hard to tell, but I think there were little pieces of bone mixed in with the ebonized oddments of wood and tarred patches of burnt newspaper and a few singed scraps of metal. As I tamped it down with the tongs, the last vestiges of live fire flew up in tiny fluttering orange dots like zipping lampyrids, leaving only a smoking mound of char. I grabbed the fireproof broom and swept it all away into the pit below the grating, which led somewhere deep under the house that no one would ever see; I always wondered exactly where.

Smoke continued to pour up from the hole; I would have to leave the flue open for a while. I wasn't thrilled about this, as it would be an unsecured opening to the house, though nothing much larger than a raccoon could realistically fit through.

Fond as I am of a hearthside fire, there is something inherently melancholy about a burnt-out one, something about the bitter-smelling murky emptiness where there had once been a vibrant and bustling blaze, that touches upon my own interior hollowness and leaves me feeling exposed and desolate, that forces me to face what I would rather avoid, though I am not sure exactly what that might be. Maybe I am amiss to avoid the fact that there is nothing to avoid. Maybe it's easier to believe there is something there, deep inside, a hidden core, an unsullied nucleus of being, even if it should prove to be something horrible or terrifying or disgusting. As long as it is there and it is you. But maybe the most terrible thing would be if there were nothing at all, nothing good or evil, positive or negative, just nothing, the scorched open barrenness of a used-up fireplace.

I sat on the smooth marble ledge before the fireplace and peered into the ashen void, watching without clear focus as phantom whirls of smoke eddied up through the air, and before I knew it, there were tears again. Maybe I was tired. Overtired, probably. The best thing to do would be to sleep. I couldn't cry in my sleep.

But sunlight was invading my room, pushing back the darkness too fast for me to escape into slumber, and my thoughts were starting to gang up on me until I felt on the verge of bursting. I lay there staring at the ceiling, waiting for sleep to overcome me. It wouldn't.

I threw back the covers and walked several steps to the mirrored closet door and stared into it. Naked save for my black CK boxer briefs, I began massaging my penis over the underwear with my left hand while flexing my opposing bicep. Then I turned my arm over to accentuate the tricep. The early mix of sun and shadow presented me in a way that reflected well on my muscle tone, but in spite of this, it was a vain endeavor, as useless as the attempt at sleep. My penis remained flaccid. I felt a surge of panic. My fingers clenched and my right fist shot out and slammed into the mirror, smashing the chin of my image so that the shattered glass created a vortex of ill-fitting slices of my face, like a jigsaw puzzle where incorrect pieces are shoved together.

My knuckles bled. There were slivers of mirror stuck in them. I was watching myself in this small circle of crushed glass, which had something of the effect of a disco ball, scattering light and throwing back a distorted likeness. I examined my hand. There was no serious damage; the blood made it look worse than it was. I turned on the iPod, which was connected to my bedside Bose Soundock, and clicked on a live version of "Open Up and Bleed." I smeared blood on my chest and chin, cheeks and arms, shoulders and stomach. Iggy screamed:

> I been hurt
> I been shut inside
> I've even tried to fix and die
> But I'm just gonna kick out through that door

A passionate urge—almost electrical—to smash the rest of the intact mirror flooded over me, but I successfully defended against it; the mirror was a loss, but if I brought further injury to my knuckles I wouldn't be able to spend time with the heavy bag, which was an integral, absolutely essential part of my daily existence, so I resisted, instead pulling down my shorts and stepping out of them, lubricating my penis with the warm wet sap from the back of my hand, and working it up into a sturdy erection. I moved closer to the mirror as the music picked up in intensity and my erection surged until it was obvious I wasn't going to be able to hold back. I wiped some blood on the glass and pushed myself up into it, hard and cold and smooth against my yielding flesh. My tongue lashed at its own image (instinctively avoiding the sharp-edged chips), and I pressed my penis against the glass. I licked and caressed the glass. I thrust into it until the door rattled on its hinges. I was close. I leaned back and gripped my penis hard with my blood-soaked hand and jerked. A spasm of semen came pulsing out, spattering the mirror in gloppy, dripping clumps.

After the ecstasy, I sank back to where I had been, maybe a half-step deeper. The moment was over, leaving me only my muddle. And the cleanup. It is always the same story. Whether it's a load of dishes after a good meal or the scattered remains of a sliced-up baby or the sticky mess of blood and semen and glass shards, there is always a price.

I showered and bandaged my hand with an underlying layer of Neosporin, wiped down the mirror with Windex, swept and mopped the floor. Then it was all I could do to lumber back to bed. It was just past eight a.m., when most people would be on their way to work, ready to keep the machinery of the world in motion, crawling through rush-hour traffic while catching up on the morning news or sitting in stuffed commuter train cars on their way to the city for another nine-to-five odyssey. Just before I drifted off, I thought about how lucky I was not to have to deal with any of that. I slept. There were no dreams.

   •   •   •

I woke at 3:03 p.m., dry-mouthed and groggy, hand throbbing, penis sore. It was a grim day. Dark and windy and rainy and unseasonably cool, even more depressing in contrast to the almost artificial loveliness of the two preceding days. My room was submerged in a sinister kind of daylight darkness, where you know the sun is there but it's too beaten to push through the atmospheric murk. Nothing would have been better than to go back to sleep, but it was not to be.

I lay on my back with the covers drawn up just past my chin and listened to Chopin's *Preludes*, and as the wind-driven wetness pounded the windows and shingles and roof with what seemed a personal vendetta, I kept my eyes upward. I would not have been surprised if the ceiling collapsed in on me. But it didn't. And as "The Raindrop Prelude" finished, I was crying again.

I needed to get out of bed. There were things to do. Or at least, *a* thing to do: buy a new mirror for the closet door. Having a mission for the day was good. I rose and headed straight for the shower, but then I realized it was a shave-day. I shaved every third day, setting my schedule out on the calendar with a big black S written with a Sharpie Ultra Fine Point Permanent Marker. I double-checked the calendar on the inside of the closet door opposite the broken mirror (stealing a full-bodied peek at myself). One more thing to do.

Shaving has always been more for me than the simple everyday routine I imagine it is for most men. It is a much more involved affair that lasts at least an hour. I start with the face, dry-shaving with an Andis T-Outliner, which is a professional close-cutting buzzer that I prefer to a traditional razor because it causes less irritation and doesn't cut quite as close, leaving me the faintest shadow instead of that baby's-ass smoothness that they're always touting in commercials for the newest multi-blade disposable razors. Then, also with the T-Outliner, I proceed to the scalp, which I do on the same day as the face so as to ensure symmetry. Next, I enter the shower with my Philips Norelco Bodyroom Pro, an electric shaver designed specifically for men. This device is a godsend. I had been using the Gillette Mach3 for years, which never failed to nick and cut my torso and nether regions, no matter how slowly and carefully I ran the blade over my body. After it almost sliced off a nipple, I decided to research other methods. The Bodygroom Pro is water-resistant and capable of running in the shower, which is where I take off my chest hair and the few strands that sprout up on the top of my back and shoulders (I'm lucky enough not to have that werewolf-tufted back, like some guys), working down the fuzzy trail on my lower stomach and finishing in the groin area, which can be a bit tricky.

I took my time, plugging my iPod into the bathroom speaker unit and letting the *Preludes* finish while I sheared the unwanted bristle from my body and followed up with a warm, soapy shower, lathering and rinsing a couple of extra times to ensure there were no loose hairs sticking to me. I exited the shower clean and shiny smooth, and I took some time to admire my dripping, glabrous front in the large vanity mirror above the sink: a fine job, with minimal irritation and maximal depilation.

Feeling the day was taking a turn from its dismal beginnings, I clicked on Iggy's "Lust for Life" and did a naked jig in front of the mirror. Still moving to the beat, I dried and powdered and liberally applied some post-shave healer—followed by a light, fragrance-free mois-turizer—re-bandaged my hand, and dressed.

The rain had eased to a drizzle, but cloud cover persist-ed. It was one of those days when the most you can hope for is a few breaks of muddy luster between periods of general dankness and blustery downpour. Though it was well past lunchtime, I made my coffee and Farina with blueberries and poured a half-glass of grapefruit juice. At the kitchen table, I took a few prudent sips of coffee (getting mostly froth) and, bolstering myself, snapped on the news—a national cable network. I wondered if the rest of the country had been alerted to the harrowing reports from our otherwise quiet and bucolic suburb.

For a full fifteen minutes, more than ample time to twice polish off my Farina (I have been told that I am a "fast eater." To the extent that this is true, it is perhaps a result of so often dining alone and rarely having to pace myself among company. I do not feel this charac-terization is particularly accurate, however, as I have hardly ever rushed to get through a meal. I chew my food well because I savor its flavor, and it's not as though I am starved for breath between mouthfuls. If I were to concentrate on eating with such excruciatingly deliberate slowness as custom dictates, this would only detract from the pleasure of eating. I believe I eat at a fine tempo. It is the others, those communal diners, who waste time with talking and laughing and gesticulating and looking at each other when they should be focusing on the matter at hand—the plates in front of them.), it was the usual: healthcare, job loss, a deadly home invasion in Sarasota (five fatalities, one in custody, two on the lam). Debate over deploying more troops to Afghanistan. A Taliban attack on a police station in Pakistan. Another Iranian Mullah denying the Holocaust.

I was simultaneously relieved and disappointed that my crimes seemed to fly under the national radar. I switched from MSNBC to CNN to Fox, half hoping that my deeds would be discussed and roundly condemned, if only to provide a space of agreement for the fiercest of political adversaries. But there was nothing, not even a thirty-second filler. I wondered over this. Could it have been some kind of ploy by the authorities to flush me out by limiting my exposure and jabbing at my pride? An attempt to avoid copycats? Or did a couple of kidnapped tots make for lower ratings than overseas suicide attacks and snarky senators trading barbs? Maybe I had overestimated the greater effect my acts would have. This seemed the proper conclusion.

I finished my coffee. Then, as I was about to move on to the juice (which I always save for last, as I prefer to let it lose the overnight chill it retains from the refrigerator), there was the tease. Just as the rim of the glass met my lips, a winsome Asian afternoon anchor on MSNBC was about to break for a commercial, but not before she left her audience with the enticing promise of a "disturbing" story that "no parent could afford to miss."

Only after the first commercial—a fifteen-second spot for a new low-cholesterol spread that offers a money-back guarantee if you can tell it's not butter—was I able to tilt the glass back and take my first small drink of juice. This turned into an extended, three-gulp downer, the cool, astringent fluid racing through my gullet and coursing straight to the stomach, causing me to wince at the sudden acidic bloat and slam down the glass as if it were a shot of tequila.

After a three-minute break that felt like an hour, she was back with the story. There was another pitifully inaccurate sketch—a villainous young hooded guy with Mephistophelian eyebrows (my eyebrows are indeed thick, but they are not pointed at such an exaggerated angle) shadowing a pair of dark and beady eyes (my eyes are dark but rather large, and the presence of eyes in the sketch was, in my case, absurd; I never took off my glasses) with a few bangs of close-cut hair falling on the forehead like that Caesar coiffure George Clooney had popularized during his star-making tenure on *ER* (but my head was buzzed almost clean, per my shaving ritual; it had not been close to that length in a decade), and strangely, one of those disgusting patches of facial hair centered just below the lower lip that has come to be known in the vulgar colloquial as a "flavor savor" (I would sooner be drawn and quartered than allow such an unseemly splotch to sprout from my face).

I considered that they might be trying to get at me through my vanity—a potentially effective ploy—and I found my fingers tightening around the empty juice glass. Fortunately, I was able to rein myself in before breaking it and further damaging the hand that had punched the mirror, but not before the strain caused a little blood to seep through to the surface of the bandage.

The anchor tossed the story to an on-site reporter, who was standing at the very spot where Juanita was abducted, right in front of her home, with her aunt in the car, etc. Then came the familiar sequence: a few interviews from neighbors (nobody I knew or recognized), reiterated police statements, notice for citizens and especially parents to be exceptionally vigilant, a toll-free police hotline for tips, and mention of a reward for information leading to the retrieval of the baby and/or apprehension of the suspect. The reward was a nice new touch. The rest was uninspired.

I switched to CNN, where I found more of the same pap, but when I landed on Fox, there was red meat. One of the network's overly testosteroned shit-flingers was talking about how I should be made to suffer—indeed, *tortured*—before being strapped into the electric chair and left there to fry longer than usual. I found this very entertaining, so I continued to watch the animated simpleton effuse and yell about the awful abuse he would like to personally inflict on me. And I watched him perform with his invited guests, asking how society can produce a person like me. One "expert" provided an absurdly erroneous profile of me as a sad loner who has trouble in social situations. Another speculated that I probably worked a menial job and that I had always wanted children but couldn't find a woman to have them with. Further, I was informed that my meager achievements had been constantly overshadowed by those of my siblings in my formative years.

They were never going to find me.

I laughed as the round-table discussion grew in vehemence and concluded with a collective prayer for the families of the taken babies and a plea to anyone watching who might know something, anything useful, to call the authorities at once. Finally, the red-faced, riled-up host thanked his guests for their insight but resolved that, despite some thought-provoking theories, he was convinced only of the fact that I had been "born bad," that nothing had made me the way I am, and that nothing could have prevented me from being the way I am. "Some people are just bad apples," he reasoned, flipping his palms up. "And there's only one thing to do with a rotten apple. Throw it out of the orchard."

His metaphor made me think of how I hate fruit.

The talking heads continued jabbering on a new topic, but the sound hardly made it into my mind as I stared out the kitchen window into the backyard, where the sun, though nowhere to be seen, was somehow sending its light through small cracks in the cloud cover, slowly burning off the afternoon gloom. I watched a stray cat saunter in search of a meal. I watched the wind lift a browning leaf off a high branch and settle it slowly down on the grass among countless others.

•   •   •

The television droned on, but I didn't register anything until I heard his voice.

It was Chief of Police Marcus Michaelson, now speaking on the national news, looking no worse for wear despite the long, sleepless hours spent in his unflagging dedication to the task of apprehending me. His dress blues were nicely starched and creaseless. His head was polished to a clean, glossy finish. His determined little black eyes (which actually resembled the sketch of the perpetrator more than mine) lasered forward as he reiterated his promise to *capture the childnapping fiend and bring the full weight of the law down on him*. He raised a tight Stalinesque fist to punctuate his words. *The Baby Snatcher will find no quarter in our community, and he will see justice. He will see retribution. This is the promise I make to you today, and to him*—Michaelson looked directly into the camera, directly at me—*if he's listening*.

．　　．　　．

This was the first time I heard the term "Baby Snatcher." I assume it was coined on the spot by Michaelson. The reporter repeated it in her summation of the interview, and the anchor said it again during his closing segment. I was not happy. As if the sight of Michaelson's bulbous figure on television were not sufficient to stoke my murderous fire, he had now branded me with a name that I found distastefully prosaic at best, and painfully patronizing. And it was already catching.

I flipped through the news channels, including the local ones, and was dismayed to see that the name was spreading like crabgrass. I wished that Michaelson had a newborn son so I could *snatch* the suckling child from his mother's breast. I imagined the mother—Michaelson's trophy wife, a short, zaftig blonde badge bunny that he met as a young uni in a neighborhood cop bar—chained to a structural beam in my basement, being forced to watch as I flayed her precious infant and made a dead skin mask out of his hide (just for effect, not for use).

And I would make Michaelson bear witness as well, after taking out his knees with my bamboo kendo sword (known as a *shinai*, purchased on a less memorable trip to Chinatown on the assumption that I would take kendo lessons, which I never did) and waking him from unconsciousness to have him view up close the slaying of his boy, the spoliation of his seed, before finishing him off at my leisure, perhaps with numerous slices from my katana—"death by a thousand cuts," as the Chinese used to do so artfully. Then I would sit back and watch as he slowly bled out (being sure, as a matter of course, that a large tarpaulin was in place to protect the carpet). I wouldn't grant him the satisfaction of seeing me rape his wife, of letting him think I wanted anything he had. But I wouldn't let her go, either.

I powered down the television and headed for the basement. Pain shot through my right hand each time it made contact with the heavy bag, but I thought of Michaelson and pushed through the hurt. When I removed the gloves, the bandage was soaked in blood and my hand was trembling. I showered and watched the watery red drain away through my toes as the hotness washed over my wound and Miles Davis trumpeted through "In a Silent Way." But the image and voice of Michaelson returned, unbidden. *Baby Snatcher, Baby Snatcher, Baby Snatcher*.

I was slow to regain my composure, but there were things to do. Above all, I had to go to Home Depot for a new mirror. Even one day without it would be too much, and it was a fine reason to get out for some air.

Then came a more satisfying thought, a way to rectify the account with my adversary: I would call the police

hotline and demand that they immediately stop referring to me as the Baby Snatcher. Could it be that simple?
Of course, it would be necessary (and probably fun) to
disguise my voice, perhaps by using one of those vocal
distortion gadgets, like in *Scream*. I mulled this plan,
weighing the risk it would entail against the potential
dividends, and concluded that it was worth the effort.
I would place the call from a pay phone and give them
something to let them know I was their person of interest. Then I would warn them. *Stop using that abhorrent
name or more babies will be killed. Not snatched, killed.*

•   •   •

My mood brightened as I dressed and mentally laid out the remainder of my day, and another domino fell in the right direction when I remembered that there was a small party store in the same strip mall where the Home Depot was located, an unrenovated throwback to the suburbia of my youth, before megastores and national chains replaced virtually all of the small independent shops. My mother would take me there every fall, as early as mid-September, to begin our search for the perfect Halloween costume. I always looked forward to Halloween; it was the highest holiday of the year for me. I would parade around the school during our annual party, then come home and stroll through the neighborhood collecting candy in my plastic pumpkin, though I was forbidden to eat the treats until one or both of my parents inspected each piece for evidence of tampering, i.e., syringe marks, hidden blades, etc. I thought of my sixth-grade ninja outfit, which I acquired a couple of months after I got my Chinatown katana. I begged my parents to let me carry the sword while trick-or-treating, but they unconditionally refused, despite my logical argument that the sword would add a vital touch of authenticity to my costume. My father rebutted this very skillfully, explaining that it would actually *detract* from the authenticity, as ninjas used ninja swords, or *ninjato*, which were shorter and straighter in the blade than the katana, and as the samurai were blood-sworn enemies of the ninja, no self-respecting shadow warrior would be seen carrying his rival's weapon (he had apparently done some research). This did make some sense to me, although I considered countering his reasoning with the hypothetical wherein I was a ninja who had bested a famous samurai on the battlefield and appropriated his sword as a victory trophy, parading it around for all to see and admire. But I didn't hold out hope of this argument swaying him, so I relented and agreed to carry a *bokken*—or wooden training sword—instead.

It was late rush hour when I got on the road, and though I would normally never be out in traffic at this time, the snarl provided well-needed cover. My first stop would be the Depot. I had to have that mirror. I needed it off my list so I could have a clear mind. Breezing through crowded aisles lined with shelves and racks fully stocked with rakes and wrenches, handsaws and hacksaws and jigsaws and table saws, hundreds of screws and nails of various shapes and sizes, hammers and screwdrivers and box cutters and lawnmowers and weed whackers and ground tillers and hand axes and power drills, my stomach fluttered with excitement.

I asked a buoyant young clerk named Drew where I might find what I was looking for. Not only did he tell me both the aisle and bin numbers, but he happily invited me to follow as he escorted me right to the spot where a full row was dedicated to mirrors of all kinds. Trying my best to match his courtesy with the appropriate responses, I smiled and told him how much I appreciated his solicitude. I was then delighted to find the same model of mirror as the one I had destroyed, and I gleefully placed it in my carriage and wheeled it to the checkout counter.

Next was the party store, which was eerily unchanged from how I remembered it. Even the smell, a blend of over-brewed coffee and candies and structural oldness, was the same. Or maybe it was my antiquated memories that were conforming to its current state.

It turned out the voice disguisers were popular, as evidenced by their prominent display up front near the checkout counter—on sale for $9.99. To mitigate any semblance of nefarious design, I purchased an adult *Scream* costume as well, though the goth-girl cashier was so absorbed in texting that she hardly looked at me or my items while ringing me up. On the way out, I saw a Michael Myers mask and almost turned back to buy it. I probably would have, had there not been more pressing matters to attend. I made a mental note.

As I stepped out to the low jingle of overhead bells, I heard a female voice calling: "Sir! Sir," and I froze for an instant. Turning around, I saw the clerk leaning over the counter and looking right at me. Reminding myself that I had done nothing to suggest ill-intent, I walked back in with a mild smile.

"Yes? Did I not give you enough money?"

"Oh, no." She smiled with a warmth that was absent seconds ago and spoke in a soft, solicitous voice that was inconsonant with her image. Underneath her blackened eyes and pasty makeup was a classically pretty face of refined features and youthful allure. "But you're gonna need *these* to make that voice thingie work." She was holding a package of AA batteries.

My gratitude was sincere. "Thank you so much," I gushed, as I rushed over, deeply relieved, and placed my cash on the counter.

When she handed me the change, the flat of her fingernails grazed my upper palm, and a strange sensation vibrated through my entire body. It is exceedingly rare that I have any kind of physical contact with other humans.

"Happy Halloween," she said in parting.

"You, too."

• • •

It seemed cheaply made (in China, like everything else), but that didn't matter as long as it worked. There were three settings: "Scary Monster Voice," "High Alien Voice," and "Amplification." I slipped in three AAs, lifted the mic to my mouth, and tried out each one. "High Alien" was comical, like a campy space invasion movie from the sixties. "Amplification" was the clearest, but I worried that it was too close to my actual voice. That left "Scary Monster Voice," which sounded somewhat like a cross between Boris Karloff and Bobby Picket narrating "The Monster Mash," but lower and more distorted. It wasn't perfect, but it was clearly the best option. Scary Monster it would have to be.

I thought about the comely cashier one last time as I pulled out of the lot, peeking into the rear-view at the storefront before merging into early evening traffic. Such musings were for another time, another life. Nothing could be permitted to cloud my mind. Nothing could be allowed to tear my focus from the business at hand.

The first step was to find a suitable public phone, one that wasn't too close to my home or to the stores I had visited. Not too secluded, but private enough that no passersby could pick up my distorted words. The task was complicated by the increasing scarcity of pay phones in an era of ubiquitous touch-screen devices, whereas I am among those few Americans who have never owned a cell phone.

Cruising to the Rolling Stones' *Exile on Main Street*, my heart filled at finding a nice old-fashioned glass-enclosed phone both outside another small strip mall consisting of a 7-Eleven, a Chinese takeout, a stationery store, and a dry cleaner. There were some teenagers in ripped jeans and heavy-metal concert tees sucking down Slurpees and trying their best to look meanly aloof as they crouched next to their ten-speeds in front of the convenience store. Apart from that, the coast was clear. There were only two other cars in the lot and no foot traffic. I had a pocketful of change taken from my makeshift piggy bank, a large metal Bolla wine gift box into whose top my father had carved a coin-friendly slot. He would drop his day's change in every evening upon returning from work. Once a year, usually around my birthday, we would count all the coins, stick them into wrappers, and cash them in at the bank. It usually amounted to around $100, sometimes a bit more, and I remember coming home every year feeling like a wealthy man.

Parking a few spots away from the phone, I sat in the car to gather my courage. The aroma from the Chinese kitchen was strong and savory, and though I general-ly avoided such cuisine, I was tempted to break for a serving of chicken chow fun and fried pork dumplings. I repressed this desire. There was a security camera lodged under the cornice of the 7-Eleven, but it was pointed toward the entrance of the store, so unless it swiveled, I felt confident it would not frame me. No other obvious surveillance devices were visible, though there was no accounting for random cell phones and traffic cameras, or such other miscellaneous implements of technological scrutiny that always manage to capture the perp on *Law & Order*. It was a chance I had to take.

After a few minutes, I headed over to the booth. To avoid resembling the sketch in any minimal way, I did not wear my sunglasses or raise my hoodie. This made me feel vulnerable but less conspicuous. As I strolled casually over those few yards of pavement, I kept an eye on the kids, who seemed far too wrapped up in their own affairs to take any notice of me. By the time I was safely ensconced in the opaque Plexiglas booth, I was sweating and trembling. It was a reasonably spacious enclosure, probably of '80s vintage, with a hard blue plastic bench and cloudy walls further obfuscated by graffiti and bird droppings and all manner of stains and smudges. The thought of pressing the earpiece against my face disgusted me, but it had to be done. I took my trusty travel bottle of Purell and wiped down the phone as best I could, lathering a mess of the antiseptically pungent liquid all over the keypad and handle and earpiece, anywhere any part of my unclothed body would have to come into contact with.

I withdrew a few quarters and rubbed them clean of prints with a Purell-moistened tissue (probably unnecessary, but there was no harm in being overcautious). Then I realized that the hotline number, which I had memorized, was toll-free and would not require payment. A minor but mindless mistake. A shiver ran through me. I had a premonition that such a silly little oversight would be my downfall. I slid the quarters back into my pocket.

Shaking off my malaise, I readied the voice disguiser, testing it out again before the crucial moment. Then I looked around one last time and dialed the number, holding the device's speaker up against the mouthpiece.

It barely got through one ring.

"Police hotline."

Despite my rehearsals, I was strangely aphasic.

"Hello. Police hotline. Hello…"

It was a rather rough male voice. Was it a cop or just some jaded receptionist?

"Hello… Hotline…"

"I am not the baby snatcher." I lowered my tone so that it sounded still more distorted through the device, despite the instructions on the packaging advising users to "speak clearly and in a normal voice."

After a pause, the voice said, "Okay, I'm going to have to ask you not to call back. We need to keep these lines open." Then he hung up.

I had run through various scenarios, but this was not one of them. I took a beat, looked around again—the kids were now gone, the lot practically deserted—and redialed.

"I am not *snatching* them," I said.

"I'm sorry? Could you repeat that? I'm having trouble understanding you." It was a different voice—younger, female, more articulate.

I cleared my throat and tried to speak more normally, but my lips were quivering and my larynx was lumped.

"I am not snatching them. I am *killing* them."

"What? What is your name, sir?"

I felt myself regaining calm, retaking a bit of the control that had seeped away from me. "You know who this is," I continued with composure. "You people are making this sound so cheap. I do not *snatch* babies. I *kill* them. They are *dead*. I am *killing* the babies. The first one, Jake, the *champ*..." I slipped in this detail about his clothing because I discerned that it might have been withheld from press accounts.

"Please just tell me who you are, sir."

Did she really think I was going to divulge my identity because she asked politely?

"The second one was a cranky Hispanic in an adorable little onesie, while her aunt was bending to get her phone."

I provided still more specifics.

"Okay... okay..." She was struggling to keep a cool head and a calm tone. There was a pause between her words. Clearly, she was trying to draw out the call to complete the trace. I knew that if I didn't move things along, units would be dispatched to the source and I would be surrounded within minutes.

"...Okay."

I imagined her alerting her superiors with frantic hand motions and panicked, widened eyes. Computers were already being set in motion, plotting the possible coordinates as they tried to triangulate my position via satellite.

"Get it right." I was emphatic. "No more Baby Snatcher, or there will be more." (I was fairly certain there would be more anyway, but I had to play my hand.)

"Okay... fine, whatever you need. Just tell us—"

"Tell Michaelson I called. And don't use that fucking name!"

∙　　●　　●

My heart hammered. I walked fast—but didn't run—back to the car, passing it twice to make sure no one was there before getting in (which might have looked fishier than if I had just gotten in). I fought the instinct to race out of the lot, instead rolling smoothly out onto the road. Soon, I was driving on quiet residential streets toward home, and my pulse normalized.

I switched on the radio to hear if there were any reports about my call, though I doubted the police would publicize it so soon. I landed on the traffic and weather report. Traffic was at low volume. Gorgeous fall weather was in the forecast for the next few days—"perfect weather for one more backyard barbecue."

For a second, I rejoiced at the idea of spending some time at the park, but this spark of excitement was summarily doused by the realization that I could never safely set foot in that public space again, never again amble idly around the little lake or sit on a tree-shaded bench to read. And if I were so cavalier as to revisit the scene of my virgin crime, I would never feel totally at ease. I would always be looking over my shoulder, wondering if someone suspected who I was. No, there was no going back.

The top stories were announced. I was the lead.

No new evidence in the Baby Snatcher case, frustrating authorities and inflaming public anger as citizens band together to protect their communities. The Baby Snatcher has kidnapped two infants so far, and despite the combined efforts of federal and local law enforcement, officials admit they have little to go on and are reaching out to the public for assistance.

This was followed by a snippet of a news conference where an infuriatingly monotone FBI agent referred to me twice as the Baby Snatcher.

I was fuming. Though only a few short blocks from home, I put on the Stooges' "Gimme Danger," made a wide, reckless U-turn without checking for cars around me, and sped back in search of a different pay phone, determined to put a definitive end to this. I drove faster than I should have. I couldn't help it.

> *There's nothing left alive*
> *But a pair of glassy eyes*
> *Raise my feelings one more time*

It was almost evening. Though it should have been brighter at this time, clouds shrouded the sky and a delicate veil of mist rendered the lower atmosphere murky. Headlights gleamed like low-hung stars on the roadway. Windshield wipers began their rhythmic flow. I was anxious and furious, but I couldn't let my emotions steer the ship. When I got to a main artery, I managed to slow down and keep cruising at a steady seven miles per hour over the speed limit. The cops would be out in force, looking for any excuse to pull over vehicles at random, jumping at the slightest behavioral anomaly.

I spotted a quaint little open-air public phone outside of a supermarket, a good distance away from the entrance, near the back of the lot. I pulled in and parked several spaces away, monitoring the comings and goings, checking for cameras, security guards, parents on patrol, nosy nobodies with nothing else to do but eyeball the actions of others. This was not a market I frequented. I had been there maybe two or three times in my life, when my local stores were out of something I needed. I could have used a gallon of milk and some Farina, but it probably wasn't the smartest idea to go in. There were sure to be cameras. The police would trace the call to the outside phone and analyze the surveillance videos and coordinate them with the time of the call, and I would be dragged away in cuffs.

This was the first time that any serious thought of capture entered my mind. I envisioned a phalanx of officers leading me away through a hungry throng of reporters, enraged parents screaming for blood, and the merely curious, all clamoring for a brief glimpse of the latest true-crime celebrity before going home for dinner. They would tell their families how normal and nonthreatening I looked. I could have been their neighbor's grown son, the one who still lives at home and has never had a girlfriend but always waves and smiles; that contemplative nephew who barely talks at family gatherings but surely has a heart of gold; the young divorced dad who lost custody of his kids and now lives alone in the big house down the block, but who just as surely has a heart of gold and would do anything for his children. I would make them question everything and everyone around them. I would make them question themselves.

As I watched the mothers push carts of groceries through the automatic doors, with their children clutching at the hems of their jackets (the smaller ones snuggled into the specially designed seats up in the front of the carriages), I knew I could never allow myself to be apprehended. I grew suddenly suspicious of everyone around me. How had I not foreseen the possibility of arrest? It had simply never entered my mind that I could be captured, that they could extricate me from the life I had known and guarded for so long. Crooks and criminals got collared, but I was neither. I was a warrior, a philosopher of the deed. I had summoned the will to act on the strength of my conviction that life is wrong, that life is pain, sadness, and calamity, that human existence is tragic, an evolutionary error, a baleful malfunction in the machinery of the natural order, and that it is better to cut the cord before the cord strangles you. It is even better never to have been at all, but second best only to be for a short while. So I was doing a service to society. I was acting in the best interest of the babies, saving them from lives of longing and dashed hope, sparing them years of disappointment and disillusion, the anguish of heartbreak, the agony of sickness, the indignity of old age. I had become an artist, a visionary, a mystic. I was the good guy, but would anyone else see it that way?

I continued to scold myself. How could I not have taken precautions against the eventuality of capture? I thought of spies who carry cyanide caplets that they can snap open between their teeth if taken by the enemy. I should have had something on me at all times, a knife or a gun (both of which were in the house), something with which to defend or end myself, if need be. Anything was better than life in a cage. They would not take me. Not ever. Not alive.

•   •   •

The shopping crowd was light. Most people were probably home having supper. Nobody was paying attention to the pay phone, that antediluvian relic destined to go the way of the telegram and the tape deck. It was nothing more than an eyesore.

I walked over with the voice disguiser in my pocket, inconspicuously checking out my surroundings. The phone was enclosed in a weather-worn perforated metal shell, providing minimal concealment and less auditory privacy than I would have preferred, but it would have to do. I hunched over and readied the device and dialed the number.

Two and half rings this time.

"It's me again."

Something was wrong. I sounded like a demented clown on helium. I realized the switch had flipped to the *High Alien Voice* setting. I fumbled it back a notch and repeated.

"It's me, the one who called before."

Still wrong. I had switched it to *Amplification*, so it was basically a loud, echoing version of my own voice. I sounded like an enraged Olympian god, which might have been appropriate, but definitely not smart.

It was hard to see in the dimness, so I held it up right up to my face and managed to get it back to *Scary Monster*.

"Hello. Is somebody there?" Another woman. She had a deeper, older voice.

"It's me."

"Me who?"

"Don't be foolish."

"You're telling me you're the Baby Snatcher?"

"Yes. I mean, no. I mean, I'm the one you're calling that, but that's not me. That's why I called, so you won't call me that anymore. I'm the one you're looking for, but I refuse to go by that ridiculous name."

"Uh huh." Pause. "And what color was Adam's hat?"

I wondered how many pathetic men had already called, claiming to be me, only to be summarily dismissed by this rudimentary ruse.

"If you mean Jake, he wasn't wearing a hat, cunt. And I hope you people haven't ruined my Faulkner."

Another pause, this one pregnant.

"Okay. Just calm down and let's talk."

"I'm done talking. Just tell Michaelson that if I hear the term Baby Snatcher one more time, just one more time, I will go on a baby-killing rampage, and I will make sure the press knows he could have avoided it but chose not to out of vanity and stubbornness. I'll make sure everyone realizes that all that baby blood is on *his* hands."

"Please… tell us why… it's not too late…"

She was doing her best to extend the call, apparently convinced I was the genuine article.

"*Why*?" I repeated mockingly.

I hate that word. I loathe its vacuity and rabbit-hole implications. *Why* do we feel the way we feel? *Why* do we do the things we do? *Why* does the universe work as is does and *why* is it here in the first place? There is no fucking *why*.

But I wanted to give them some cud to chew on. With any luck, they'd choke on it.

"Because I want to make the world a better place. Now do what I say. Stop calling me by that name."

"What do you want to be called?"

It was a good question. It seemed inexcusable not to have an answer, to be so woefully unprepared.

"I don't care," I said. "Just not Baby Snatcher."

But I couldn't leave it up to them.

"Fine. The Baby *Killer*. You can call me the Baby Killer. And also tell Michaelson…"

I drew a blank. There was so much I wanted to tell him, to do to him, but there was no time. I was cutting it too close as it was.

"…tell him…tell him he's a *douchebag*."

I slammed the handset onto the cradle.

I was shaking.

∙   ∙   ∙

The call went longer than I had planned. Maybe her initial disbelief was merely an act, a coy stratagem to buy time as her colleagues raced to the site. And maybe it worked. Maybe those extra few seconds I took to threaten Michaelson would end up costing me dearly.

I power-walked to the car, half-expecting a fleet of squad cars to encircle me at any moment. I imagined my response, my evil smirk as I slowly slipped my hand into my pocket as though reaching for a gun, forcing them to issue one last warning before opening fire. And the police do not shoot to wound; they are trained to neutralize the aggressor and end the threat. Suicide by cop would be the result. I probably wouldn't feel a thing. They'd kick my corpse to make sure I was dead and find that I was only reaching for a voice disguiser. *All the better*, they'd say. *He deserved no less.*

I drove away undetected. My fear, though warranted, had been for naught. After a few blocks, the sweeping sound of distant but approaching sirens invaded my space, joined in a beat by a frantic blue and red strobe. My stomach knotted as several cruisers rushed by, cutting through traffic like a sudden gale. I could only think they were headed to the supermarket parking lot, where they would scour for evidence of my presence. The CSI team would search every square inch of the phone booth and the immediate environs, interviewing employees and customers and anyone who happened to be on scene, hoping for the tiniest breadcrumb that could lead them to me. They would find nothing. The waning sirens transformed into a happy, wholesome sound—such mellifluous music, knowing that I was safely away. My mood elevated and my nerves sweetly melted. I put on Sinatra's "Zing! Went the Strings of My Heart," doing my best to keep in tune with the Chairman as I drove home, thinking about dinner and my new mirror.

Everything was so pretty and pleasant as I pulled onto my street and slowed down to stretch out the experience, relishing the pallid radiance of the street lamps with their yellow halos concentrated around the bulbs and spreading weakly through the mist like aerosol. I observed the lush, ghostly silhouettes of the heavy treetops swaying like drunkards in the low sky and casting silken shadows upon the house fronts all lit and locked up for the night with families safely inside, TVs working their spells, children doing homework before dinner, Dad having that after-work cocktail, Mom checking the chicken, teens texting their friends. The world was exactly as it should be, despite all that it is. The world was just right, as right as it always was and ever will be. Things could never be other than they were just then, at that moment. Things were as perfect and complete as a riddle that provides its own answer.

Bumping over the uneven bricks of the driveway apron, I realized it was happening again. I was crying. But there was nothing upsetting about it this time. It was something pure and immaculate, an elemental, untouched innocence in the heart of being. There is a primal kernel of existence that will forever remain an intact infant, spared the trauma of maturity, the tribulations of adulthood, the horrors of a ripened life. That kernel was still somewhere inside of me, repressed by the accumulation of years. It had been waiting in the darkness.

As was I. Sitting in the silent car in the dark garage with the ignition off. Waiting.

•   •   •

I turned on an AM news station. Sports. I despise sports. It's not that I have no interest in sports, nor merely that I am bored by the spectacle—it is an affirmative and infernal hatred. Thinking about sports makes me angry. The idea of grown people behaving like children, playing at work, or working at play, running and jumping and throwing balls around while all involved—the players as well as the spectators—take such frolicking nonsense seriously, infuriates me. Sport is the illusion of recreation lost in the reality of work. The opposite of fun. The true death of childhood.

After an excruciating minute of scores and condensed recaps, I shut it off. I sat there and waited another minute—then another few seconds, just to be safe. Then I turned it back on. Good timing.

…a man claiming to be the Baby Snatcher has contacted police demanding that he be referred to as—and you might want to take a deep breath—the Baby Killer.

Cut to Marcus Michaelson:

We've had contact today from an individual who we believe is indeed the... uh... Baby Killer... or is perhaps someone with intimate knowledge of these crimes.

It was rapturous to hear him squirm through these words.

Now, I'm not going to take questions, and I want to stress that we have no hard evidence that the abducted infants are deceased. We are doing everything in our power to find and to stop this criminal before he can commit any further atrocities.

Back to the newsman:

There you have it, the Baby Snatcher is now the Baby Killer. So please, if you have any information or notice anything suspicious, please call—

I killed the radio and remained in the car, conflicted over how I felt about this development. It hadn't gone exactly as planned. Nothing ever does. At least they weren't calling me the Baby Snatcher anymore, but I wasn't sure about the new appellation. It had a sharper edge, but it was a mere modification. This was my fault for not being ready with a better hook, for not being prepared with a more assertive suggestion. I considered making one last call to put a period on it, but this was far too risky. The cops probably had pay phones staked out within a wide radius, and people were really going to be on their guard now; a *killer* trumps a *snatcher* on the evolutionary scale of evildoers. I would have to live with the Baby Killer. There were worse things.

Entering the dark house, I was greeted by the glowing green *Clean* light on the face of the dishwasher's control panel. I do love a machine full of clean dishes, almost as much as I love a dryer full of warm, softener-scented clothing (I was reminded that I should do a load of darks soon). I opened the dishwasher's door, inhaled the balmy, vaguely soapy scent, and started unloading. The heated ceramic and silverware felt good in my hands as I sang Sinatra's "It Happened in Monterey," humming through the parts I had forgotten.

After washing and re-bandaging my injured hand, I went to the basement and did a long, slow, and very deliberate Dynamic Strength routine. Then I rushed up to install the new mirror. The screwed-in brackets were still in place, so all I had to do was slide it in and give it a quick once-over with some Windex. I posed and flexed before the new glass while my body was still sleek with sweat, then masturbated—this time without climaxing— and took a very long, very hot shower.

It was burger night. While I didn't often slip into indulgence, I found the best way to maintain discipline was to reward it occasionally with reasonable extravagance. This meant three 90% lean beef patties broiled to a perfect medium rare, topped with fat-free American slices and a dollop of ketchup, nested between the golden brown halves of a lightly toasted potato bun. I also allowed myself the caloric excess of sour cream and onion flavored kettle chips and a sliced deli pickle from the jar.

While eating, I watched the news. There was nothing new concerning the Baby Killer. No leads, no clues, no witnesses. There was only the queue of experts speculating on my psychology, or giving tips on how to ensure the safety of "our" children in these troubled times. The sales of home alarm systems had spiked, and gun shops were doing swift business—they might have been the only ones not rooting for my apprehension. It was all so boring and banal. The news media worked from an old script to normalize the emergent crisis, to pare the horror into digestible bites, suitable for mass consumption. The only interesting new development was a report on the unofficial formation of neighborhood watch groups throughout the area, where teams of men walked a beat around their blocks to prevent the Baby Killer from disturbing the unrippled surface of their tranquil domestic ponds. I chuckled at the macho display of vigilance, but then I realized that this might make it difficult for me to continue. With people so on edge, it seemed only a matter of time before the mob would project its suspicion on anyone who displayed the least aberration. The villagers were restive.

The danger was heightened, yet I had to continue. I could *not* just stop. It was impossible. I had felt the rush, flown the heights, and I could never go back to the way things were. Maybe for a day, a week, a year, but not forever. The thought of living without this newly acquired taste was unbearable. I chewed my burger, listless at the idea of how empty my existence would be, lacking my passion. My life was irrevocably altered. There was no choice.

I finished my meal and was tired enough for sleep, which often happens when I get up too late in the day. My whole equilibrium is thrown off. I resisted the urge to slumber, deciding it would be better to make my latte, though it was a bit early, and take it easy for the rest of the evening. I sipped my coffee while checking my email, which I only did a few times a week. Rarely did I receive anything of importance. Never would be more accurate. I had no friends with whom to exchange correspondence, and no professional connections.

I scrolled through some porn-related spam and came to an offer for a free trial membership on a dating site with a money-back guarantee promising that if you join and don't "find love" within six months, they'll return your payment. I had received such solicitations before, but I had yet to take the plunge.

Maybe someday.

•   •   •

Technically, I am a virgin. I say technically because I don't think the concept of virginity should apply to a man. A female is penetrated, opened. Her hymen is broken. She bleeds. She is *altered* and is never quite the same afterward. But what is the difference between ejaculating into one's hand or into a woman's vagina? There is no marked physical consequence for a man, no deflowering. I have never felt the need to insert my penis into a female. My carnal desires can be well satisfied on my own, and I take pride in being self-sufficient where other men are in such bondage. The brain is the most erotic of organs. Nothing in reality can match that which is imagined.

I kissed a girl once, at a college party that I had been reluctant to attend until I was coerced into going to by a classmate from a course on Kant. She was drunk. I was curious. It was a disgusting and degrading experience, our tongues sliding slimily over one another like slugs, noses deformed against our faces. Teeth tapping teeth. A kiss entails the exchange of microscopic food particles, and overlapping oceans of bacteria. Her breath smelled of liquor and marijuana and cigarettes. I pulled away, smiled wanly, lifted my hands in a sort of anemic apologetic gesture, and left the party without a word.

· · ·

After the few minutes required to clean up my inbox, I logged off. I went downstairs and watched recorded episodes of *Law & Order* and *Criminal Minds* and back-to-back reruns of *Family Guy*, both of which I had seen several times but nonetheless found amusing. It was still a little early to turn in, so I read for while in bed. I missed my lost Faulkner. To assuage the hurt of the loss, I chose a beat-up paperback copy of *Sanctuary*. After an hour, my eyelids started drooping. When I had to reread the same paragraph several times, I put the book down and turned off the lights, but my mind was aswarm with the events of the day, and of recent days, and sleep would not come. This is why I do my utmost to keep to the same daily routine and avoid deviation, because even when I find something positive, something that makes me feel good, something that I like to do but for some reason cannot do with regularity, the result is frustration and heartache. I believe the Stoics knew best when they taught that the simplest and mildest pleasures are to be preferred, and that once one graduates to more complex and intense indulgences, the specter of disappointment intrudes, like a vampire invited into the holiness of one's home.

For years I had avoided this, living in flatline tranquility with precious few ups and downs. I cultivated habits and rituals to satisfy every basic need and followed my unwritten rules with the ardent devotion of a novitiate in a cloistered monastery. I was left wanting for nothing. But now I had partaken of the serpent's fruit, and I wanted—*needed*—more. I could no longer be sated with simple human aliment. I felt like a junkie. I twisted myself up in the covers and buried my face in the pillow. I tried every technique I could think of to break the beast inside and attain the replenishing comfort of unconsciousness: deep, concentrated breathing; counting to 100 and back; envisioning myself in some bucolic landscape, a dark enchanted wood or a deserted beach in winter. I put on Chopin's *mazurkas*, then some soft Gregorian chant, then a live recording of a Japanese *shakuhachi* performance at a Zen monastery in Kyoto. Nothing. I stared at the ceiling and carved out imaginary shapes in the darkness. Nothing. I lay there for well over an hour, restless and frustrated and farther from sleep than I had been before.

It was pointless. I got up and walked over to my new mirror and stared at my body in the moon-dim darkness, to which my eyes had grown so acclimated that I could see quite clearly. I began stroking myself, hoping it would help me relax. But my mental space was invaded by visions of that long-ago night at the college party, when I exchanged saliva with a girl whose name I have forgotten, if I had known it in the first place. I recoiled at the unsolicited recollection of that moldy brown dorm suite sofa and those drab, beer-stained carpets, and I felt her spongy, milk-warm tongue exploring my mouth, her moist cheeks grinding against my face, those clammy hands curled around the back of my neck. No matter how I tried, I could not blot out this intrusive memory, so relentless in its assault. I stared at my taut biceps and abs, but she would not leave me be; she would not release me. There was no escape from this waking nightmare. I couldn't get to the part where I picked up and left— maybe I never did. I was trapped in the afterlife of her embrace, stuck in an endless loop of those immeasurable minutes of horror. The punishment of an eternal kiss.

Penis shrunken back to limpness, I sat hunched on the edge of the bed, looking down at my shriveled genitalia. Then my gaze returned to my full reflection in the mirror, the new mirror that seemed so perfect when I had hung it earlier in the day, reflecting a precise and accurate representation of me, a clean and clear photographic image of my body. But now something was wrong. My body in the glass seemed warped and twisted in spots, normal in others. I was a misshapen mishmash, a Frankenstein's monster made of unrelated body parts that didn't fit together. Instinctively, I looked down at myself to ensure there were no actual deformities, then leaned forward and squinted, suspecting it was a trick of the light—or lack of it—that was causing this illusion. Or perhaps my physical and mental fatigue had finally gotten the better of me, deceiving my vision into seeing something other than what was there. Try as I might to right the image, this vague deformation persisted in my reflection. My face was lopsided, like that of a stroke victim, with one eye slightly larger and their sockets uneven with each other. A shoulder protruded up an extra inch or two—giving a faint, Quasimodo cast to my outline—and the right pectoral drooped in an almost feminine way. I grabbed at my breast and squeezed worriedly, tightening my hand as hard as possible. It was firm and solid as always. Pure muscle.

I sighed in relief, but when I turned back to the mirror it was worse. My mouth hung half open in a dumb-lipped gape, and the shrunken eye was now almost fully closed as though I had been punched. Both cheeks were raised and swollen in facial elephantiasis, and my abdomen was transformed into a stretched and flaccid spread of fat, like pulled putty. My evenly shaved head showed patches of raw red baldness, like a patient hastily shaved in preparation for brain surgery, and my arms hung, apelike, down to my knees.

I was aghast. I feared for my sanity. I knew I could not resemble this deplorable creature that stared back at me, yet the wretched likeness would not dissolve. I had never experienced anything like a hallucination, but I was starting to doubt my senses, to question reality.

There was only one way to make it go away. I rushed the glass and slammed it with a trio of robust, rigid rights, shattering it more thoroughly than I had the first mirror. Then I flipped on the lights, ready to deliver more punishment. Through the fissured glass I saw my body as it should be—as it *was*—unscathed and inviolate in its flawlessly toned excellence, the poised and tense musculature more pronounced than ever as it stood ready to defend against any further affronts to its dignity.

I bent and leaned and turned and inspected myself from every angle, comparing the image with the flesh;

there was absolutely no discrepancy. Only after a few minutes did I register the pain in my hand. No fresh glass had succeeded in cutting the knuckles, but the impact must have reopened the wounds, causing a decent seepage of blood through the bandage. It throbbed. I went to the bathroom to clean up, apprehensive about looking into another mirror. But as soon as I hit the lights and peered at myself, I was relieved to find that all was well and back to normal. I washed and slathered my hand in antibiotic ointment and dressed my wound anew. The pain, however, did not subside, so I did something I rarely do, something I save for only the most extreme situations: I took a couple of Tylenol PMs.

· · ·

I categorically detest putting any kind of drug or chemically altering substance into my body. I do not drink alcohol and I have never smoked a cigarette. Though I am well aware that most people find over-the-counter pain medication to be innocuous, it bothers me acutely to corrupt the temple of my body with any such pollutant. But there are times when drastic measures are called for, which is why I keep the bottle of Tylenol on hand.

I am an extremely hale and strongly constituted person who seldom contracts so much as a seasonal cold or mild flu (though I did get the chicken pox at thirteen). Yet there are chinks in my armor. I am susceptible to headaches, for example. And then there is my insomnia. Even as a baby I was a bad sleeper, or so my mother used to tell me. My parents didn't get a full night's sleep until I was nearly two, and even then, sleep remained an issue for me. I wasn't able to spend the night in my own room before the age of ten, sleeping instead in my parents' king-size bed, tucked at the edge of my mother's side. I did this until it became infeasible and awkward and cramped. Still, my parents didn't force me from their bed. They probably would have let me sleep with them forever, but it was time. I eased through the transition by spending many nights nested in a sleeping bag at the foot of their bed before finally settling into my own room for good. Once there, I found it so spacious and comfortable that I wondered why it took me so long to appreciate this.

I have often reflected on this period of my life, the years spent in my parents' bed watching the eleven o'clock news and the first few minutes of *The Tonight Show* before falling off into the safety of sleep. I was not afraid of the dark, nor did I fear being alone, so I don't know what compelled me to sleep with them. I only remember the security of that big high bed, and how untouchable I felt once I climbed up onto it and ensconced myself in the soft cool sheets and fluffy down comforter. And I remember feeling the warm presence of my parents' bodies next to me as I let the day's events ebb into dark forgetfulness, confident in the promise of tomorrow, sure in the shelter of the now, protected from whatever creeping threats lurked in the night. When I woke, the sun would be streaming through the gauzy white drapes, and my father would be shaving with the radio on, and my mother would come over to kiss me good morning and ask what I'd like for breakfast.

Even then, I wasn't a great sleeper. But I was a much better one than I am today.

I took the Tylenol with a little water (not too much, lest I get up in a few hours with the uncomfortable urge to urinate) and went right back to bed, where I waited impatiently for the effect. I felt the burden of thought pushing up against the bulwark of my mind, and I hoped to be unconscious before it was torn down. For a second, I considered sleeping in my parents' bed. I closed my eyes and imagined how it would feel to pull myself under those long-sealed covers and lay my head on the pillows undented by human shapes for years. If the pills had not already anesthetized my limbs and clouded my mind, I probably would have gone and spent the night there. But by the time the thought came to me, I was already adrift. As I dropped steeply into a deep, drug-abetted sleep, I felt tears creeping down the sides of my face onto my pillow.

•   •   •

Twenty-three minutes after noon, my eyes opened, but I was not ready to get up and start the day. This is why I hate taking sleep-inducing pills: it feels more like a coma (or what I then imagined a coma would feel like) than restorative slumber, and I invariably awaken feeling groggy and, while not exactly sleepy, poorly rested. Unpunctuated by dreams or intermittent moments of wakefulness, sleep is like eating without savoring flavor.

I need those occasional breaks, when I rise to the surface of unconsciousness and look down to see where I am, like a remote-viewing or near-death experience where the soul floats up and observes its waning body but knows it is not yet time and flits back in, leaving a uniquely psycho-physical sensation. When I sleep through without such lacunae, it is as if I have been anesthetized for an operation, knocked out one minute only to awaken the next to be told it's all over and everything went smoothly and I can expect soreness, weakness, and a little nausea but otherwise should be fine. Montaigne said that when we are unconscious, we are not wholly ourselves, we cannot appreciate the true value of experience, cannot be wholly invested in our lives. He loved his sleep, but he regretted not being able to fully taste and luxuriate in its pleasure, so much so that in his younger days he came up with an interesting method to glean more active enjoyment from sleep. Thus the Lord of Montaigne commanded his servants to wake him during the night and inform him that he was indeed asleep. I imagine he would then smile dreamily and reply with something like, "Why yes, I am, how exquisite," before sinking back into beautiful oblivion.

But when I take these pills, it is as though I have been knocked out with a blow I never saw coming.

The sun surged strong through the blinds, striping the walls of my room with blazing bands of yellow-white light. I lay with my head heavy on the pillow, arms paralyzed at my sides, legs planted in place like soggy driftwood half-buried in sand. I couldn't get up but knew I couldn't go back to sleep. I felt as if I had been slipped one of those Haitian voodoo zombie concoctions where all observable signs of life are reduced to such faint impressions that the person is presumed dead and promptly buried, all the while being acutely aware of everything happening to him, feeling the physical pain and excruciating mental anguish as he is shoved into a box and planted underground, only to regain control of his body and scream and claw at the casket in agonized futility until his nails break off and his throat is ripped with burning and he is unable to emit another sound and all he can do is lie there and hope death does not delay.

To make matters worse, I thought about what lay on

the agenda: nothing. It promised to be another lovely day, but I could not risk going to the park. Even strolling around the neighborhood might have proven dangerous with so many bloodthirsty suburbanites on patrol. Had I, through my deeds, inadvertently nullified the suburban pact of ask no questions lest ye be asked? Perhaps it would blow over with time, but for now, the dogs were sniffing for a scent, and any hint of one would set them barking.

At one o'clock I told myself I would get up at 1:15. When 1:13 came I knew there was no way I was getting up in two minutes, so I granted myself a half-hour extension. At 1:45 I still wasn't ready, but I told myself that only death would prevent me from exiting the bed at two. When I suddenly awoke at 2:43, I didn't punish or chastise myself for missing the deadline. I fought through the lethargy and heaved my body up and into the shower, where I sat for more long minutes under streaming hot water before washing.

Breakfast happened just after three. It was an inexcusably late start, for which I was having trouble forgiving myself as I ate my oatmeal and figured on how to fill the coming hours. I considered heading back to Home Depot for yet another mirror. I could put the one I had destroyed back in the box and exchange it, claiming it was broken when I opened it. This cheered me a little, but it would amount to a minor distraction. I needed something major. I thought about calling the police hotline again, to correct them once and for all and supply them with the perfect sobriquet, but this would be a dicey move. Plus, I could not even think of what I would say. I spent at least ten fruitless minutes sitting at the table trying to conjure up another name, something more artful and a little less direct, maybe a touch more mysterious and a skosh less aggressive. But after racking my brain and ending up with nothing to show for it but the onset of a minor migraine, I realized that I had already stumbled upon the perfect name. I was the Baby Killer. I was born to be the Baby Killer. I was nothing if not the Baby Killer.

And anyway, it was smarter to stay away from public phones. I was assuredly not one of those serial killers who harbored some sort of repressed, unconscious desire to be caught. Then again, if it were subconscious, I wouldn't know about it. So maybe I did.

Without waiting the requisite hour for digestion, I did the only thing I could think of to stop me from thinking: I worked out. Shunting my thoughts with the Stooges and sweat, I put in an hour of dynamic strength and ten rounds with the heavy bag, six sets respectively of push-ups and crunches and pull-ups and chin-ups, plus three ten-rep military sets of concentrated dumbbell raises (a U.S. Marine Corps technique I had learned from an old issue of *Men's Health*—it works the entire body in one intense exercise, starting from a crouch and lifting two thirty-five pound dumbbells slowly up and over my head, holding them there for a count of three, then slowly bringing them back). I usually didn't like working with weights, but once in a while it was a nice addition, especially when I needed a little extra burn.

By the time I finished exercising and took another shower, it was after seven. I wasn't hungry or sleepy, there was nothing good on my DVR, and I didn't feel like returning to Home Depot. I considered making another fire, but I knew it wouldn't be the same—without the *ritual*, without Juanita. Strangely, I found myself missing the little brat. I sat on the sofa in the dark for a while. After long minutes, I turned on the television.

I was hoping to lose myself in a tedious sitcom or some histrionic police procedural, but I settled instead on one of those hour-long nightly news segments where they count down the top stories of the day, from mildly interesting tidbits to utterly crucial ignore-at-your-own-risk reports. The host seemed perpetually vexed as he worked his way down from innocuous political indignities to major issues like the never-ending debate over healthcare reform, overseas wars, and foiled domestic terror plots. I shuffled to the edge of the couch in anticipation, wishing I had made some microwave popcorn (which I did, on occasion, especially when watching horror films). Sadly, there was no corn to be popped, so in lieu of this, I treated myself to a cold can of Coke (which I absolutely love but seldom drink because all that sugar turns right to fat if you don't burn it off immediately). The final story approached. I couldn't possibly make number one on a national prime-time news program, could I?

After torturing me with delay, the host finally returned with the number one story of the day:

…a truly horrific account from the Northeast that has the whole region, the whole country even, beside itself; the unspeakable acts of the self-proclaimed Baby Killer. We warn you, this report is not for the faint of heart, and you may want to remove your children from the viewing area.

I leapt to my feet. This was a thrill. There is something indescribably satisfying about being famous while remaining anonymous. I had taken my place on a nationwide stage while resting comfortably and safely on my living room couch. I had roused the hatred of millions yet remained free and immune from retribution. The host went on to relate the "unspeakable" details of the case—*my* case—explaining that, despite the name, it was not known with certainty if the babies were indeed—here he paused—killed. All they knew for sure was that two babies with no apparent relation between them other than both being younger than a year old were abducted from their caretakers by a man fitting the same description. And then they flashed another sketch. This one bore a vague resemblance to the Unabomber, yet it was somehow the closest to what I actually look like. There was the black hood and the dark glasses, which did appear to be Ray-Bans.

It irked me that I was referred to as the "self-proclaimed" Baby Killer, but I had to leave it be. I had done what I could to set the record straight. I would not let myself get mired in minutia, however vexing. Not now.

Still standing, I watched the rest of the segment. Hordes of furious parents protested in front of the police station. Burly, beer-bellied men in their T-shirts and baggy jeans and khaki shorts stood on neighborhood corners talking about their need to pick up where the authorities had failed. Terrified young mothers blubbered on cue. And finally, there were the police, who reiterated their tireless determination to catch this ghoul, to stop him by any means necessary. Though reference was made to the head of the local investigation, Chief Michaelson did not make an appearance. I was pleased by this. I was running the show, not him.

The segment ended with some brief closing remarks by the host, who appeared teary-eyed beneath his glasses.

He said that in his twenty-five odd years in the news, covering everything from sports to politics to international affairs to natural disasters, nothing had so chilled him to the core, nothing had appalled him as much as this story. Nothing had ever made him mourn so for the fate of humanity. He said, "the mighty hammer of justice must be brought down." He said, "We must remain strong and cling to each other." And finally, "that light will overcome the darkness, that good will defeat evil, and that the perverted acts of one deviant will never, ever succeed in diminishing our belief in the basic goodness of the human spirit."

I sized him up as another self-righteous little man with a splash of influence and a platform. I thought about how I would have liked to tweeze his dick off with my fireplace tongs and toss it into the flames and force him to watch it char to ash as he bled to death while I sat there, legs casually crossed, nursing a cup of hot cocoa with Cool Whip, keeping one eye on the screen and flipping through channels as though to emphasize that I was not particularly interested in or entertained by his suffering. This fast-talking loudmouth was going to spoil the rest of my night.

I would not allow this. I couldn't, not after all I had gone through. I bounded out of the room and down the basement stairs, turned up The Stooges, stuffed my fists into my gloves and worked the bag brutally. Thirty consecutive minutes. No breaks for rounds. It was a personal milestone. My fists were deadened, hanging like rocks attached to my wrists. I could not lift my arms.

Physically spent, I struggled to remove the gloves and crawled back up the steps, picking up my clothes on the way as though they were a trail of breadcrumbs leading to a long-awaited destination. As I walked through the kitchen to dump them in the hamper, I noticed the red message light blinking on the answering machine.

Carter

·   ·   ·

It was rare that my phone ever rang, let alone that I would receive a message. From time to time I might have gotten a wrong number or a solicitor—even though I am on the government's "Do not call" list—someone calling for Harry or Brenda or looking to rent an economy sedan or to find out what time we close. But I couldn't remember the last time someone had called to speak to me, or left a message.

For the first few months after my parents' death, I received periodic calls from family friends. They were "checking in on me," or "seeing how I was holding up," or "letting me know I was in their thoughts and prayers." Invariably, they would assure me that if there were anything they could do for me I had only to reach out. "I wasn't alone," they told me. "We're here for you," they vowed. I suppose it provided some solace at the time, but I realize now that they were only calling out of morbid curiosity, to see if I was falling apart (and hoping I wouldn't call their bluff by taking them up on their empty offers). Then there was my aunt. She pretended to care for a brief period after I left her custody, which was deeply in her interest as my closest living relative, considering my fortune. She would give me the obligatory Christmas/Easter/Thanksgiving/Birthday calls for a few years (never going so far as to invite me over for a holiday, which I would have declined), and the odd check-in every now and then. But this eventually stopped. So I usually don't pay attention to a ringing phone. It's nothing personal.

I approached the machine warily, as though fearing it might be booby-trapped, and my finger hovered above the blinking light for a few seconds before hitting the play button. It was a female voice. Light and lilting and warm. Kelsi, from next door, of the Kelsi and Marlowe duo. "Hey there, neighbor! Marl and I wanted to know if you'd like to come over for dinner tomorrow night. I'm making my famous duck *à l'orange*—well, famous between the two of us…" (a squeaky little giggle there) "…and we'd really love it if you could make it. I know it's short notice, so if you can't, we totally understand. But we really hope you can! Call us either way, K? Hope all is well. Bye now."

Her voice was inordinately chipper. Could she really have been so happy about the prospect of having me over for duck?

I fought through my exhaustion to process this information. It had been years since I had interacted socially with peers, ages since I had received any kind of social summons. Now I had been invited to dinner by my new neighbors, a bright and good-looking young couple with a beautiful six-month-old baby boy. The child would surely be in attendance, but I had no designs on him.

To invoke an awful blue-collar cliché: one does not shit where one eats.

Marlowe and Kelsi had moved in at the beginning of the summer. I formally met them shortly thereafter. I was walking down the driveway to get the mail and Kelsi was plucking some weeds from a once-lush lawn that the former owners had lazily let languish, while Marlowe was carrying the last of the cardboard moving boxes from the car to the house. She was a petite and pretty blonde with shoulder-length hair that frequently flopped in her face so she had to keep pushing it back behind her ears—an adorable mannerism that perfectly reflected her perky, upbeat persona. She couldn't have been more than twenty-five, a young mother with perfect teeth and a Colgate smile. She told me she was a second-grade teacher, that she was taking the year off for maternity, that she was hoping to get a job in the district once they settled in. She seemed so thrilled to be in her new house and so very happy to meet me, the first of her new neighbors, that when she shook my hand I felt as though I had won a prize. While we chatted there at the boundary separating our properties, Marlowe came waltzing over. He was a big brawny guy with Black Irish good looks, probably about my age but older looking because of a protuberant beer gut pushing up under his T-shirt. Marlowe was also smiley, though not as open and unguarded as his wife. He had large hands, a strong handshake, a wide fleshy frame whose bulk betrayed heavy weight-lifting without proper emphasis on definition (the opposite of my approach), and I would have been willing to bet that he had dabbled in steroids, perhaps when he played high school football. A finance guy who had somehow managed not only to maintain his career but to thrive in one of the most decimated industries in the recession, Marlowe noted that his daily commute would be extended by at least a half-hour. But he didn't mind. "It's more than worth it," he said, pulling his pretty wife close under his arm. This provoked a delightful little giggle from Kelsi.

She giggled often, which should have annoyed me. With her, it was almost charming.

They had come out here to the provinces from the big bad city because Kelsi had just had the baby and the market was ripe for buying. After several frustrating months of searching, they had almost given up hope on the perfect house until they stumbled upon this one, which had been lived in by the same family for twenty-five years until all the kids moved out for good and the husband died and the widowed wife decided to sell (despite the buyer's market) and move in with one of her sons in Pennsylvania. I never liked those people. Though we seldom interacted during those many years, I was glad when they moved, and I had stupidly hoped the residence would remain vacant. Though the house was in decent structural condition, it had not been renovated and needed some serious work, including updated appliances, new kitchen tile, wallpaper, maybe a modernized bathroom, and of course a new paint job. But in all, it was a deal that a young family simply could not pass up. Kelsi was almost ecstatic when she talked about how beautiful the neighborhood was, and how the school district was one of the top-rated in the country, how it was going to be a great new start for them. She said she couldn't ever imagine wanting to leave. She said I was very lucky to have grown up in such a lovely community. She almost made me believe it.

I offered to help Marlowe carry in some boxes and dismissed his protests until he allowed me to do so. Afterward, they invited me in for some lemonade, and to meet their newborn son, Carter, who was in his crib under the watchful eye of his grandmother. I nodded at the nondescript old lady who wore a blue muumuu and matching slippers. I took only the briefest of glances at the child. It was hard to believe that slender Kelsi could have squeezed out a baby half a year ago.

Following these niceties, I graciously refused their invitation to supper and bid my departure. I was late for a workout and didn't want to further disrupt my routine. Thanking me profusely, Kelsi forced me to take a rain check, and both spouses professed their pleasure at meeting me, saying they looked forward to seeing me again soon, and often. If I ever needed a cup of sugar, Kelsi and Marlowe would be the go-to people (though I am very specific with my sugar, only using 1.5 teaspoons per day of Hawaiian Sugar in the Raw in my oatmeal/farina).

As I walked the short way home, I wondered what they thought about me. I hadn't divulged much, only that I had lived in the neighborhood all my life (being one of the earliest inhabitants and one of the very few remaining natives, my parents having put a down payment on the house on spec, before the construction was even complete) and that I had never given much thought to leaving. Kelsi had smiled sweetly and said she thought that was wonderful. Marlowe had nodded, saying it was a great house and a great place to live.

The following Saturday, they appeared at my door with a pie. Apple. Homemade.

"Aren't *I* supposed to bring *you* a pie?" I joked.

They laughed and said it was the least they could do for my helping them with the boxes. Kelsi explained that Marlowe had recently undergone laparoscopic hernia surgery and was under doctor's orders to avoid heavy lifting, so I had done them a great favor. I told them I loved apple pie—especially with a dollop of vanilla ice cream—and that I would have invited them in to have some with me had I not been rushing out to "an appointment." I even checked my watch for effect. Yes, a medical appointment. I had already rescheduled twice, so...

They completely understood. I thanked them for the pie and walked out with them to sustain my subterfuge. Then I drove to the bookstore, where I spent an hour browsing after purchasing a green tea latte. I remember feeling as though I had escaped something dreadful. Though I liked this young couple—as much as it was possible for me to *like* anybody—there had been no one but me and a few repairmen and Mathilde the maid in that house since my parents' death. I simply could not let two people I barely knew inside. It seemed unbearable, the thought of them sitting around the kitchen table, chatting and laughing and drinking coffee and eating pie as if we were old chums. Picturing such a scene left me feeling vulnerable and uncentered. I had to do an extra workout that night to sweat it out of me. But I did treat myself to a healthy slice of pie afterward. It was delicious. Real apples. I did not have ice cream.

$\bullet \quad \bullet \quad \bullet$

But now the gauntlet had been thrown down. I had been extended an official invitation to a weekend dinner. They clearly wanted to cross the line from mere neighborliness to active friendship. And why not? I was a polite, well-spoken, clean-cut guy in their age bracket. I was single and childless, but there was nothing inherently suspicious about that. I was still young; there would be plenty of time to settle down. If anything seemed slightly *off* about me, they would probably chalk it up to a shy temperament and the inherently alienating nature of the suburbs—this is just the way people are out here. Maybe Kelsi would conspire to set me up with a cute teacher friend—the one who is tired of dating assholes, who would love to meet a *good guy* with his own home and start a nice little family. We would live right next door to Kelsi and Marlowe, taking turns at dinners and barbecues, babysitting each other's kids, going on family vacations together. There would be afternoon coffee klatches for the women and evening beers on the stoop for us men (as though I would ever waste a single calorie on beer), where we would offer each other idle commiseration over work and wives and taxes and sports and such other trifling affairs that marked our lives. We would chat about the stock market and bitch about the never-ending costs of keeping up a house. Perhaps we would insinuate our interest in the hot young babysitter who watches our children while we are out dining on Saturday nights, always with the tacit understanding that it was harmless fantasy (devoted family men that we are). We would guffaw and give high-fives and crush our cans and exchange manly handshakes before heading back in to the wives and kids for ice cream, hoping for weeknight intercourse (while imagining the hot young babysitter) before sleep.

With sweat drying on my body like a fine crust, I pictured all of this. Was it so unimaginable? I had never been a seeker of domesticity, never longed for the ideal of a happy home and helpmeet, for a flock of loving cubs and two cars in the garage. Yet there was something about this couple, Kelsi and Marlowe, something I couldn't pin down, that tempted me to wonder if I could have been like them if circumstances had been different. I try never to allow myself to dwell on such vagaries, to agonize over "what might have been" … *if* the limo driver had called in sick or hit one more traffic light on the way home; *if* the trucker had pulled over for a nap or a quick coffee before continuing his route; *if* my parents had missed their flight and stayed in Mexico an extra day; *if* I had gone away with them and been on that plane; *if* my mother had not had two miscarriages on either side of my birth and successfully delivered siblings. *If* I had been one of those miscarried fetuses instead of the one who survived.

When rumination over such stochastic contingencies succeeds in slipping past my mind's censors, I am aware that it is less than pointless—indeed, that it is more dangerous than idle daydreaming. To contemplate such alternate realities that never were, that never could have been, that never had a chance of happening, can only result in suffering. It brings to mind the Many Worlds interpretation of quantum mechanics. When broken down from its incredibly complex mathematical scaffolding, the theory states that there is a potentially infinite number of versions of the universe—or a multiverse—and that every single event, imagined and otherwise, that could have possibly occurred but didn't, at least in our current universe, has indeed happened or is currently happening or will happen in a parallel universe, in another dimension, in a different location on the fabric of space-time. Upon encountering this theory, I remember being at once excited and devastated. It was exhilarating to imagine that somewhere out there on a different astral plane my parents were alive and well, and that we were still going for dim sum on Sundays and having Mom's meatloaf on Mondays. But then I realized that, even if some alternate reality—or an infinite number of realities—existed, it wouldn't matter. It would neither help nor hurt me because I was perforce stranded in this particular reality and would never be able to hop over to see what any other one was like. I used to torture myself with contrafactuals and endless permutations of what-if thinking, until I finally came to understand that even if I could go back and try to alter the situation, change one crucial element in the mixture, it would just set off another trigger to attain identical results, over and over, always reaching the same conclusion, perhaps like Nietzsche's Eternal Cycle of Recurrence. Regardless of the arrangement of the circumstances, I believe the endgame would always be the same. My parents would be dead, and I would be alone. They would never not be dead, and I would never not be by myself. Because this is how it happened. This is how it was, how it is, and how it always will be. Things happen the way they do, exactly as they must, not because there's some cosmic or metaphysical or religious design, not for any kind of karmic payback or providential retribution, but simply because they happen. Existence needs no further justification. Things happen because they happen. Why? Not a valid question.

In a post-workout haze, I found myself standing in the middle of the kitchen in nothing but skin. I was starting to catch a chill, so I dropped my clothes in the hamper and went up for another shower, thinking about the invitation and all its spiraling implications, imagining myself sitting there at the table and eating and making small talk and laughing and trying to make others laugh and complimenting Kelsi on her cooking even if I hated it and saying how nice the house was coming along and asking with understated concern how they were adapting to the neighborhood and emphasizing how wonderful it was to have them be a part of it. Of course, I would have to bring some sort of offering. My parents would never show up at someone's house without a bottle of wine, a freshly baked cake, or a nice box of candy. And then there was precious baby Carter, which added an interesting note to the score.

I should have been honest. I should have confessed to this nice young couple that I was not the person they thought I was, that I was rather fond of them but could never be the neighbor they wanted and we should just cut our losses right then and there and remain friendly from a distance. They could count on me in the event of minor emergencies and late-night fixes, but social calls and soirées were ill-advised (and babysitting was certainly out of the question). Friendship was not possible for me; that ship had sailed long ago.

Then again, there was to be duck. I love duck. And I hadn't had it for so long; the last time was with my parents, cooked Peking style during our last Chinatown Sunday, a lifetime ago. Kelsi's recipe was sure to be different, but duck is duck, and I had a hunch she was an ace in the kitchen. How could she not be?

There was every reason not to go, and yet somehow the decision seemed already made; I would accept. I would accept gladly. I would be there with bells on. I was tempted to immediately call back to convey my emphatic acceptance and offer a thousand thanks in advance, but it was surely too late for a call. I wouldn't want to wake them, or the baby. I had never sent a text message in my life (I still haven't), but if I'd had one of their mobile numbers (or owned a cell phone), I would have sent the following two-word, all-caps sentence: *I'M IN.* I would accept their invitation and accept them as neighbors. As one of the original residents of our picturesque suburban development, I would be acting as a plenipotentiary for the neighborhood welcoming committee. It would be nothing short of a blast. I would love them. They would love me.

Wait, I spoke out loud, stepping back from my burgeoning excitement in an attempt to isolate and analyze it. Why was I so titillated by this scenario? What was I expecting to glean from this, or from any, encounter with other human beings? I could never have *friends*. Certainly not now. For all of my adult life, the concept of human companionship in any form had been completely foreign to me, so unspeakably alien, in fact, that it was impossible to imagine anything vaguely resembling… *friendship*. This wasn't a business dinner. It wasn't a date. The only hoped-for outcome could be friendship. It was too much to process, especially in light of all that had happened, that was still happening. And yet I couldn't stop myself. Visions multiplied before my mind's eye, scenes of us becoming neighborly friends, friendly neighbors. Perhaps at some point I would have an affair with Kelsi. This I saw very clearly. With Carter in Kindergarten and Marlowe always working late, Kelsi has grown bored with her domestic lot. And there am I never having to work at all, until one day when she calls me in a panic because the pipe under the sink is leaking and flooding the bathroom and she doesn't know where the water main is. I rush over and shut the valve and take a look at the pipe in question—even though I have absolutely no plumbing skills and am not sure where the water main shut-off is in my own home—and see that it's just a loose washer. I find the channel locks in a hardware drawer and save the day, whereupon she, effusing with gratitude, insists that I stay for coffee and a crumpet and one thing leads to another and before either of us knows how it happened we're entwined in her marital bed. When it's over, we lie sweating in semi-awkward silence, not quite knowing what to say but knowing quite well that this is just the beginning, and that it will not hurt our relationship as friends and neighbors but, if anything, will strengthen it, she being a more fully satisfied woman and therefore a better wife and mother; perhaps the latent guilt and underlying shame even makes her overcompensate and become more attentive to her family, drives her deeper in her devotion to son and husband; and perhaps it leads to me being a more invested and devoted friend. And who knows whom Marlowe is fucking on those late nights *at the office*, anyway?

After an extra-long and deeply contemplative shower, I strode out of the bathroom, draped in a towel, and put on Sinatra's "Strangers in the Night." Slipping off my towel, I waltzed up close to the glass and slow-danced in front of the shattered mirror. I thought of the hit I was going to be at dinner. I casually rehearsed witticisms and clever conversation, imagining the way they would listen in rapt appreciation and how they would later talk about me with adulation while washing the dishes together.

I grabbed my erect penis and worked it up to a near climax, successfully stopping at the last possible instant before drying myself and putting on my pajamas.

I made my latte and watched *Goodfellas* on DVD. This is my favorite film. I've seen it dozens of times and could probably recite it nearly line by line—I've even performed the Billie Batts scene for myself in the bathroom mirror, doing all three characters—yet it never fails to swallow my attention whole. That was what I needed just then. I needed to be distracted. I needed not to overthink the immanent event. I had been running on overdrive and the strain was taking its toll.

After the movie, I went up to bed and read for a while. I shut the lights a little earlier than usual (around 2:30), opting for some Mahler to send me off. I was first exposed to Mahler through my father, who listened to Beethoven and Mahler almost exclusively, declaring a slight preference for the latter after years of studious comparison. As my father explained it, Mahler is like fine European espresso as opposed to the strong, straight American cup of Joe that is Beethoven. A symphony seemed too much of an investment for the time of night, so I chose the shorter *Kindertotenlieder*, which translates from the German as *Songs on the Death of Children*. (The irony did not elude me, though it was assuredly unintentional.) In this version, Leonard Bernstein led the Wiener Philharmoniker and the famous baritone Thomas Hampson. I didn't have it loaded on my iPod—lengthy classical compositions use up too many gigs, and the genre itself seems less amenable to digital technology—so I had to use my CD player.

As the doleful notes hovered around me, Hampson's booming, low-toned vibrato rode behind the spare instrumentation like a funeral procession, and I thought about the tragic story behind this piece, and how gloomy old Gustave would come to regret its composition, while his young wife Alma would blame its curse for the "three hammer-blows of fate" that would ultimately and inexorably disfigure their lives. In a poignant twist, shortly after composing the music to *Kindertotenlieder*—the words are actually by the German poet Friedrich Rückert, from a series of 428 poems documenting his own agonizing experience with the deaths of his two children—Mahler's oldest daughter would die of diphtheria. Following this tragic event, Mahler essentially disavowed the music. Soon after, he succumbed to pressure from his critics and resigned from the Vienna Opera. Mahler was then diagnosed with severe heart disease, which compelled him to significantly limit his movements to the degree that every step had to be counted with a pedometer. He died at the age of fifty.

Kindertotenlieder proved an effective sedative. Though the words were incomprehensible to me, the exquisitely sorrowful orchestration, coupled with the deep, intrinsically grief-stricken voice, cast an ineffable spell. I felt the burden of mentality, of intellect, of personal concern … lifting.

A flow of tears traced a path from my eyes to the pillow. I didn't bother wiping them.

I woke at 10:03—fairly early, a propitious omen—to a mellow brightness pushing in at the window and the buzz of a lawnmower next door. The lawnmower had probably awakened me, which would normally have set the day off badly, but not on this day. There was plenty to do in preparation for the evening. The first thing, after my shower, was to confirm.

I hung up before the first ring. In my haste, I hadn't formulated my words, and extemporaneous speaking is not where I excel, so I decided to keep it simple and straightforward: *Thank you for inviting me, Kelsi. I would love to come to your house for dinner.* I considered writing the words down, but this seemed absurd. I could handle two sentences, especially after a few rehearsals.

She answered just after the first ring, as though she had been waiting all night by the phone. I said "hello," and she must have recognized my voice (my number is blocked and does not show up on Caller ID) because she responded by cheerily announcing my name.

"We haven't seen you in forever. How *are* you?"

I paused, bypassing her question. "Thank you, Kelsi, for inviting me to dinner for your house. I would love to come there. To your house. To eat dinner… at your house…"

How could I have botched that? I sounded like an outmoded automaton, my delivery so weak and wooden it was as though I were reading from a malfunctioning teleprompter.

"Great!" She graciously disregarded my verbal tangle. "I'm sooo excited. I hope you like duck."

"Oh, I love duck," I blurted. The truth comes easily, as long as it's kept short.

"Excellent! How's eight?"

"Excellent. Eight's a fine time. That's when I usually eat. Earlier than eight's not really dinner, I feel. But eight is great. If I had to pick an ideal time for dinner, it would be eight."

She hesitated for a second or two, maybe three. "Great!"

"Great. Can I bring something?"

"Just you and your appetite!"

"Something for… Carter?"

"Oh, that's sweet, but he's good, really. There's too much of his stuff around the house already, and he won't be dining with us," giggling.

"Mm."

"Super. Then we'll see you at eight?"

"Yes. At your house for dinner… at eight."

"You remember how to get here, don't you?" She laughed first. I followed mechanically. "Bye now."

I tried not to assail myself too harshly over my less than laudable performance. I hung up and stood by the desk, telling myself I had the whole day to relax and coach myself into readiness. Telephonic communication was awkward for me, and I would make a much better impression in person. Before giving myself the chance to negate this thought, I prepared breakfast and ate with exceptional slowness, practicing for dinner. I watched a home improvement show where a young couple leaves their modestly disheveled house for a few days and lets a team of decorators and their crew totally renovate it at their discretion. The couple returns to a posh new palace that barely resembles their previous space. In this particular episode, the young Indian couple didn't seem thrilled with the work (I wasn't overly impressed either), but they were too polite to voice their dissatisfaction.

It was difficult, but I avoided the news.

After breakfast and a requisite interval for digestion, it was time for my workout. My hand ached more than it had since the initial injury, but I muscled through; it was important to be pumped for the evening. Then I posed in front of the broken mirror, showered, and posed again before the bathroom mirror. While flexing, my hand had started bleeding again; its knuckles were swollen and rough with crusted blood running in jagged lines, and a bit of blood had somehow landed on my face. I went back into the shower and washed it thoroughly with soap and hot water. The antiseptic sting felt good as it rinsed away the dead clots and left a clean wound site. After my second shower, I posed one last time, being careful not to further aggravate my wounded hand.

I have a fairly extensive wardrobe, which occupies a walk-in closet and three chests of drawers, and I spent a full hour selecting my outfit for the night. I settled on a nice crisp Ralph Lauren Oxford shirt (purchased several years ago but never worn, as I was saving it for an occasion), off-white with thin, sharp dark gray pinstripes, and a pair of deep-dyed blue-black Polo jeans. Whenever possible, I like to keep the ensemble designer-consistent. This makes me feel balanced and comfortable.

I laid out my clothing for later, threw on a T-shirt and jeans, and set out on my errands.

Presently, there was the question of what to bring. I had some difficulty narrowing my choices, so I opted for the lot: a bottle of red *and* white wine, a bouquet of fresh flowers (from the florist, not one of those cheap supermarket deals), a box of assorted Swiss chocolates, and a yellow cake with chocolate buttercream icing, which was my second favorite dessert growing up. First place is reserved for my mother's homemade carrot cake with cream cheese frosting. After all these years, I can still taste that moist, dark cake, still feel that sweet tang filling my mouth when she would let me lick the unusable remnant of icing off the spatula. I would scrape up every bit of its velvety whiteness from the walls of the metal mixing bowl, and she would invariably quip that I had saved her the trouble of having to wash it, and then I would sit impatiently at the kitchen table, inhaling the aroma as the cake baked at 350 degrees for 1.25 hours, after which I could barely contain myself from devouring it, though my mother would never let me touch it before it cooled, so she could properly apply the icing. Adrift in memory, I was overcome with pathos. I would never taste my mother's cake again. I could have carrot cake, maybe even one similar to my mother's, made with the same recipe and the same brands of ingredients, baked in the same oven and served on the same plates. But I would never again eat a cake baked by her.

The initial rounds of shopping went smoothly. There was a noticeable police presence in the mall (and surely even more plainclothesmen camouflaged within the general populace), but no one bothered me. No one seemed to notice me at all. I was the invisible man, the wolf in sheep's clothing, the serpent slithering unseen through the children's garden. Everyone was solicitous and friendly. The wine salesman helped me choose two nicely priced but perfectly respectable bottles of table wine and even gave me a couple of those specialized wrapping paper slips to fit around the bottles. The florist personally put together a striking array of lilies and carnations, garnished with leafy sprigs of green and delicate white baby's breath. The woman at the chocolatier let me sample several pieces of candy and a delicious block of peanut-butter fudge (a piece of which I guiltily bought for myself, thinking that one must reward oneself sometimes, and if this week hadn't qualified for such, then nothing would) before picking out the perfect selection of truffles in an adorable little golden gift box that she tied with a shiny red ribbon.

All that remained was the bakery, right on the way home. This should have been the easiest stop, as I was in the habit of going there as often as several times a week for fresh dinner bread, but something felt queer as I rolled into a front spot. I almost pulled right out and opted for a supermarket loaf (which is often just as good, as long as it's from the bakery section and not pre-packaged). Instead, I waited in the car a minute or so, listening to "Raw Power," the title track.

If you're alone and you got the fear
So am I baby let's move on outta here
Raw power will surely come a-runnin' to you

There was a small bespectacled woman standing outside the door of the bakery, maybe mid-forties, with wild stringy hair like shredded straw. She wore a long, faded blue floral house dress and fluffy bunny slippers. At first, I took her for a panhandler (something you don't often see in affluent suburbs), but then I realized she was handing out flyers that I assumed were religious propaganda of some sort.

"Please sir, please help us stop the evil," she implored, shoving the paper at me.

I smiled and took it without looking as I entered the bakery, certain that she was referring to Revelations and the End of Days, the beast whose number is 666 and the Rapture and the Battle of Armageddon and all such insanity that would be very entertaining were it not for the fact that so many morons believe in it so literally. The jingling of a wind chime attached to the door announced my presence. There were no other customers in the bakery. I had been frequenting this establishment for as long as I could remember, this bland little bakeshop in a glass-encased storefront wedged into the corner of a mid-sized strip mall, and though ownership had changed several times over the years, nothing much else about it had. It was like a time capsule: the same name and antiquated signage, the same display cases rife with ample varieties of old-fashioned cookies and biscuits, pastries and tarts; lining the rear wall were shelves of full-sized cakes and pies, while the upper half of the wall was devoted to loaves of bread, from French to peasant to cinnamon raisin sourdough to Italian to semolina to white and wheat and seven grain. My mother would take me to this bakery after school for an oversized chocolate chip cookie or a fresh fudge brownie sans walnuts (I never understood the need for nuts in a brownie). Though I am a sucker for sweets and baked goods, I have incredible will power and will only allow myself to indulge on infrequent occasions. Still, every time I set foot in there, that warm confectionery scent would envelop me like a superior foreign power, and it took all I could muster to refrain from amassing a bagful of treats.

The clerk was new, or at least I had never seen him before. He was a slight and slim young guy with sharp features and darting eyes. He smiled and came over to lean against the counter while I surveyed the encased goodies, focusing on the three chocolate cakes on the shelf behind him. I asked for one with yellow inside. He turned and analyzed them and turned back to me with a worried look, biting the corner of his lower lip.

"Sorry, we're out of yellow." He frowned slightly, a display of sympathetic disappointment. Then he suddenly perked up to point out the alternative: "But… I can give you a chocolate. Same icing only chocolate cake inside. It's soooo yummy." He amplified his eyes to emphasize the degree of the cake's deliciousness, crossing both hands over his heart as though overcome by the very thought. If he wasn't gay, he was doing a fine job of pretending to be.

"I'm not too sure about chocolate on chocolate," I said. "It's a bit monochromatic."

"Well," he scoffed, turning bitchy on a dime, "it's not exactly interior design we're talking about here!"

"Mm. Good point."

It wasn't a good point at all. It was a stupid and rude remark, and it merited a severe reprimand. But I needed to buy a cake.

"I'll take one then."

His brightness returned. "Trust me, you will *not* be disappointed." He gushed as though my purchase had made his day, zipping around to pull a cake from the shelf while happily humming "My Heart Will Go On."

Hoping to avoid the too-close-for-comfort temptation of the pastries, I glanced at the flyer that the zealot had handed me on the way in, expecting to see an invitation to an anti-abortion rally or some other dreadful Christian gathering. Instead, I unfolded the paper and lost a breath when I saw the (still inaccurate) sketch of the Baby Killer. In bold block letters above the sketch were the following words:

> STOP THE EVIL BEFORE HE COMES TO YOU'RE [*sic*] HOME. NO ONE IS SAFE!

There was also a little comic-strip image of what I took to be the archangel Michael crushing the satanic serpent under his foot. The figure was rendered with bulging cartoon muscles and a blond bob that reminded me of He-Man from the *Masters of the Universe* animated series. He brandished a mighty sword above his head, presumably in readiness to decollate the devil, while the snake's tail was coiled around one of his bulbous calves. It was not a bad drawing; it resembled something that might have appeared on a power metal album cover from the eighties. At the very bottom was the name and address of a huge Evangelical church just a few blocks from where

I stood. I knew the place. It looked more like a sports arena than a house of worship. I always wondered what went on in there.

The flyer did unnerve me, but I assured myself there was no cause for worry. After accepting her offering, I had walked right past one of these concerned citizens without so much as a hitch in my step, had I not? With perfect indifference. Was that the behavior of a baby killer? I took a deep breath.

"Anything else?"

The cashier's girlish voice pierced my concentration.

I ordered an oversized chocolate chip cookie, a brownie, and an assortment of pastries.

• • •

Never before had I eaten in the car, but I couldn't resist. I broke off a piece of the cookie, then another piece—a larger one. And then another, until the entire cookie was gone and my shirt and lap were sprinkled with crumbs. I was disgusted with myself. Worse, thanks to the chirpy choirboy in the bakery, I had the theme to *Titanic* stuck in my head.

I cued Slayer's *Reign in Blood* as I pulled back into traffic, cranking it up until my seat vibrated and the windows shook. The opening riff of "Angel of Death" shredded the air. I felt energized, but also calm. Then came the bridge, a slower but nonetheless driving section of chugging guitars and pounding bass that would have had me headbanging like a demon, if there had been any hair up there to bang. But when the band starting building toward the tumultuous climax—a chainsaw buzz of distortion enveloping an unrelenting thrash of snare and kick drums—my heart sank slightly as Araya screamed the closing lyrics.

Angel of death
Monarch to the kingdom of the dead
Infamous, butcher
Angel of death
Angel of death

A pang of regret pierced me. A spasm of jealousy bolted through my body. Would not "The Angel of Death" have been a more apposite name for my brand?

·   ·   ·

Slayer had successfully booted Celine Dion out of my head by the time I pulled into the garage. I unpacked my goods and set them on the kitchen table, regarding the fine display of generosity and gratitude that would surely make me a guest to be remembered.

There was still plenty of time, and I was craving a nap, but I resisted this impulse. I had already indulged in the cookie, so another workout was most definitely in order. It wasn't as intensive as the rage-driven sessions of recent days, but it was enough to reinvigorate me, and I felt a lively spring in my step as I headed up for another long hot shower, listening to Coltrane's *A Love Supreme*, which documents the magnificent performance at the Antibes Jazz Festival in the summer of '65. It is the only extant live recording of the four-movement suite by the classic quartet.

I must have stayed in the shower too long. As I exited, I noticed that my fingers were pruned almost down to the palms, and my body had become reddish, like… like a *lobster*. Thinking about my time with Jake brought me such nectarous warmth. But it already felt so far away, as if it were one of those long-ago occurrences that had fundamentally shaped me—a perfect reel of memorialized experience, cauterized into my consciousness to be revisited throughout my life as a touchstone of strength, an anchoring base to cling to when the storm tossed me about.

This was not the moment to get lost in fond recollection. It was almost time to get ready. With the event horizon so close, the reality of the situation took hold of me. I tried to assimilate the raw fact that I would soon be sitting at a table with other human beings, supping and drinking and engaging in conversation. I would breathe the same air as my hosts, and I would be expected to share a part of my existence with them. My life would be temporarily joined with theirs, if only for a few hours. It would be the first night since just after college that I had dined with anyone. The last time had been a casual dinner with my old neighborhood pal, Brian, on his last trip home before he moved out to Seattle to work for Microsoft. We went for Sushi and shot some pool before saying our final goodbyes. We promised to keep in touch. We didn't.

I took several deep breaths and looked at my naked self in the fogged-up bathroom mirror. The extra work-outs and increased time/sets had made a difference. My already steel-cut body was becoming a precision-crafted whole. I studied the exquisitely detailed muscular compartments, each toned to a degree of perfection rarely seen outside of fitness magazines and anatomical illustrations. It had taken years of discipline and sacrifice—physical, mental, and emotional—to attain this level of corporal refinement, and I was very pleased. I posed and flexed, admiring myself from many angles, but I resisted the strong urge to masturbate.

Putting on *Amnesiac* by Radiohead, I leisurely dressed as Thom Yorke droned.

> *After years of waiting, nothing came*
> *As your life flashed before your eyes*
> *You realize*
> *I'm a reasonable man*
> *get off my case*
> *get off my case*
> *get off my case*

The outfit was perfect. Young and hiply casual, yet neat and respectful—just right for such an occasion. I topped it off with an unconstructed three-button black slim-fit sports jacket (not Ralph Lauren, unfortunately, but Calvin Klein; close enough) and a gorgeous pair of gray suede high-top Saint Laurent sneakers (with black contrast laces). Dress shoes are a concession I refuse to make under any circumstances. Those rigid wooden soles make me feel as if I'm treading barefoot on a boulder. The last time I wore anything like them was for my Confirmation at age thirteen, and I remember cursing under my breath as I walked down the church's center aisle in a strangling tie and brand-new unbroken-in tasseled loafers, looking up at the larger-than-life crucifix hanging on the wall of the apse and thinking that at least Christ didn't have to worry about uncomfortable footwear as he traipsed over the Via Dolorosa. By then I had long stopped believing. The breaking point had come shortly before my first Communion, when my catechism teacher told us, in solemn seriousness, that the imprinted wafer and cheap wine we were going to eat and drink were (really, actually, physically, literally) the body and blood of a two-thousand-year-dead crucifixion victim from the suburbs of Jerusalem. Out of all the preposterous biblical fairy tales (the parting of seas and the walking on water, the bushes burning and the feeding of thousands with a little fish and bread), to say nothing of the stupid rules (not eating meat on Friday and not being able to say *goddamn* without bringing down the Lord's ire), it was the concept of transubstantiation that finally got me to quit the team. But my apostasy was not yet manifest as I approached the dying Christ on the way to the confirmatory alter while thinking about how much I hated my shoes. In that moment, I felt culpable, remorseful, ashamed. A sinner.

The time was approaching. I spent a very long while in front of the mirror, checking myself out and making minor adjustments to my clothing. Most notable was the partial-tucking of my shirt, the highly stylized quarter-tuck. This is where most of the front of the hem is tucked into the pants with painstaking care in order to seem utterly nonchalant, while the back and most of the sides are left to hang out as though one couldn't be bothered to finish the job. The effect is twofold: it conveys the impression of youthful insouciance (while showing some effort toward orderliness), and it gives the chance to show off a nice belt buckle, which would otherwise remain hidden under the flowing ends of a completely untucked shirtfront. It is not an easy affectation to pull off. A touch too tightly tucked (or conversely, too loosely) and it all falls apart. Like a well-done bed-head, it must present the impression of being unplanned, a spontaneous and unintentional outgrowth of inherent nonchalance, even though astute observers will understand and appreciate that it requires the utmost attention to get it just right. Anything less than just right will leave one looking foolish.

. . .

It was time. Nerves jumping, I concentrated on getting the gifts in order, putting the wine and cake and candy in a doubled-up shopping bag and cradling the flowers in the crook of my left arm. My legs felt hollow as I locked up and stepped outside. It was inexplicably strange to be walking across the lawn to the house next door. It was something I had never imagined myself doing.

The night was cool, but I was already sweating a little. As I walked over the grass to their porch, I was astounded at how lush and green and healthy their lawn was. The hedges were trimmed back low and neat beneath the front windows, and multi-hued rows of fall flowers spurted from patches of smoothly layered mulch where vibrant, newly planted ornamental bushes burgeoned: miniature corkscrews and a blue-tinted Norwegian spruce and a flowing little Japanese cherry. It was as though the entire property had gotten a makeover, revitalized by its youthful inhabitants. Even the trees seemed happier. The cedar shingles on the house had been power-washed and returned to their original brightness. The roof had been redone with imbricated architectural shale. The dusty old Venetians had been replaced by delicately drawn lace curtains and light-filtering cellular blinds. This was not the place I had grown up next to.

There was a weatherproofed cherry wood bench beside the front door, polished to an unblemished shine as though inviting visitors to relax and take a load off while they waited for the homeowners to come out and join them with a carafe of chilled lemonade and a tray of mixed-berry scones. I would have liked to sit there a few minutes and watch the darkness deepen over the silent street, listen to the night birds rehearse, close my eyes and take an early evening nap while the air cooled around me.

Boxing back last-minute jitters, I stood before the door a few seconds, then turned back to my house and looked at it forlornly, as though it were a faraway haven that I would never see again. For a split second I was ready to drop everything and run back and lock the door and shut all the lights and possibly never come out again.

I rang the bell.

A patter of feminine footfalls grew steadily louder until the locks snapped and the door opened and there was Kelsi's bright, smiling face, ushering me in with a wrap-around hug and a smacking kiss on the cheek.

"Hey there, you. So happy to see you."

She did seem genuinely glad to see me, which was very strange. No one has ever seemed glad to see me. Marlowe soon followed, coming up to me with a firm shake and a lipped grin, his left hand grabbing under my elbow.

"Awww, you shouldn't have brought all this," Kelsi said with a simper, looking at my gifts.

"Really, man, what is this, Christmas?" Marlowe patted me twice on the back with fraternal manliness and relieved me of the bag.

"It's nothing, really. So nice of you to have me over. Here. To your house."

"Here, let me go put these in some water." Kelsi took the flowers and brought their petals to her nose and closed her eyes as she inhaled their scent. "Oh, they smell wonderful,"—giggle—"and they're soooo pretty. Thank you, thank you. It's been a minute since anyone brought me flowers." She squinted sidelong at her husband and elbowed him playfully in the love handles as she scurried off into the kitchen.

"Why would I get you flowers?" Marlowe called out after her. "We've already had sex."

"Har har," Kelsi yelled back.

Marlowe looked at me and laughed. It took me several seconds to realize he expected me to laugh back. So I did. Then he draped a meaty arm around my shoulder and led me through the foyer. "Come on in. Let me show you what we've done to the place."

I had been in this house only once before, when the neighbors' poodle strayed over into our backyard and my father ordered me to bring it back. The former residents were so grateful they invited me in for chocolate milk and 'Nilla Wafers. I was fourteen. That might have been the last time I had 'Nilla Wafers, sitting at their kitchen table with a cookie while mother, father, brother, and sister lovingly stroked their returned dog. The layout was much the same as our house, much the same as the rest of the homes in the development, except those that had been renovated. This likeness offered little comfort, however. I felt I was on foreign soil. If anything, it was more unsettling to find myself among these similarities, as though I were visiting a bizarre kind of alternative universe, one of those Many Worlds that exist on some other dimensional plane, just not mine. It was like being in an alien landscape, not knowing if the aliens themselves were really as friendly as they seemed or were hiding some nefarious agenda beneath the veneer of their hospitality.

And now I was back in that house. Kelsi and Marlowe had maintained the basic structure of the interior, the partitioning of the rooms and such, but the amount of cosmetic renewal was stunning, especially considering how short a time they had been there. The clean white marble tile in the foyer was new, as was the textured mauve wallpaper running floor to vaulted ceiling. They had ripped up the shag carpeting on the stairs leading up to the second level, stained white the underlying hardwood, and shellacked it to a dazzling finish, with a rich black runner coating the center (which Marlowe informed me was Persian). The kitchen was also tiled in white, with freshly painted white walls and new raw wood cabinetry and a butcher block kitchen table with matching chairs, all very modern and minimal, making the space seem larger than it was. And all the appliances were the latest state-of-the-art models: the Sub-Zero Pro fridge/freezer combo, the Bosch stainless steel built-in dishwasher, the Kenmore chef's double-wall oven and a sleek black glass-top stove, which was working on all burners as Kelsi fluttered around stirring and seasoning what simmered in pots and pans.

"Oh, you guys are making me nervous," she chastised us, giggling, as we hovered about the kitchen watching her work. "Go watch the game or something in the den for a few minutes while I get the food ready. Too many chefs…"

Marlowe laughed and I followed suit. It had been a long time since I had laughed in a social setting, but I turned out to be a quick study. We retreated into the den, which had been redone top to bottom with naturally colored varnished wood floors and a light beige paint job. A large, dark tan leather sectional, which could probably seat ten people comfortably, wrapped around a modern amorphous sofa table of black granite, and the whole setup rested on a large black area rug and faced a 60" hi-def widescreen television built into custom-made cabinetry that perfectly complemented the couch.

"Wow. This is a hell of a room," I commented, genuinely impressed.

"Let me tell you something: if I could stay in here forever, I would. I got all the sports channels. Literally, all of them." He paused to let this sink in. "And this TV lets you split the screen into four. Imagine watching the Superbowl on this thing."

I expressed requisite awe, which seemed to satisfy him. I pictured several young suburban fathers sprawled about eating chips and dip and drinking beer and yelling at the screen and fist-bumping while their disinterested wives huddled in the kitchen talking about their kids and the new Korean manicurist and the latest additions to their homes and complimenting each other on their clothes and jewelry and hair. Hell could not have been much worse. "Some job on this house. Very impressive."

"Oh yeah. And we're just getting started," Marlowe said, clapping and rubbing his hands like a plotting scoundrel in an old-time movie. "Once we're done, you'll never know some old fogey empty-nesters lived here before us."

"Out with the old…"

"You said it. What are you drinking?"

"Water for me."

"Really? You didn't drive here, did you?" Laughing again at his own joke.

"No. I only drink water. And coffee. Lots of water and coffee."

"Okay." He paused, searching my face for clues. "I bet there's some kind of story behind that."

"No story. I just don't like the taste of alcohol."

"You're a strange guy, aren't you?" He cocked his head and fit this comment into an amused smile that concealed an underlying seriousness.

"People are strange, when you're a stranger.'"

He didn't seem to get the reference. He paused again, then snapped out of it with a clap. "Alrighty. Ice water it is."

I strolled about the room while Marlowe went to fetch our refreshments, looking at pictures of the couple at their wedding, on vacation someplace tropical (Kelsi comely in a pre-maternity bikini and Marlowe already showing some early signs of a married-man paunch), and finally a slew of photos of the completed trio: a confused Carter sandwiched between his loving parents; a bemused Carter being held overhead by his father like an infant Superman; a sleeping Carter being softly kissed on the forehead by his mother; a disinterested Carter just sitting there posed against a wall of pillows in a banded jacket, breeches and jodhpurs, looking bored and a bit baffled and none too happy with the ridiculous outfit he has been dressed in.

I feel your pain, Carter. You didn't ask to be here. They took it upon themselves to bring you into this world and now you're supposed to be perpetually thankful for it, to see life as some kind of unique gift, something so special and wonderful, to be savored and cherished and valued above all else. Believe me, nobody feels your pain like I do.

• • •

Marlowe and Kelsi returned with a tray of drinks and a platter of cheese and crackers. My water was nicely chilled with chipped ice and served in an expensive crystal goblet. We clinked glasses and took our seats on the couch, the two of them snuggled up against each other across from me with matching glasses of red. I rarely allow myself the indulgence of cheese, but I had a couple of slices of brie and camembert on some whole wheat crackers, and then a few more.

"Where's Carter?" I asked conversationally, between bites.

"He's upstairs taking his nap." Kelsi turned her eyes upward as if she could see him through the ceiling.

"Sleeping is what he does best," Marlowe said, right before swallowing an entire cheese-covered cracker.

"Not unlike his father," Kelsi quipped.

"Yeah, I sleep like the dead," still chewing his cheesy cracker.

One can only be so lucky.

"He's a pretty good pooper, too," Kelsi added.

"Not unlike his father."

They laughed. I followed suit.

"So, you've been here all your life?" Kelsi asked me.

"Where?"

"In this neighborhood?"

"Oh. Yes. I was born here. My mother actually gave birth to me in the house. Long story. I've spent almost every single day of my life there. Except for a few vacations when my parents were alive."

"Oh. I'm sorry. They're both…"

"Dead. Yes. It happened a long time ago."

An awkward silence followed.

"Mm. That must've been tough, losing them when you were young."

I gulped down the rest of my water. "You'd be surprised what you can deal with when you're forced to. Especially when you're young."

A few more seconds of silence. Even more awkward.

"Well, here you are." Kelsi brightened, as though my very presence were testament to my strength in the face of adversity, my mere existence a victory in itself. Which, in a way, I would agree with. But it was a Pyrrhic victory at best, a temporary, hollow victory, a false finish that we so often convince ourselves is sufficient, as if the *miracle of life* is itself an adequate bastion to fend off despair, to banish the ultimate hopelessness of it all, dying from day one, decaying from the get-go, sentenced before we emerge from the womb. And there was no better example of such naive optimism than this unsullied couple in the blooming springtime of their lives, basking in the warm enclosure of their fresh familial circle (into which they had invited me for a brief visit), comfortable in their confidence in a bright future, in their credulous certainty that good things will happen to good people like themselves, that the just will get their desserts despite the inevitable hills and vales along the way, the bumps and bruises we all must endure. They believed that everything would work out for the best, even if we can't initially see how. They blindly trusted the contour of life. They accepted. But that was only because existence had not yet shown them its true face. Whatever hardships and tragedies had been thrown at them were of insufficient severity to dissuade them from the belief that life was anything other than beautiful, that it is worth living at all costs, that in the overall balance of things the good outweighs the bad. They had not come close enough to the kernel of suffering.

I wished they could be spared. I liked them, despite everything. I liked their guileless positivity and open friendliness. I wish we all could be spared. But none can be.

After a few minutes of small talk (mostly on their end), a couple of refills of wine for Marlowe, and two more goblets of water for me, we moved into the dining room, whose regal decor I found a bit ostentatious (or at least less tasteful than the rest of the house). The walls were a flat yellow with a grand golden chandelier hanging over a large wooden rectangular table with ornately carved legs and matching chairs padded with red velvet cushions.

"What a lovely room," I said.

"Thank you." Kelsi, smiling as always, placed the serving dishes on the table. "We like it."

"This is the one room I had a say in," Marlowe boasted.

"It does seem a little more… masculine."

"Exactly what I was going for."

"Almost kingly."

"Well, it is my castle. Now serve me my meat, Queen." To punctuate the joke, Marlowe grabbed his knife and fork in either hand and banged their blunt ends down next to him.

We all laughed. Then Carter joined in on his baby monitor, which was sitting next to Kelsi on a side table.

"Oops, looks like you woke the young prince, my liege. Very nice." She shot a faux dirty look at her husband while laying some serving spoons and forks in the dishes. "You boys help yourselves while I go check on him."

"I'll get him, Kels." Marlowe started up but was gently pushed back into his seat by his wife, who was already heading away. "As you wish, my queen."

"Looks like marriage agrees with you guys," I comment- ed, once Kelsi was away.

"We met when I was a junior in high school. She was a freshman. As soon as I met her I knew she was the girl I was going to marry."

I hate lines like this.

"How did you know?" I couldn't help asking.

"I don't know… you just know."

"No. I really don't know. I've heard people say this and I'm not sure exactly how… how you know from the moment you see someone…"

Marlowe twisted his head upward in search of an answer. "Can't really explain it. Just one of those things."

"One of what things?"

Shaking his head with puckered lips, he looked at me, bewildered, as though his expression were explanation enough.

"Like the universe itself." I filled in the blank for him.

"Yeah. In a way."

"Random but somehow making perfect sense."

"Exactly. The way it is because of the way it is."

"Like God: He is, always was, and always will be."

"Amen," said Marlowe.

Then Kelsi returned with a groggy Carter pressed against her breast.

"There he is," Marlowe cried out to his son. He made a funny face and held out his open arms.

"Would you get the crib, hon?" Kelsi requested, holding Carter back like ransom.

"Sure thing, babe. You mind if the little killer here hangs out while we eat?" he asked me, halfway out of his seat.

"I could think of nothing more delightful."

While her husband went off to fetch the crib, Kelsi brought her child over for a formal introduction, bending down so our faces were level, inches apart.

I was enraptured, wholly bedeviled by this amazing little creature. He was physically beautiful to a degree that set him above the multitude of bald, bland infants who resemble each other to the point of indistinguishability. But there was something else about the child—as if he were in possession of a nascent self-awareness, a kind of heightened intellect gleaming in his ocean-deep eyes that reminded me of the stories of Guatama Siddhartha emerging from his mother's womb without crying, a kind of transcendent understanding quickening his timeless face.

"He's… he's… remarkable." I barely managed to get the words out of my mouth.

"Say hello, Carter. Say hello," she instructed, beaming at her infant boy.

Perplexed, he looked from her to me, and then we locked eyes, his, wide and brown, seeping into mine as he sized up this curious visitor to his realm from the safety of his mother's arms. His parents were fine-looking people who had surely passed on their superior genes, yet he looked nothing like them, neither in outward aspect nor inner radiance. There was something exceptional inside this child, something rare and unparagoned, and I couldn't help feeling it resonate with something inside me, something that had nothing to do with Kelsi or Marlowe or the rest of the world. There was something inexpressible between us, something unbreakable. I know he felt it too, in his own infantile way.

"Hello there, little one," I greeted him in a perfectly adult voice. "Nice to meet you." I gently took his warm, moist, doughy palm between my fingers, offering a caricature of a handshake.

"I think he likes you," Kelsi whispered.

He looked at me in knowing silence.

"The feeling is mutual."

"He usually cries when he meets someone new."

"So do I, but I do my best to wait until I get home."

She laughed and playfully slapped at my shoulder.

"Okay." Marlowe returned, situating the crib between him and Kelsi. "Drop him in Kels, and let's get to the eating part before it gets cold."

"Look at this, Marl. I've never seen him take to someone like this before."

The connection was indeed extraordinary. Even his mother recognized it. I retain a perfect memory of little Carter gripping my hand, refusing to lift his eyes from mine, calmly and intently staring at me as though linking up with something inside me, something primal, preliterate. It was a singular communion, as if we shared pieces of a lost evolutionary structure calling to each other from across a great distance, like wayward magnets drawn together after centuries apart.

"Yeah." Marlowe was not impressed. More likely, he did not want to show it. "Cute. Now what do you say we dig into this duck before it turns into a goose?"

"What the hell is that supposed to mean?" Kelsi turned to him, laughing. Carter's hand slipped from mine but he still held it out, like Adam's hand reaching for the divine touch of the Creator.

"It means scoop me some grub, woman."

"He gets so cranky when he's hungry," she excused her husband. "He's worse than a baby." She placed Carter in his crib, out of my view, and proceeded to fill our dishes with succulent slices of orange duck and wild rice and buttery mashed potatoes.

We stopped talking and started eating. I was careful to measure my pace. For a few moments the only sounds were the clinking of silverware and the occasional cooing of Carter serenading us as we chewed and swallowed and washed down our food. The baby's presence was monopolizing my mind, so I said something simply for the sake of breaking the hold. "This is quite a feast, Kelsi. Everything is really delicious."

"Thank you. We're really happy to have you. It can be a little scary moving into a new neighborhood. You never know who you're going to be living next to."

"And thanks for the wine." Marlowe held up a glass of the red I brought. "Sure you don't want some, just a taste?

"I'm sure. Water is my wine." I toasted the air with my glass.

"For a guy who doesn't drink, you sure can pick 'em."

"Everything is really delicious." I repeated myself verbatim. I felt stupid for the redundancy, but I wasn't lying. The duck was lean and juicy and flavorful. The rice was cooked to a flawless consistency, and the potatoes were whipped to a brilliant fluffiness that perfectly complemented the meat. Even the bread was fresh, and bread is something I know well.

We ate and chatted while Carter lay quietly in his crib, out of sight but not at all out of mind. They talked mostly about themselves—which was a relief, as I didn't have much to say about myself—about their first little apartment on the second floor of a private house, where the crazy old landlady would complain about every step they took on the creaky hardwood floor, and even if they flushed the toilet too late, in response to which Marlowe claimed he would get up in the middle of the night and flush a few times "just to piss her off." They had planned to get a larger apartment, but between the housing crisis shooting down prices and sending mortgages to historic lows, and the tax credit for first-time buyers, they figured this was an opportune time to become homeowners.

"Never too soon for the American Dream," Marlowe said. He gave a corny wink, laying a large hand on Kelsi's shoulder and massaging it a bit. "What happened to your hand?" he then asked, scooping a heaping forkful of potatoes into his mouth. Some of it fell out and dropped back into the dish. He quickly scooped that up and into his mouth as well. Had he only just then noticed my bandage?

"Oh. I slammed a door on it." I lifted it for display. "Looks worse than it is."

"I thought maybe you got in a scuffle or something."

I laughed. "I'm a suburban kid. Never thrown a real punch in my life. Not like you city boys."

"Well, the mean streets aren't as mean as they used to be, but I've had my share of *fisticuffs*." He said the word with sarcastic affect, then put his hands up beside his head and rolled them around in shadowboxing mimicry.

"Yeah. A real fighting Irishman." Kelsi tousled his hair teasingly.

"Seriously, though. I did a little boxing when I was younger. My uncle was an amateur middleweight. Almost made the Olympics. He's got a gym down by the bridge. Sometimes I go there to work the bag and blow off some steam. Matter of fact, I'm thinking of putting a bag down in the basement one of these days."

"Maybe you could give me some pointers," I suggested. "Forget the city, the suburbs aren't as safe as they used to be."

"Tru dat," Marlowe affirmed, lapsing into poorly played street slang as he chuckled into his raised spoonful of rice. "A man's got to know how to handle himself."

"More duck?" Kelsi rose, the ever-attentive hostess detecting an empty plate.

"I shouldn't, but I must."

She was already filling my dish with meat and potatoes. "We never eat leftovers, so have as much as you can fit in."

"You haven't asked me about my name," Marlowe interjected.

I looked up and halted my chewing. Had I done something unintentionally inappropriate?

"Everybody asks about my name."

"You mean… the spelling?"

"No, silly," giggled Kelsi, grabbing my utensil-less hand and squeezing. "Don't you think Marlowe is an unusual name? Have you ever heard it before?"

"Well, there's the playwright Christopher Marlowe, but that's a surname. Marlo Thomas?"

"That's a chick, man."

"A *chick*?" Kelsi sat back and smiled with semi-serious indictment at her husband. "I didn't realize we were in guy talk mode now? Just pretend this *chick's* not here and you *dudes* can talk however you want."

"Sorry, language Nazi." He leaned in and smiled at her, then turned the smile on me. "I meant," with exaggerated politeness, "is not Marlo Thomas of the female persuasion?" He bowed his head at his wife for approval.

"Very nice." She tapped the top of his head approvingly.

"I believe she is, yes," I said, swallowing my food and preparing another forkful. It was no Peking duck, but excellent nonetheless.

"My name is spelled M-A-R-L-O-W-E. My mother was a huge fan of hard-boiled detective fiction, and while she was pregnant apparently all she did besides eat was sit around reading Raymond Chandler novels. So one day my father said that she was going to give birth to a little Phillip Marlowe. And a few months later, *voilà*."

"I guess they could have named you Phillip. Or Raymond. Or even Chandler."

"Sure. But would it have been as dramatic?" He wagged a forefinger before his face. "I think not."

"Interesting." I nodded and raised an eyebrow.

"I tried to read one of his books once. Eh. Couldn't get into it. Stopped after, like, five pages."

"My husband's not much of a reader," Kelsi critiqued with a sour expression.

"What? I read the Internet all the time."

"See?" She looked to me in mock shame.

"Reading is reading. Get off that high horse, babycakes." He turned to me as though we shared an inside joke. "She goes to a mommies-only book club once a month and thinks she's a professor."

"I was an English major in college," Kelsi defended herself. "I love to read. But it's hard to find the time nowadays."

"Time is… very hard to find."

"Reading's overrated," Marlowe protested. "You should live life, not read about it. Or see the movie."

"Well, I'm going to make sure this guy loves his books." She turned to her beloved child.

"And I'm going to make sure he can throw a football. You a fan?" he asked me expectantly, as though there were clearly a correct answer.

"Uh…"

"Hey, what's with the Fritzes?" Kelsi rescued me with her interruption, jumping with interest at the first possibility of neighborhood gossip. She looked from her husband to me.

The Fritzes were an older, childless couple who lived on the other side of Kelsi and Marlowe. They were known for their eccentric complaining about every neighborhood peccadillo, such as the way someone's trees overhung the roadway, or how another's car engine revved too loudly, or how another's unkempt lawn was dragging down property values. At least, this was what I overheard when my parents were still active in neighborhood politics. But the Fritzes had never bothered me.

"They've always been a bit… off." I smiled. "The suburbs can do strange things to people."

Marlowe swallowed quickly and wiped his mouth. "Fucking old bugger rings the doorbell and tells me my sprinklers, which I just paid three grand to fix up, were spraying onto his lawn. Have you seen his lawn? It's a goddamn patch of dry weeds! He should be thanking me." He pointed at himself. "He should be paying some of my water bill."

"What did you tell him?"

"I said I'd adjust it," irritably mashing some grains of rice into his potatoes.

"I've heard they've been here forever," Kelsi chimed in. "What are they still doing here at their age in that big house with no kids?"

I shook my head in ignorance.

Marlowe was riled up. "I mean, you've got to know when to say when. They've lived their lives. What do they need a house like this for, with a backyard they probably never use and all those extra bedrooms? They should sell and move to a nice little senior condo community. These homes were meant for families, not retirees."

I nodded in agreement. Then I said: "Like Dylan says: 'Your old road is rapidly agin'. Please get out of the new one if you can't lend your hand, for the times they are a-changin'.'"

They looked at each other quizzically. I felt a blush rush up from my neck.

"Dylan who?" Kelsi asked softly, as though trying not to hurt my feelings.

Now I looked at them quizzically. "Bob Dylan."

"Oh, man," Marlowe leaned back and guffawed. "My uncle listens to all that stuff. You ain't no dirty hippie now, is you boy?" It was an impressive redneck imitation.

Kelsi slapped him on the arm. "I think it's nice to appreciate the old stuff."

"You saw that, right? You see how she abuses me?"

Evincing no shame over their cultural ignorance, they exchanged menacing looks of love, Marlowe pretending his arm was hurt, Kelsi making a baby face and rubbing and kissing the spot she'd struck a moment earlier. Their marital interaction and badinage were precious. I do not say this with the slightest condescension. There was something so honest and authentic about their syrupy displays of affection, as though it were like this every day and not merely put on to impress their guest. They seemed to maintain an air of freshness and sparkle even as their long-term relationship had become moored in security and familiarity. Knowing the quirks and foibles and exasperating eccentricities of one another's personality, being able to finish each other's sentences and all but exchange thoughts without speaking, having memorized the maps of their respective psychical, spiritual, and physical geographies, they still wanted to explore no other country. But they were young, and there was plenty of time for life's bitterness to poison the parfait. The statistics on divorce are clear. Countless unpredictable events can blight even the most sublime union. But for now, for this moment, everything was right. Nothing could be better. And now was all that mattered.

"You guys… you… you're beautiful," I found myself saying.

"You all right, bro?"

I was crying.

Luckily, it had only just begun, a weak dribble out of one eye while the other welled in preparation.

"Sorry, excuse me." I coughed to camouflage what was happening. "I think I went a little heavy with the pepper." I drank some water, dabbing my eyes with a napkin.

"Are you okay?" Kelsi looked from me to her husband to me.

"Fine, good." I gave them a thumbs up. "I'll just go…" I shot to my feet, nearly knocking over my chair. "Where's the bathroom?"

Kelsi accompanied me down the hall, though I knew exactly where it was; the blueprints for our homes were identical. Indeed, the strange sense of an otherworldly parallel was starting to push me off the tracks I had so prudently ridden upon all evening, staying in place even when a few sharp turns had almost flipped me over. It would have been a shame to lose my way now. I just needed a quick *timeout*, as suburban parents say to their overheated and unruly offspring—a swift snap of solitude to regroup. This was more company than I had had in a lifetime.

Dazzlingly clean and smelling of mild pine forest potpourri, the bathroom had been tastefully redone in small rectangles of beige flooring with bamboo wall tiles and a white marble sink with gold-trimmed fixtures. I ran the cold water and splashed some on my face. I was not sure why I was doing this except that I had seen people in movies do the same in moments of tribulation. And it did help. Mostly, it made my face wet and chilly, but it also succeeded in washing away the saltiness. Leaning over the sink with my elbows on either side of the basin, I stared deeply at my reflection in the bright, spotless glass before me. This was something I did often and for extended periods at home, but never in a foreign mirror. My reflection seemed different, variegated. Raising a timid hand to my cheek, it felt as if I were touching another, a wax statue, a lukewarm, insensate thing, neither subject nor object but some indefinable in-between. I tried to be as still as possible, analyzing the angles and curves of my face for clues and points of reference, landmarks of self-remembrance, but the more I looked at myself the less recognition I felt; the more I studied my features the more they melted into odd deviations of what I thought they were, minor variations on what I had come to expect with such surety whenever I looked in the mirror, not so profound as to make me seem a stranger but altered to the point where I could have passed for a brother, an impersonator, a doppelgänger that was going to stray off into his own independent actions at any moment. And there was something else. I discerned someone strangely specific staring back at me. What I was seeing was the sketch on the news, the picture on the photocopied page. The Baby Killer was there in front of me. But he was not taunting or daring, not threatening to take the reins and lead us off into the dark forest from which there is no egress. He was not the snake under Michael's feet, the evil tempter determined to lead me astray. No, he was appealing to me in the most heartfelt and human of terms, communicating in a reasoned, honest, and quietly impassioned way that made pellucid sense of all the swirling chaos around me. He *was* the conquering archangel crushing the beast underfoot. He was the way through the forest, the light in the darkness.

• • •

I don't want to be misunderstood. I don't want the all too simple diagnosis of latent psychosis or some other species of psychopathology to cloud the picture. Of course, I harbor no doubt that all manner of theories will be advanced in explication of my "unsound" mindset— theories that will be tossed about like soap samples, hypotheses that will be raised and rejected, argued and antithesized. The psychologists and mental health professionals and sundry experts will see to this, espousing their positions in newspapers and journals, the more prominent ones perhaps getting to air their thoughts on some evening news special devoted to me. People are constantly seeking the tidy explanations, and there are always an abundance to choose from. This is not to say that one or more of these explanations will not provide some useful insight into my mental turmoil and monstrous actions. They would probably attribute most of my deviance to "dead-parents-syndrome," if the DSM permits such a diagnosis—and surely to a touch of that convenient catch-all, clinical depression. My life and mission would be reductively descried as the sad result of years of self-imposed isolation and social deprivation. The one who slipped through the cracks. It would be asserted that cases like mine are hard to see coming, and worse, nearly impossible to prevent, thus absolving the experts from any blame. In the parlance of popular media, I would be one of those "ticking time bombs," dormant for years, decades, until one day they explode without warning. They might even manage to frame my account in cautiously sympathetic terms, once all the cards are counted. It will be a matter of determining what factors contributed to my abominable behavior, or led me to this precipice. Maybe they will make a movie out my story. It's a shame that Johnny Depp is too old to play me.

But I was not hearing voices or seeing things. Nothing imaginary was guiding my actions. I was in full possession of my faculties and in firm control of my conduct. I knew that I was looking at myself, and only myself, in that bathroom mirror. If I heard anything, it was my own internal voice, the submerged and suppressed speech of the self bubbling up from the recesses of being like a lost underwater treasure slowly being revealed. What it was telling me wasn't clear, but the insinuation was obvious.

"Everything all right in there?"

It was Marlowe, breaking the sanctity of my solitude.

"Be right out."

"You fall in or something?"

I heard Kelsi's admonishing voice in the background: "Marlowe!"

"Just washing up. Don't wait for me."

Another stupid thing to say. I was a font of foolish

statements. Wait for what? Of course they were going to wait for me. I was their guest, the centerpiece of the soirée. I dried my face and hands with a couple of monogrammed paper hand towels that were stacked in a Lucite holder next to the sink. They were soft white cotton with a large embroidered silver letter R in the middle, flanked on either side by an M and a K floating at the upper edges. Then I wiped down the puddles and streaks I had splashed on the countertop and dripped down the cabinets. I took a fresh paper towel and stared at the R in the center and wondered what their last name was. I wondered about their heritage, what their parents were like, how they were as kids. The front of my shirt was dark with wet, but there was nothing I could do about that, so I patted myself dry as best I could, took a last look at myself in the mirror, folded the unused paper towel and slipped it into my back pocket, and opened the door.

The dinner plates had been cleared, the table was swept of crumbs, and dessert dishes and coffee mugs lay before our places. My hosts were waiting patiently in their chairs, trying not to betray any manner of concern about my extended bathroom hiatus. Marlowe sat at the head of the table. Carter was planted on his mother's lap, sucking steadily on a blue pacifier and staring at me with placid intensity as I took my seat across from him.

I tried to explain away the time spent and the wet shirt. "I sometimes get hot flashes."

"Ah. I didn't realize you were menopausal."

Marlowe's alcohol-tinged quips were starting to dance on my nerves, but I laughed and excused myself again for taking so long. We sat back to digest a spot before digging in to dessert, relaxing in a post-dinner lull where everything seems to have slowed and quieted and the senses are focusing on absorption and little else. Marlowe sipped a tumbler of cognac and did his best to foist one on me, trying to guilt me into it by saying how he hates to drink alone and Kelsi can't join him because cognac is a man's liquor. I stuck with water.

"Carter hasn't cried at all this whole time," I said.

The kid turned to me as though he knew I was talking about him.

"Yeah, he's a trooper. Doesn't like to cry in front of strangers."

"I'd hardly say I'm a stranger anymore."

"It's really amazing," Kelsi commented with genuine astonishment. "He hardly ever cries. At first I was worried that maybe something was wrong with him, but… he's just a good baby. We got lucky."

"Yes. You're very lucky."

"Coffee's brewing. Should be ready in a minute."

"You do drink coffee, don't you?" Marlowe questioned.

I had already told him I did. "As long as there's no liquor in it."

"Well, this is an Irish household, but we'll make an exception this time." Another joke. "What's your beef with alcohol anyway? It can't really be that you don't like the taste." He leaned in as though he were on to my secret and I should just give it up.

If he wanted a story, I would give him a story. I took a deep breath and looked into my empty plate as though reluctantly dredging up a few crates of backlogged pain for display.

"Well, the truth is, my parents died in a plane crash." I paused. "It turns out the pilot was drunk, so…you know…I guess I have a negative association. I just…" I put up my hands to finish the sentiment, tightening my face against the pain of the real memory that hovered behind my embellishment.

Kelsi turned her face down so her chin rested softly on her son's pale pate. Marlowe looked at me in shame. A cumbrous silence hung over the table.

"Shit. I'm so sorry, man. I really… can't imagine… I had no idea… shit." He pushed himself back from the table in what I interpreted to be a confused display of self-flagellation.

"No worries."

"No, I feel awful, really." He looked to Kelsi for support, but she only glowered at him with reproach. "I'm so sorry," he said.

"Don't be. It was a long time ago."

"Seriously, I feel terrible."

"Seriously. Don't. I'm just kidding."

His jaw dropped.

"You're *kidding*?"

"Not about them dying. That's as true as the truth gets. But I'm pretty sure the pilot wasn't drunk. Maybe the copilot. But what does he really do anyway?" After a pause, I added: "Regardless, it was a car crash. No planes involved."

Marlowe looked at his wife, then back to me. "Well, I am sorry about your parents," he said.

The atmosphere suddenly shifted. With one wrong turn, our conversation had veered off track and onto uncharted terrain. Kelsi, owing to her excellent grasp of etiquette, did her best to steer us back. "Okay, how about some cake?"

She shot to her feet, smiling at each of us before handing off Carter to Marlowe, who accepted his charge with quiet reserve.

"Hear that, little man? It's cake time!" Marlowe rubbed his large straight nose against Carter's flat little button, provoking a screech of delight that brought a smile to all of us.

The uneasy mood had been fractionally dispelled by a baby's laughter and the promise of cake. The grim haze was held at bay by the bold beauty of new life, its tolling bells drowned out by Carter's saccharine squeal. There remained an undertone of awkwardness, however, which was amplified when Kelsi left the room.

"I love cake," Marlowe said, grinning sheepishly. He was barely able to meet my eyes.

"Same here. Big-time cake lover."

She returned with the cake I had brought, displayed on an expensive-looking Lennox cake dish—along with a glass bowl of fresh fruit and a wooden dish filled with candied walnuts. Just as she set the dessert ensemble in the center of the table, the phone rang. Kelsi's voice was hushed and serious and calmly forceful as she addressed the caller, as though she were talking someone off the roof of a building. She hung up and stood before us with a strained apology on her face. A wisp of hair fell between her eyes.

"I'm sorry guys. It's my sister with some kind of crisis. I have to talk to her for a few minutes." She flattened her hands in supplication and bent slightly at the knees. "I'm so sorry."

"Not a problem." I waved her off. I wanted badly to fix the fallen lock in the middle of her face.

"Take your time," her husband seconded. "We'll have some nuts. I'll have a few extra because I know Sister Sappho doesn't like them."

She gritted her teeth and twisted his ear. "I'm gonna take it upstairs. Back in a flash." Her delicate footfalls soon passed overhead, ending, presumably, in the bedroom.

When his wife was safely away, Marlowe said: "Crazy fucking family she's got."

"Oh?"

"Seriously. Her sister's a lesbian who can't keep a woman to save her life because she's so goddamn insane. Kind of hot though. Between me and you…" He looked both ways, as though making sure no eavesdroppers were near, and leaned over the table to grab a grape, pushing Carter softly against its edge. "Sometimes I fantasize about her. You know, like having her join us in bed sometime." He rolled the grape around in his fingers before tilting his head back and popping it into his mouth. "Hey, family is family, right?"

"So they tell me."

"Any siblings?"

"No. I'm an only child."

"You're probably better off. My kid brother's a pain in my ass. I mean, I love the guy and all, but I've been bailing him out of shit since grade school. It's really getting old now. Can't keep a job *or* a woman. He's worse than my lesbo sister-in-law."

I nodded and sipped my water.

Marlowe sipped his brandy. "It's a shame Kelsi's sister's a pearl-diver." He snapped off a piece of vine with several grapes attached and pulled them off one by one.

"Otherwise I'd hook you up. She's not butch or anything. She's actually *very* hot." He shook his hand as though cooling a burn.

"Too bad I'm not a lesbian."

"Nobody's perfect."

He downed the last of his cognac and quickly refilled his glass. "Have a grape. Some nuts. She could be on that phone for hours."

He took a walnut for himself and held the dish out to me. I waved him off.

"Thanks. I don't like nuts."

"Then maybe you *are* a lesbian."

He was amused with himself. And very drunk.

"But I will have a grape," I said.

The grape was delicious, possibly one of the best I had ever had. It was large and plump, sweet and juicy, and it seemed somehow to transcend the essence of grapeness. I have mentioned that I do not typically enjoy fruit, yet I grabbed a few more, and as I bit into the third and felt its skin explode between my teeth and its juices splash back against the walls of my mouth, I heard Marlowe's voice come at me from across the table. In the most casually conversational tone, he said: "So how about that fucking Baby Killer?"

He said this while holding his son's arms out, as a puppet master would, and playfully bobbing them up and down.

I stopped short in my chewing and stared into the dripping innards of my cloven grape. The tiny edible seeds within glistened darkly. "Mm. How about that?" I responded, before laying the second half in my mouth and letting it sit so my tongue absorbed the fullness of its flavor.

"Man, would I love to have five minutes alone in a locked room with that sick piece of shit."

He was shaking his head, gritting his teeth, and lightly pounding a fist into an open hand, which drew Carter's attention.

"Mm," was what I said to that, finally chewing and swallowing and readying another grape. As I said, I abhor fruit. I hate the very idea of it. But these were good grapes. "And what would you do with this person—in a locked room?"

"Ohh oh." His head-shaking increased in rapidity. His fist pounded harder against his palm. His teeth clenched tighter. "First of all," he said, "I wouldn't even call him a *person*. And let me tell you, only one of us would be coming out of that room alive."

I paused, took one last grape and ate it quickly. "Okay. But what *specifically* would you do? Say you had a chance right this instant to be alone in a room with the Baby Killer. What would you do?"

"Shit, I don't know." He unraveled the fist. "All I know is that he should suffer, and I'd like to be the one to make it happen. And jail's no answer—our tax dollars providing this scumbag with a bed and three squares a day."

For an instant, I wondered if I could get oatmeal and Farina in prison. Oatmeal seemed possible, but it was unlikely to be Quaker Oats. Probably some generic prison-issue.

"Even solitary confinement's too good," Marlowe went on. "He should be killed. He should be nothing but dead. Erased from this Earth. No trial. No appeals. Straight to the gas chamber, or I guess it's lethal injection now." He stopped for a second and stared at the side of his son's face. "Nah. Even that's too humane. Firing squad. Electric chair. Stripped naked and greased up with monkey pheromones and thrown into a locked room with an angry, horny four-hundred pound gorilla."

"Interesting scenario, but I don't think gorillas mate with monkeys. Or humans."

"You get the point."

"Well, who knows? Maybe you'll have your chance."

"Yeah." He laughed it off. "I could only be so lucky. That coward probably never comes out of his house, except when he's stealing babies. Probably some fat, lonely, pimple-faced loser who's never even fucked a woman." He swirled his cognac around in his glass with his right hand and patted baby Carter's belly with his left.

His profiling wasn't entirely wrong.

"Man, if anybody ever tried to take my son…" He looked down at Carter and squeezed him close against his body, eliciting a breathy harrumph from the little one. "…I'd stop at nothing to make sure that was the last mistake that fucker ever made."

"Mm."

"Just thinking about it makes my blood boil."

Marlowe looked out into an imaginary distance with fatherly concern, then took a long swig of cognac.

I was worried he might be holding Carter too tightly.

"Yeah, I know what you mean."

"Well, yeah, but you can't *really* know." He finished his drink, got up, and walked over to place Carter in his crib, which was off to the side of the room, then went into the kitchen and returned with an uncapped bottle of Guinness. "I mean, until you have a child, until the nurse hands you this little life that you created, until you hold it in your arms and you look at each other and feel this amazing, amazing…" pausing in search of another word, and failing, "this amazing *bond*."

He was starting to tear up. His voice thickened. "I'm sorry, but you just can't understand."

"Mm. I understand. I understand that I can't understand."

"But someday you will. You dating anyone?"

It was too late to revert to buddy-talk, too late for offhand. He had let a hurricane come through and there was no shutting the door on it now.

"Uh, no. Not at the moment."

"Because Kels has some pretty smokin' little teacher friends who are looking for a good man to settle down wi—"

"I really wish you could tell me exactly what you would like to do to the Baby Killer if you found yourself alone in a room with him. I mean specifically."

"What? I told you. I don't know. Beat the shit out of him, I guess."

"Mm. That's as creative as you can get?" I rolled a grape around my palm with a finger of the opposite hand.

"Smash his head in with a bat? Stab him in the heart? Kick him in the balls until they're mashed to jelly?"

"A little better," I encouraged him, eating the grape and leaning forward to intensify the interrogation. "But what if you saw him trying to take Carter? What if he did it right in front of you? Took your only son while you were right there watching it and knowing what he was planning to do? What would you—what could you—do to stop him?"

At this, Marlowe eyeballed me oddly, as though an inchoate distrust were building somewhere inside, but then he broke whatever skein of suspicion was coiling, laughed a little uneasily, and took a hearty slug from his bottle of beer. "Ha. You're creeping me out, man. Let's stop talking about this, okay?"

"Mmm…" I turned my eyes upward as though deciding whether I was "okay" with the proposed change of subject. Then I looked at him directly. "Nah. Let's stay on point. I like current events."

"Well, there are other current events, aren't there? Health care? The troop surge?" He was desperate in his attempts to push me off base, and his hostility was palpable. "The fucking World Series? You a Yankees fan?"

"I hate sports," I declared. "And that other stuff is so dry, so bloodless. None of it really affects us personally, does it? I'm sure you have an excellent health plan through your employer, and there's really no chance either of us is going to fight overseas. But someone snatching and killing infants, right here in our own area? Right under our noses?" I leaned forward. I paused. Then I pulled back calmly and tapped the table with a forefinger several times before speaking. "Now *that's* an issue that hits home, especially for you. And for him." I turned my focus on Carter, who was diligently working the pacifier and ogling me through the bars of the crib. "I mean, it could be anyone. We have no idea. They have no leads."

"They might," Marlowe objected. "They can't tell the public everything, you know. Maybe they're closing in. And we're not even sure he's killing them. That's just what he says. Maybe the sick fuck's just taking them because his wife can't get pregnant, or he's impotent or something. Probably a limp-dick little faggot motherfucker."

"I thought you said he probably never fucked a woman in his life. Now he's married? And gay?"

"Jesus! What does it matter?" He lurched forward, almost yelling. Then he grabbed the sides of his head as though a pulsing headache had gripped him. In the next beat, he attempted to regain his composure, smiling tautly, nostrils flared. He said: "I really, really wish we could get off this topic. It makes me uncomfortable. Bad enough this shit is happening. We don't have to let it into our homes."

True. You didn't have to. But you did.

"Fair enough." I pretended to back off. "But you're the one who brought it up."

"I know. I know. My bad." Hand on heart. Curative slug of beer.

"No. No, it's me." I shook my head. "I don't have a child, so I can't possibly understand how sensitive this issue is. I shouldn't have pushed. In fact, I don't even remember what it's like to be a son, so what right do I have to talk about any of this?"

"No… I mean… yes… kind of… but I didn't mean… it's not a *bad* thing or anything." He reddened and rocked back and forth in his chair, watching himself peel the sticker off his beer. "Fuck, I really put my foot in my mouth, didn't I?"

"Don't sweat it, Marlowe."

I rose casually and arched my back as though in need of a good stretch, then walked over to the crib where Carter now lay on his back, sleeping. "Looks like our conversation didn't interest him."

"Like Kelsi said, he'll sleep through anything, that one."

Anything?

"What the hell is she doing up there?" He turned irritably toward the stairs, no doubt hoping that his wife would come down and diffuse this awful tension with her abundance of natural charm and comforting femininity.

"Oh, so if I pick him up…" reaching gently into the crib, slowing slipping my hands in underneath and lifting with care so that he wouldn't feel the motion, "… he won't wake up?"

"No—well—you probably shouldn't—" Marlowe rose and took a couple of unsteady steps toward us.

"He's okay, see?" I carefully cradled little Carter in my arms and angled his unconscious face toward his father. "Don't worry. I'm really good with babies. They're kind of my specialty." Looking down lovingly at the peacefully sleeping child, I rocked him tenderly, twisting the upper half of my body like a slowly rotating mechanism.

Marlowe stood there with a look of suppressed panic, as if he couldn't fathom why my innocent handling of Carter should disconcert him. Yet he surely sensed, perhaps only as a parent can, that there was something not quite right about the situation, that his child was potentially in some kind of danger. Still, he just stood there, vaguely nonplussed, trying to make sense of the raw data his instincts were feeding him. I felt I should clarify, if only to ease whatever confused worry was accumulating. I felt I owed him that.

I looked down at Carter and then back up at his befuddled father. It was important for me to grant him direct eye contact during my confession.

"Okay, however we've gotten here, I guess we've come to this point, so, here goes." I inhaled deeply and slowly exhaled. "Marlowe, I want to tell you, man to man, that I didn't plan any of this. In fact, I really hoped this wouldn't happen, which is why I considered declining your invitation. But you guys are so sweet—especially your wife. I just couldn't say no. And it's been so long since I've been invited anywhere. I just…" I found myself caressing the baby's head. It felt like a fuzzy little melon.

"What are you talking about?"

"I'm talking about what I have to do. What must be done. Some things simply must be done. They have to happen."

"Do me a favor, give me my kid."

He was suddenly sober and stern, but he remained exactly where he was, unmoving, standing before me like a gunslinger readying himself for a shootout.

I paused as though it pained me to refuse. "Can't do it, Marlowe." I shook my head regretfully. "I just can't do it."

He waited before responding, shifting his weight as though about to move on me, but still he held back. "I'm not asking."

"You could ask if you'd like. You could try to stop me. You *will* try to stop me. But you won't succeed."

"Put down my son." He didn't raise his voice so much as harden it, stressing each syllable of the command and taking three small steps forward, until he was standing a couple of feet away. There was more deference in his voice than directive, as though he were politely pleading rather than demanding.

We stood staring at each other for several stretched seconds. His fear fed my resolve, despite his best efforts to keep it from showing.

"Fine." I dangled the word in the small space between us and looked down diffidently before turning and laying

Carter in his crib. Then I turned back to meet his stare head-on.

"What the *fuck*, man?"

His display of indignation over the poorly chosen stunt that I had played out for far too long remained fraught with nervous uncertainty. He moved forward. I could smell the alcohol and dry nervousness on his breath. I think he meant to intimidate me. Perhaps he should have. He was four or five inches taller than I, and he had forty or fifty pounds on me, yet I sensed he was overcompensating for the fact that he was so obviously cowed by a smaller man, by a man with no wife or family or attachments to the world, a lesser human being. Or maybe he was conflicted by self-reproach, by the fact that he had taken such a pitiable person into his home, shown him the utmost in hospitality, and had been confronted by this twisted joke, which he was having trouble getting past.

Or maybe he knew just who I was, what I was going to do. Maybe he knew that he could not stop me, even if he was hell-bent on going down trying.

I would oblige him.

He pouted like a chastised teen, backed up a step and put his beer bottle on the table. "That wasn't funny." He raised a finger in my face, centimeters from my nose. "You don't fuck around with a man's son."

"Actually, that's exactly what I do. It's really nothing personal."

I do hate when people use that expression. I felt sullied, just saying the words. Everything is personal. Nothing is *not* personal.

He extended his arm, indicating the way out. "Please leave. Now."

"But we haven't had dessert. I brought cake."

His flustered face reddened still more. "Now, please."

His use of the word *please* irked me. He was commanding me, pure and simple, basically throwing me out of his home, uninviting me, not asking me politely to do something for his pleasure. *Please* was a poor word choice. It was disingenuous. It was a lie. I let his arm hang out there, studying the dark spots on his sclera, the pores of his face, the burgeoning stubble that probably hadn't been there in the morning.

"You know I can't, Marlowe." I tried to affect the soft contrition of one who is morally compelled to do something for the greater good, something that he knows will adversely affect another, even if that is not his primary motive. I almost wished I could have explained to him why I needed to do it, and how, ultimately, it was to his son's benefit. If I could have calmly reasoned with the man and patiently presented my case, perhaps he would have seen the inherent altruism of my trespass. How could he not have? But there was no time for that. And he would never understand, anyway.

"You know who I am, and you know what I have to do. I have to take your son. I have to."

"What the fuck are you talking about?" Here was rage.

I tilted my head slightly, fanned out my open hands, and pronounced: "This is your chance."

$\bullet$ $\bullet$ $\bullet$

There was a moment where everything seemed frozen, a second or two of unsullied stillness, a flash of pure nothingness where both matter and all things immaterial—thoughts, emotions, words—ceased to be. Particles seemed to stop swirling. Sound was sucked up by silence. We were at once there and not there, joined by the space between us instead of separated by it. I think Marlowe felt this too.

It passed quickly.

Moving with surprising swiftness and coordination for a man who had imbibed so liberally, Marlowe lunged forward, grabbed me by the collar, and pushed me back against the wall, jutting his face up into mine so our foreheads all but touched and I could smell the musk of the day on him. He pulled hard on my shirt so that it came up in front, ruining the meticulously executed quarter-tuck I had spent so long arranging.

"I don't know who you think you are, but you get the fuck out of my house right fucking now." Spittle sprayed over my face. His nose grazed mine, and he held me there for a moment before releasing with a dramatically forceful unclenching of his fingers.

He was glowering down at me, tall and hostile, a big gruff bully with the home field advantage pressuring the lesser visitor. To the casual observer, I would have seemed no match for him, but in my mind I saw where it was going, saw exactly where we would be in a few minutes, as though the script were written and the lines already memorized and all I had to do was recite on cue.

"Okay," I said. "Okay." And I arched back a fraction and sprung forward like a prodded cobra, the bony flat of my forehead smashing with unyielding power into the bridge of his nose—they were aligned so perfectly due to our height differential that I hardly had to aim. I felt his cartilage cave in beneath my solid ridge of bone, and I watched the larger man stumble back as tears blinded him and blood squirted from the center of his face and his hands rose to address the explosion there.

I was transformed. Beyond rage. Taken over by a presence I could not explain. It was the image in the bathroom mirror that was acting now, moving my limbs for me, steering my body, animating my flesh. The energy pulsing through me was like nothing I had ever felt. There was no hatred or malice, but I was unstoppable and would not relent, would extend no quarter to my foe, would show no mercy. Marlowe was merely an object in my way, a potential threat to the security of my ends, and he had to be neutralized. I would not stop until he was completely and thoroughly immobilized, until he was rendered incapable of hindering my mission. I swung back and struck his left check with a hard right roundhouse, stepping into it, swaying him down to one knee. Then I connected with a left-right-left jab combo, flooring him. He groaned and moved around on his back, dazed and writhing. I stood above him, watching the blood spread over his face as though a pipe had burst from within. I bent down and straddled his waist and pummeled him with five more unchallenged rights straight into his destroyed nose, which was now more like a mound of flattened flesh than a distinguishable facial feature. He was barely moving. Strange sounds issued from his mouth, and bloody drool dripped liberally out of one corner. I leaned over and dragged him up by the collar, holding him against the same wall where he had previously pinned me. He was a heavy man, but I lifted him as though he were weightless.

"You've got to know when to say when, Marlowe," I whispered directly into his ear, then let him drop, lifted my right foot, and stomped down hard onto his midsection, feeling the sole of my Saint Laurent sneaker crack through things internal.

Here is where it became something other than utilitarian. Because I could have stopped. The man was unconscious and leaking blood from more than one orifice and surely suffering some permanent damage. He was, for all practical purposes, well out of my way. Yet I was driven to continue. This was not out of personal animus. If I had to pin a reason on it, I would say now that my violence spawned from a deeper odium, a gnashing contempt for all that Marlowe represented, for his soft suburban lifestyle, his idyllic domesticity, his thoughtless, bourgeois approach to the world, his selfish sense of entitlement and his welcome embrace of all that had so easily been granted him. He was a man, like so many others, who believed he deserved what he had just for being who he was, for the mere accident of his birth. This is, I should admit, a retrospective account; at the time, I only knew that I could not stop. I slammed the side of my foot into his kidneys again and again until he was absolutely still. Then I halted, pegged into place as though waiting for further instructions from some unseen source, and laid into him again until my leg cramped up and I was compelled to stop. I had to bend down close to see if he was breathing, which he was, though obstructedly.

What seems odd now is that when I finally relented, despite my exertion and the waning adrenaline surge, I was barely winded, touched with only the faintest layer of sweat, and utterly composed. I even took a few seconds to redo the quarter-tuck.

Not unexpectedly, the commotion had disturbed Carter's slumber, for just as I turned to him, he started crying and rocking restlessly in his crib, waving his limbs like an inverted cockroach.

I hovered over him and spoke softly. "It's okay. It's not your fault, little one. Don't worry. It's all going to be okay."

His face was scrunched up in a weeping rictus, and he reached out with clawing hands in search of something he couldn't have been aware of. I grabbed his fists and gently enclosed them in mine, which seemed to placate him. Then I lifted him into my arms, holding him so that the front of his body was against my chest with his head just above my right shoulder. I remember lightly patting his back, thinking he needed to be burped. Maybe he just wanted to be held, to feel himself supported in human arms. Whatever it was, once I had him, he stopped crying.

Grabbing my sports jacket from the back of my chair,

I took one last long look at the dining room, which now included Marlowe's slumped form, and walked slowly toward the hallway.

When I heard Kelsi approach, her rushed footfalls sounding softly on the hallway stairs, I put my jacket back on the chair. I had been so hoping to avoid this.

"Okay boys, sorry about that." She had apparently heard nothing of the ruckus and bounded back into the room with glee, rubbing her hands together in eagerness to rejoin the revelry: "Who's ready for dess—"

She stopped short on entering. Her face instantly locked up and her mouth drooped with a slight quiver. She took in the tableau, without, I am certain, comprehending it. I think she first saw her unconscious husband, bloody and bent on the floor. Then her eyes shifted to mine—to ours—to the bewildering sight of her infant son in the guest's arms. She might have wondered why, in the midst of carnage, I seemed so coolly vacant.

"I'm afraid I won't be staying for cake," I said.

"What—what's going on?"

She tried not to sound panicked, as though this would all be revealed as some sort of elaborate gag that had gone too far. It was a lot to take in.

I took a deep breath. I felt like a doctor summoning the fortitude to deliver a terminal diagnosis to a patient he is particularly fond of.

"I think I should give it to you straight, Kelsi. The hospitality you've shown me deserves at least that."

Another breath.

"I'm taking your son. Marlowe tried to stop me, so I had to put him down. But he'll recover. Eventually. For the most part. Please don't make me do the same to you."

She stood rooted in place like a wax statue. A deep pallor came over her face.

"Wh—" The remainder of the word puffed out in a gasp: "*Why?*"

I was so hoping she wouldn't ask that question. She, of all people.

Deeply disappointed, I shook my head and pursed my lips, like that same doctor faced with the impossible challenge of answering the unanswerable. It is one thing to explain why—in medical terms—a disease is fatal, but why the patient has been stricken with it is not a question worthy of scientific interest. It is no kind of question at all. "Why indeed, Kelsi."

As she stood before me, struggling to understand the ramifications of all that was happening, feeling perhaps that she could better cope if she could at least attach some reason to the apparent madness, she could do no better than repeat herself.

"But *why*?"

There was a sudden rift in her composure. Her shoulders sagged and her knees bent, and it appeared as though her whole body were on the verge of melting. She began to sob.

Why? Who the fuck knows? Why do I prefer Farina over Cream of Wheat? Why do I like Quaker Oats more than the imported Irish steel-cut brand? Why was I not born with Sinatra's voice and Johnny Depp's hair? Why did my parents die in a fiery crash on the doorstep of my adulthood?

She knew what I was. Yet she did not attempt to attack me, nor did she rush to the aid of her husband. She stood there, an amalgam of emotions, mostly fear, I would imagine—the worst and most primal fear a mother can experience—but the fear was mixed with confusion and anger and perhaps a measure of self-recrimination. She had invited the vampire into her home, had welcomed this hungry lion into the den where her cub sleeps. Almost single-handedly, she had brought this ultimate horror upon her family. What were the odds, she might have wondered, of moving right next door to this man? It was as if I could see the negative conditionals multiplying in her mind, regressing to the point where I could never have entered their lives. She should not have invited me to dinner. She should have never talked to me that day while plucking weeds. She should never have moved her family from the safety of the city to this suburban death trap. If only they had chosen the other house. If only they had waited another six months, maybe this one would have been off the market. If only the economy hadn't tanked, they would never have been able to afford this place.

"There's nothing you could have done differently," I consoled her. "This was going to happen."

It wasn't easy for either of us.

"You're *him*."

She had to verbalize the realization.

With a shy shimmer of a smile, I tilted my head in affirmation, like a celebrity being recognized despite his public disguise. It was oddly pleasing.

She clamped a hand over her mouth and looked down at her demolished husband, then back up at Carter and me.

"For what it's worth," I said, "I think you're a nice person."

"Give me my baby."

She finally moved, inching toward me, reaching out with one hand and speaking calmly but firmly. I think she was trying to appeal to my humanity. But she had it all wrong; I was doing the humane thing. I was offering mercy.

There was no point in trying to explain this to her.

"I cannot. You know this."

"You're a monster!" she shouted, her voice breaking on the final syllable. She held out both arms in desperation and took a tentative half-step forward.

"Shhh." I censured her harshly. "You're going to upset him." And yet Carter remained perfectly tranquil. "I'm not here to argue, Kelsi. All I can tell you, again, is that it is out of your control. It's all out of *our* control. And it's for the best. I know you can't see that, but I hope someday you will."

"No. No. No. No." She dropped to her knees, bawling. "Give him to me. Just give him back to me. It's not too late."

"I'm afraid it is. It was always too late." I patted Carter's head. "And it's about time we shuffled off."

"No."

"Yes."

I waited for her retort. There was none.

"It was a wonderful meal. Thank you. Really a rare treat for me. More than you can know."

"Please. Please don't do this. It's not too late."

"It's already done." Carter stirred in my arms, emitting a few incipient cries, which I shut down with some easy back rubbing. "You see? Now you've disturbed him."

Bringing the baby up closer to my face, I swayed him to and fro, shushing softly, coaxing him back to sleep.

"You sick bastard."

There was then a difference in Kelsi's voice, and I sensed that anger and maternal instinct had begun to overcome fear. She was snowballing up the courage to make her move on me. "You are not taking my son," she nearly screamed, as though trying to convince herself.

A tiny, fatherly smirk came over my face. I tried to speak with quiet yet firm resolution, like an elder telling a child that he doesn't want to punish her but is prepared to do so if she leaves him no alternative. "Carter is coming with me," I said, "so please step aside. Please."

I sincerely had no desire to hurt this woman, even as she looked around for something to grab, some kind of weapon with which to assault me (a dull dessert knife or a fork seemed to be the only available options). It was best to get out before she forced my hand. There had been enough collateral damage.

"Goodbye, Kelsi."

I gave a polite little bow, clutching Carter tightly to my chest, and I started to leave through the second entrance to the room—which led to the kitchen rather than the hall, a bit of a roundabout way, but better if I wanted to avoid confrontation. As I made my circuitous progress, she shrieked in a way I would not have thought possible for her and took a mad run at me.

I had to admire her selfless valor, the willingness to put her safety on the line for her child. She stepped over her husband and rushed me with two tiny balled fists, her French-manicured nails begging to claw at my face, teeth set to plunge into my hands and arms, knees ready to rise up into my testicles. It was anything and everything she could do to save her only son. She was a lioness facing down an intruding male from another pride, ready to lose her life in exchange for her child's.

Alas, it only works that way in storybooks, in cautionary tales told to children in order reinforce their trust in a mother's power to protect them, to make them feel safe and guarded under their parents' loving care. In reality, no one can protect another from life's peril; we cannot even protect ourselves.

"Don't," I managed to say before she came flailing toward me, her pretty face mangled with fury. Timing it perfectly, I shifted Carter into the crook of my left arm and rotated my upper half sharply counterclockwise to shield him from his mother's onslaught, then reached back in the same direction with my right arm and whipped it around in a punishing closed-fist backhand blow that connected beautifully, felling the mother with swift impact. She bounced off my fist and landed in a lump, right next to Marlowe. I took no pleasure in hurting her, but she had left me little choice.

"I'm sorry, Kelsi. I did warn you."

She picked herself up and came back at me. And again, her face met my fist, and again her body hit the floor. Once more, she struggled to her feet, but this time I was proactive, pouncing too quickly for her to react. I smashed her face two, three times. Then I stomped on her ankle to ensure she wouldn't attempt a third sally. There was no audible crack, but if I didn't break bone, I certainly caused enough damage to keep her from coming.

"Just stay down." Now I was the one pleading. "Don't make me do worse to you, because I think you know I will. Don't make me be the bad guy here."

She lay on the floor, crying and holding her face, repeating through her tears: "Please... please... don't take him... please... I'm begging you... please... please God..." The words sounded weirdly distorted. I might have broken her jaw.

"God has nothing to do with this. I'm the one holding Carter."

"Oh Jesus, please, please, Jesus."

Pick a god, any god. What have you to lose? She went with Jesus and his father. Why not Allah? Why not give Zoroaster a shot? A Hindu would have had a whole host of deities at her disposal.

I couldn't stand the pleading, her pathetic petitions to a higher power that was not there or simply did not care. I should have just left. I had obviously overstayed my welcome. But her tireless appeals to my better nature, her endless entreaties to the merciful lord above, merited a response, even if the response I gave her would not be what she'd adjured. With Carter (now bawling) snugly secured under my left arm like a football, I stepped over Marlowe and leaned down to Kelsi, grabbed her by the chin, and held her bloody face inches away from mine. My hand moved to the back of her head and down to her nape. I looked at her lovely young features and smooth, perky skin, luxuriating in the feel of her neck's creamy flesh, its veins pulsing warmly against my palm.

"I'm not going to kill you, Kelsi. You're a good mother. Bad things just happen, even to good mothers. And really, who's to say what's good or bad? It's important not to judge. We don't have that power. We're too small, too limited to know what's good or evil, right or wrong. These are just words."

She still smelled good. So good and clean and motherly. Like soap and baby powder and light perfume and girlishness. Closing my eyes, I leaned in and inhaled and was momentarily transported to another time, a safer place, a place I had long forgotten but somehow never left. I listened to her congested breaths next to my ear, her sniffling whimpers and muffled sobs.

"Shhhhhh." I rubbed my cheek against hers, wet and warm and so, so soft.

"Shhhhhh." I kissed her cheek. I would have given anything to stay there with her. But I couldn't.

When I rose, I realized that the wetness was not only coming from her; my face was striped with tears as well.

In a sad last-ditch effort, she dragged herself over and shook her downed husband's shoulder. "Please. Marlowe. Marlowe, wake up."

"I don't think he can hear you," I said. "But don't worry. He's breathing."

She collapsed her face onto his back and let her tears soak into his blood-blemished shirt.

"Okay, then," I spoke with quiet reverence. "I'll leave you two alone now." I took one last look at the couple before heading toward the hallway.

I almost couldn't believe it, but as I stepped away, a hand gripped my ankle. A masculine hand. I turned and looked down at Marlowe struggling to push himself up to a sitting position, his face unrecognizably battered, his body crooked in strange, unnatural ways but still obeying the orders of his brain. From his position of weakness and defeat, he somehow managed to throw a feeble right at my midsection, but I easily caught his fist in mine (his hand was quite a bit larger, so I couldn't totally envelop it, but I still grabbed it tightly) and squeezed as hard as I could, bending his wrist backward. He winced and leaned back with the painful pressure. I felt like Sho'Nuff, the Shogun of Harlem in *The Last Dragon*. I wanted to hear myself say, "Who's the master?" Instead, I pushed until he fell backward like an uprooted bush, and then I proceeded to kick his flanks as he clammed up in a shell and struggled to cover his soft parts. Unfortunately for him, he was unable to block my quickly striking feet from smashing mercilessly into his ribs and back and buttocks.

"No, no, no!" Kelsi screamed.

She laid her head on her husband's back and cried.

I hurried from the room and was almost at the door when I heard a body scrambling to its feet. I turned to see Kelsi, wobbly but determined, limping out of the dining room with a vicious, teeth-baring expression. She lunged at me with whatever reserve of strength she had left. Not wanting to damage that face any further, I dodged her incoming assault with a quick jerk leftward and slammed her with a short fast one to the ribs. She crumbled to the floor, coughing, her eyes wide and unfocused. I waited a minute or so to make sure her breathing returned to a functional state. It did, although she might have had a cracked rib or two from how it sounded, flat on her back and wheezing, her shirt pushed up to reveal a few inches of firm fit belly (she surely did yoga or pilates or some other intense workout routine to return to shape so soon after giving birth) rising and falling in unmeasured rhythm. It was nothing she couldn't recover from. At least physically.

Carter was squirming under my arm and crying fierce-ly. I situated him more comfortably and attempted to console him. "Almost ready to go," I whispered.

Marlowe was unconscious and inert. The problem was Kelsi. She was wounded and immobilized for the moment, but she could still crawl to the phone as soon as we left.

There was no avoiding the inevitable. I knew this was my endgame, that there was no real future beyond the order of events set in motion. Yet I could at least forestall what would come, savor this curtain call until the very last house light was extinguished. Kelsi would have called the cops as soon as I left, and I had no desire to kill her, or her husband. Even if I had murdered both of them, simply out of practical concern, the police would have traced the crime to me. She might have already spoken of my presence to her sister, or Marlowe might have mentioned it in passing to a coworker, or to that ne'er-do-well little brother of his. Disposing of them in an attempt to cover my tracks would have entailed too much effort for an unsure payoff.

It was time.

I'd had a good run, but it was time for all of it to end.

But not just yet.

. . .

I put Carter in his crib. He was crying. I promised him I would be back in "two shakes of a lamb's tail."

I rushed into the kitchen to search for some sort of rope or twine with which to bind Kelsi. I considered knocking her out or suffocating her just the point of unconsciousness, or pressing the carotid to the same end (what bored suburban kids call "the choking game"), but it was just too needlessly cruel—not to mention dangerous—so I rummaged through drawers and cabinets and closets, and the best I could come up with was a spool of white, oven-proof cotton butcher's twine. It would have to do.

When I returned to the dining room, Kelsi was on all fours, creeping toward the crib like an oversized infant. I hurried over, grabbed the balls of her shoulders firmly in my hands, and shoved her briskly forward in one strong sweeping motion, flattening her out on her stomach and knocking the wind from her so I could work with less struggle. Her chin hit the floor a little harder than I had hoped. Winded and stunned as she was, gasping and coughing in a struggle for oxygen, she fought me still. Her hands squirmed vainly at her sides like the useless legs of a squashed bug as I placed a knee on the small of her small back and pulled her tiny wrists up behind her and crossed them and encircled them with layers of string. She wriggled helplessly under my pinning knee, sobbing and pleading and begging relentlessly.

"Don't make this harder than it already is," I pleaded back, taking a house key from my pocket and using its teeth to whittle off the attached end of the string, then securing it with several knots. "I'm just doing what I have to do," which was then to pivot around and pull up her ankles. This proved a bit harder, as her legs were fit and strong, forcing me to slap at her thighs until they obeyed. "Sorry, I'm not trying to get fresh," I assured her as I quickly wrapped her ankles with tight loops of string. I knotted it, then brought her bound ankles and wrists together just above my knee, swirling a last round of string to secure her limbs in a hogtie. I recalled Kurt Cobain's lullaby.

> Polly wants a cracker
> Maybe she would like some food
> She asked me to untie her
> A chase would be nice for a few

A chase was the last thing I wanted. Cautiously removing my knee, I tested the durability of my handiwork with a few tugs. I was indeed impressed with myself, especially under such conditions.

Kelsi was now screaming. She was screaming in that piercing horror-film pitch that only a woman in distress can hit. Carter was riled by her screaming. I feared someone out walking a dog might hear, so I grabbed her napkin—considerate enough to make sure it wasn't mine or Marlowe's—balled it up, and shoved it in her mouth. Her acute shrieking was then muffled to such inefficiency that she stopped and returned to crying. All the weeping and wailing was starting to get to me; there's only so much blubbering a person can take. I scooped up Carter, his face crumpled and red and wet, and stood above the couple for one last goodbye.

"I know you're going to think this is insincere, but I really want to thank you for inviting me. Everything was delicious. I never get invited anywhere, so this was truly a wonderful and unique experience. For what it's worth, I deeply appreciate it."

I paused to let my earnestness sink in.

"Oh, and the place looks great. It's like a totally new house. Whatever ghosts of the past are lingering, I'm sure they'll be gone soon. They know they're not wanted. There's no place for them here anymore."

I took a final mental image of the scene: the slick transformations the house had undergone, the two of them, man and wife, father and mother, lying helplessly while their boy was being taken, his sworn protectors vanquished at the feet of his abductor. I closed the door behind me and walked unhurriedly over their darkened lawn toward mine, stepping carefully so as not to trip over some ambushing twig or misplaced stone, the several yards feeling like miles as I tried to avoid the bright floodlights Marlowe had affixed to the side of his house. Carter was crying. I found myself reprising the grunge lullaby, softly serenading him as we made our way home:

Isn't me, have a seed
Let me clip, your dirty wings
Let me take a ride, cut yourself
Want some help, please myself

It felt right that Carter should receive the words of this last authentic twentieth-century rock star, the one who had everything in the world and yet realized that it amounted to nothing, who understood that the light of the brightest stars illuminating the canopy of night is flying aimlessly toward us from a long-dead source, a doomed orphan emanation from an expired parent. It might as well have been born dead.

He seemed to like it. At least enough to slow his sobbing.

•   •   •

Upon reaching the garage, we were both crying. It seemed darker than usual. And quieter. I opened the door and twice plugged in the alarm code incorrectly. It started beeping and in a few more seconds would have rung out and notified the police. They would knock eventually, of that I was sure, but I needed every moment until then. I took a breath and got it right on the third try, silencing the buzzing pre-alarm warning. Then I set it again, sealing off the perimeter.

Once inside, holding Carter and looking around my house, I reflected on the ramifications of what I had done. I had precipitated the end. I had finally let it come down. And it was wonderful. Carter's tears had stopped, but I wept still as he looked up at me with what I discerned to be soft sympathy, as though he were offering comfort and compassion, instilling in me the strength I needed.

"Thank you, Carter." I planted a light kiss on the tip of his tiny nose. "Thank you."

There was so much to do that I couldn't think of where to start. I was bubbling with scarcely containable excitement. I was pixilated, overwhelmed by strange and familiar emotion. Sweating freely and feeling hot all over, as though there were smoldering coals beneath the surface of my skin, I put Carter down on the kitchen table, pulled my shirt up over my head (unable to go through the unbuttoning process), and ran my hands over my torso. Just then I realized that I had left my sports jacket on the chair in their dining room, and for a second I considered running back for it. But it was just a vestigial impulse. Strangely, the loss of the jacket meant nothing. Whereas I normally would have come unglued over such a *catastrophe*, I felt no anguish. I did not miss it at all. I realized that none of my possessions, even those I had so deeply cherished, those things I thought I felt love for, had ever meant anything. Even this beautiful body, which I had treasured and sculpted to perfection and admired for so long, meant nothing. It was not mine. *I* was not mine. I did not belong to myself. My self was not me. I saw through the illusion. There was no more *me*. I was another. And even that other did not exist.

I felt a sudden dynamism. I laughed through the tears and jumped around like a boxer before a championship bout. I had so much energy, still so much life, even then. It was like a great burst of fever before the fall. But I had to collect myself and settle my mind. I had to compose myself enough to think through my actions and carry them out with a certain degree of equanimity. It had all funneled down to this pinpoint in space and time. *Now and never. Never and forever. Always here.*

Though anything but an ordinary night, it was crucial to enact something routine, to maintain a semblance of normalcy. I had not had my after-dinner coffee. That would do.

I cued up Sinatra's timeless torch song, "One for My Baby." As those wistful, speakeasy sounds filled the space, I put the water-filled kettle on the stove, prepared the French press, heated the milk in the microwave, and frothed it up extra for the occasion. All the while I kept an eye on Carter, who was now crawling about the floor like a lost crab searching for the sea.

> *We're drinking my friend*
> *To the end*
> *Of a brief episode*
> *Make it one for my baby*
> *And one more for the road*

My latte didn't come out right. I had prepared the same cup of coffee every single night for years, using the same brand of grinds and the same French press and the same measuring spoon and mug, even measuring out my Borden skim milk with the same Pyrex cup, filling it precisely to the two-thirds cup marker. Yet with my first sip, I knew something was off. I couldn't tell if it was too strong or too weak, whether the milk was starting to turn or was under-frothed, but I drank it anyway, trying not to focus on its flawed flavor.

I wondered how long it would be before one of them would manage to get to a phone and dial 911. I felt certain it would be Kelsi. I could see her undulating across the floor like a caterpillar and somehow making it to her knees long enough to knock the phone out of the cradle with her head and press the numbers with her cute little nose. Lying on her side, she would push the gag out with her tongue in time to yell into the receiver. What would she say? Help? He's got my child? Come quick?

Forcing myself to finish the distasteful cup of coffee (what a crime it was that the last cup ever of my favorite beverage would be so unpalatable), I rinsed out the mug and put it in the dishwasher, which wasn't full enough to run. But I felt I should run it, that it had to be run, that it was the right thing to do. So I dropped in a Cascade tablet, pulled a few clean glasses and dishes and pieces of silverware from the cabinets and drawers (it's a shameful waste of electricity and water to run a nearly empty load), and started it up.

Carter had scrabbled off somewhere, and though I knew he couldn't have gone far, a frisson of panic flushed through me. Walking into the adjoining dining room, I found him moving stealthily along the wall's edge in the dark, oddly quiet and composed, exploring his new surroundings with an accepting curiosity possible only to his kind. He paused as I came up behind him, as though he knew his playful rebellion was at a close and the time for business was at hand. It was at that moment that I realized I had no idea how I was going to proceed. I needed to think of something quickly. With both hands around his waist, just above the diaper's upper limit, I lifted him from behind and held him high over my head, twirling him slowly through the unlit space below the ceiling. He giggled gleefully. I did the same.

That's when I heard the sound.

A car rolling up, its tires crunching over loosened pavement. A car that wasn't just passing by but stopping at the curb in front of the house. I pulled Carter back down to my chest and stayed as still as I could. Then came more sounds. Furtive sounds. More cars. A door opening lightly. Maybe footsteps. The brief glare of an obscure light and the unmistakable presence of humans.

They had arrived sooner than expected. Kelsi was a good mother.

• • •

Moving in the slowest achievable increments, shifting my weight with a deliberate retardation made more painful by my internal alarm, I brought myself next to the window that gave onto the front lawn and the street beyond and pressed my body flat against the wall. The sounds were a bit more distinct from this distance, and I could hear unintelligible words, low male voices speaking with grave authority in tense tones of attack. Switching Carter to one arm, I used the other to spread two blinds as narrowly as possible so that I could glimpse what awaited me. I contemplated how it could be a manifestation of my paranoia. People parking across the street for another dinner party. Some kids having a Friday night get-together, sharing forties at the curb.

No. It was them. They had come for me. And in more force than the noises had let on. The street was blocked off and there were at least ten cruisers, a couple of police vans, a small army of men in combat gear, helmets and shields, already in place beside their cars and barricades, weapons brandished. It was impressive, if not a bit dramatic. I marveled at how they had gotten it all set up so quickly and quietly. They had been waiting for this. I was big game, and all the hunters had come out to nab the prize.

I have never taken recreational drugs, but I don't believe there could have been any chemically enhanced rush greater than what I felt in that moment. An electrical shiver pulsed through my body from head to heel, lightening my limbs with an animating fluid that made me want to crash through the window and rush at that army of officers lined up to take me down, each one hoping his finger would be the one to squeeze the trigger and unleash the bullet that would lodge in my heart or brain. I watched more of them move into position. They were making silent hand signals and running around the sides of the house, crouching below bushes and positioning themselves behind trees. There may have been fifty men. My hand starting shaking. I was afraid they would see it moving the blinds.

The phone rang, jolting me back away from the window. *Unknown Caller.* I skittered out into the kitchen, shut all the lights, and answered on the fourth ring, just before the machine would pick up.

I did not say hello.

"We have the house surrounded," a dull and neutral male voice said, as if it were just another day on the job, as if there were nothing special about me, about this situation. "Surrender and come out with your hands up." I was mildly offended by his lack of inflection. Did they not realize who I was and what I was capable of?

"Are you serious?"

"Every entrance is blocked. There is no way out. Come out now and you will not be harmed."

"Really?"

"We will not shoot if—"

"No, I mean, are you seriously talking to me in that tone? I have a baby in here, and you're ordering me around as if you control the situation? Not even attempting to negotiate? Not even trying to be nice?"

A short pause.

"We're not negotiating. Leave the baby and come out."

I was infuriated. "How about you come in? Just you. You personally. I would love to meet the man behind this voice."

A slightly longer pause. Perhaps he was checking with his superiors about how to proceed.

"Come out now," was his counteroffer. "If you leave the baby and come out, you will not be harmed."

This was very disheartening.

"Okay. If that's your final offer…" I let him hang there a good ten seconds.

"Leave the child and come out. Now."

He spoke more sternly, as though the authority of his voice would impel me to comply.

"I'll think about it."

Just as I hung up, a flood of light washed against the house, like a sudden crush of sunshine against the drawn blinds. The intense brightness crept in through every crack and interstice, slices of it cutting at my legs and striping the wall behind me. High-powered spotlights irradiated the scene like a nighttime construction project, replete with barricades and flashing lights and great trucks filled with more equipment than one would have thought necessary for the extraction and apprehension of one man. I did my best to move out of the way of the searing strips of light, wondering what would be next. Smoke bombs? Tear gas? Sound cannons? No, they couldn't risk hurting the infant. The light would probably be the worst of it. Until they stormed me. Which would be soon.

This is happening, I thought, squeezing Carter, who was sucking his fingers and studying the backlit windows with calm curiosity. His collectedness was inspiring. It brought me strength. He hadn't emitted a sob since we had arrived. "You're a good man, Carter," I told him. He looked at me, reached out, and lightly touched my cheek. I smiled at him and he smiled back.

I laid him on the floor at my feet and picked up the phone. There was no dial tone. The voice came back.

"Surrender. Now."

"Yeah. About that. You've got to give me ten minutes."

"Now."

"I'll settle for five."

"Now."

I could take no more of his imperious demands. "Listen, asshole," I said, "I am trying to be nice here. Work with me. Five minutes." And I hung up.

I would have liked to flatten his prick in a searing waffle iron and listen to it sizzle to a dark golden brown as I slowly stuck flame-treated sewing needles into his eyes and asked him which of the tortures—only one, so choose wisely—he would beg surcease. But the time for daydreams of petty vengeance had passed. Every instant counted. I knew, of course, that the asshole was right. There was no way out. Yet I felt absolutely no sadness or regret or fear, only an invincible excitement. I was suffused with a kind of preternatural strength and, I swear it, a feeling of *hope*.

My life would soon be over. I was going to die.

"I'm going to die," I said out loud. And I giggled. I picked up Carter and shook him playfully and moved my face into his view. "I am going to die, little guy." He giggled back.

I was ready. I thought of the lines from *Macbeth*:

> *Nothing in his life*
> *Became him like the leaving it; he died*
> *As one that had been studied in his death*
> *To throw away the dearest thing he owed,*
> *As 'twere a careless trifle.*

I would go out boldly, welcoming death like a warrior. They would see no quivering apprehension in me as I confronted their numbers with my one, as I marched on their arms with my unprotected body and clear, unabashed soul. Words glutted my mind in their furious struggle to be the last. I thought of Whitman, and I banged my chest as I recited his towering lines:

> *O to struggle against great odds, to meet enemies*
> *undaunted!*
> *To be entirely alone with them, to find how much one can stand!*
> *To look strife, torture, prison, popular odium, face to face!*
> *To mount the scaffold, to advance to the muzzles of guns*
> *with perfect nonchalance!*
> *To be indeed a God!*

My apotheosis was nearly complete.

And there were tears again. But this time I understood their meaning. They were joyous. I had never felt so awake, so unfalteringly animate. I had never felt the wonderful weight of my limbs pulling at my torso, my head moving freely around my neck, my brain bristling in exhilaration.

I had to get in a workout.

Holding Carter tightly against me, I cantered carefully through the dark and down the basement stairs, putting on the lights—so thankful that I'd had the foresight to line the windows with foil—and setting Carter down a few feet from the heavy bag. I had somehow slipped my shirt back on, though I did not remember doing so. No matter, I tore at the collar and ripped it down the middle. The buttons popped off in rapid succession, and I think I felt some fabric tear around the collar. No matter. I yanked my arms free and threw the shirt to the ground. I peered over at my poster of Iggy standing haughtily above the crowd, indignant, defiant, his bare chest gleaming like a trophy. I would have wiggled out of my jeans, but I looked at Iggy's glutes and quads and calves and hams showing proudly under the tight denim encasement, and I opted to follow his example. I cranked up "Down on the Street," leaving Carter to his own devices (there was not much he could hurt himself with down there) while I took a last round with my bag. No gloves; only hard leather against bare knuckles. The wound on my right hand opened and bled and throbbed so wonderfully with each strike.

> *Down on the street where the faces shine*
> *Floatin' around I'm a real low mind*
> *See a pretty thing – ain't no wall*
> *See a pretty thing – ain't no wall*

It was magnificent, ecstatic, sempiternal. I was sweating and my chest glistened like Iggy's.

I ran to the opposite end of the basement, to where Carter was crawling in increasingly tighter circles around the same area of carpet. I swooped down and picked him up with a hand under the belly, pausing for a parting glance at the basement, my beloved bag, my motivational posters. Again, Walt's words whisked through my mind:

> So long!
> Remember my words, I may again return,
> I love you, I depart from materials,
> I am as one disembodied, triumphant, dead

I shut the lights and jogged up to the kitchen just in time to answer the phone.

"You have three minutes."

I huffed.

"Listen, Spock. Let me speak to Kirk."

"What?"

"Put on the goddamn captain. Get me Michaelson. You think you can threaten me? You're nothing. You're a forgettable little peon. I am the god here. I am the one who'll be remembered." I found myself poking my own chest with a forefinger. "Now stop wasting my time, and get me the chief."

Pause.

"Uh…"

"Get Michaelson now, you miserable milquetoast. You servile blackguard."

He probably didn't know the meaning of either of these insults, but the gist was clear enough. Plus, I had always wanted to use these words, and it was now or never.

"I cannot do that."

How pleasing it would have been to slowly detach this pissant's tongue with a sturdy pair of crimping pliers while holding his mouth agape with a dental prop.

"You *will* fucking do it, you pathetic waste of sperm, or I'll take this kid I have in my arms right here, and I'll tie some rope around his little neck and spin him to death like a tetherball."

It was a creative idea, and I regretted that I would never have the chance to implement it. Or would I? Was there time to gather what I needed? Carter looked at me as though he, too, thought it sounded like fun.

"Now put Michaelson on."

No response. Radio silence. I was shaking. For a second, I expected them to come crashing through the windows in full riot gear, and I braced myself. Then there was some mumbling and throat-clearing on the line. And then...

"This is Chief Marcus Michaelson. I understand you'd like to speak with me."

He sounded different on the phone. Softer, almost avuncular. Yet I knew it was him. The man himself.

I couldn't speak.

I opened my mouth but nothing came out. There was an unplaceable familiarity to his voice that froze the words in my throat.

"Hello? Are you there? Hello?"

"Yes," I said.

"Can you hear me?"

"Yes."

"Are you okay? Is the baby okay?" He sounded as

though he were genuinely concerned about my welfare as much as he was about Carter's.

"We're both fine." I answered.

"Well… that is good to hear." He seemed relieved.

"Michaelson." My voice cracked. I cleared my throat and made my pitch a little lower than normal. "Michaelson. This is… you know who this is."

"I do."

"Yes, well, I just want you to know…" What did I want him to know? Why did I even want to talk with him? "I want to tell you that… that this whole nickname debacle really pissed me off."

"Yes, we're sorry about that. I take full personal responsibility for it."

"I called twice. I did my level best to put you on the right track, and you just fucked it up even more."

"Again, we're real sorry. *I'm* real sorry."

He sounded so sincerely contrite that I considered telling him it was okay, that I would forgive him, that it was mostly my fault anyway for not being more clear about it.

"If you just come out with the child, we'll see if we can make things better."

He had been doing so well until then.

"The child, yes. You all pretend to care so much about the children. I'm the one who truly cares. I'm the one doing something." I found myself shoving my finger into my chest again. "Make things better? I mean, I realize you have to talk like this, to say things like this, but… really? Make things *better*?"

"We do our best. All we can do is try."

"Wrong answer. No one can ever make a single thing

better. The state of things always moves in one direction, from bad to worse. There's no reversing it."

"Just come out. There's been more than enough pain. We don't want anyone else to get hurt, not you or the kid."

How could he say this? I was trying to be as open and honest as I could, having a heart-to-heart with my *bête noire*, and he was hurling platitudes at me.

"Sure you do," I countered. "You said it on national TV— how you would bring me to justice at any cost and see the full weight of the law brought down on me."

He paused, and when he spoke again his tone had changed from friendliness to a sort of fatherly austerity. "I'm afraid you've brought that down on yourself, son."

Son. The word paralyzed me. My hand squeezed the handle of the phone until the blood from my ripped knuckles oozed down my arm. My instinct was to scream at him, to level every conceivable insult at this insensitive ingrate. But I kept my composure and answered in an only slightly quavering voice. "I'm not your son. I'm nobody's son." I swallowed hard. "No, that's not right. I'm everybody's son. I didn't bring this on myself. You brought it on yourselves. You asked for this. I'm just sorry I couldn't give you more. I'm sorry I couldn't take every single one of your sons and daughters and put an end to all this. All this…"

Carter squeaked. A little cough. I was crying again. I turned away so he wouldn't see me.

"Please. Just leave the baby unharmed. I'm begging you. End this."

More begging. Another *please*.

End this. That was exactly what I was going to do.

I took a few seconds to control my sobs. Then I eased

my grip on the phone, shook Carter lightly, and looked around to make sure they weren't trying to ambush me while Michaelson had my attention.

"Here's what I'm going to extend to you, Chief. A one-time, non-negotiable offer. I want you to come up, alone, and ring my doorbell. Like you're coming for a visit. I know you'll have a gun and a vest, and I know there will be military-trained snipers aiming rifles at me. Just as long as you come up by yourself. Come up and ring the bell. Ring it only once. More than one ring will make me angry. Ring it once, then step back a few feet and I'll come out. I promise. I swear on my parents' grave."

No reply. Some shuffling around in the distance. Surely others were listening, staging a plan, strategizing, laying out what the scenario would be, how exactly they would go about using this opportunity to take me down, turning my own last request into a means of capture.

"Fine," he said flatly.

"Good. In five minutes, you ring the bell, step back off the porch. I'll answer."

He hesitated for a couple of seconds. "Done."

"Start counting down now."

⚫   ⚫   ⚫

I hung up and held the handset in place. Less than five minutes to live. How strange. But five minutes is such an arbitrary interval. There are organisms for whom five minutes is a lifetime, and even a few minutes can feel like an eternity when one waits impatiently for them to pass, standing in line at the bank, watching the clock in a high school classroom as the interminable seconds tick off toward the end of the period, sitting in bumper-to-bumper traffic miles from the nearest exit with a seemingly endless sea of unmoving red brake lights dominating your purview. But five minutes doesn't feel like much when it is all that's left.

Flipping on the kitchen high hats, I looked around at all I was leaving behind and realized I would miss none of it, not one of these objects that I had lived with for so long, that I had clung to as though they were the very essence of my existence. My bliss was dampened only at the thought that my wretched aunt would get everything, that she would revel in my demise and her newfound fortune. It did not bother me so much that she would end up with my money; what galled me was that she would never know how glad I was to be rid of it all, to no longer be encumbered by all these things and this body and this life. She would simply see it as a boon to herself at my expense, the old cunt. She would congratulate herself that she had waited it out and won, when really, I was the victor.

And then I got a splendid idea: why not leave it all to the person or persons who had the most positive effect on my life, those who made my life more pleasant, or at least less miserable? Most such people were long dead, but I could think of two among the living who deserved the honor. I put Carter down and retrieved a sheet of notepaper and a pen—not just any pen, but my French-made Waterman Charleston, which my parents gave me upon entering high school, a beautifully handcrafted fountain pen out of whose gilded tip the ink (in special-ized Waterman cartridges) flows like warmed butter; I had only used this pen for special signings, legal and whatnot, so it had made contact with paper but a few times (in retrospect, I should have used it more often, as it makes the writing experience considerably more tactile and satisfying). My hand was shaking as I began to draft my testament. My entire body was all of a tremble, and this worsened my already lamentable penmanship, so I had to tear up my first effort, take a few breaths, and start again. On my second attempt, I was careful to map out each letter with precision. I left all my property and assets, monetary and otherwise, to Iggy Pop and Lou Reed (*nés* James Osterberg and Lewis Reed), to be shared equally and dispersed in any way they deemed fit. As I signed my name, it occurred to me that they might simply donate my bequest to the families of my "victims." Such a move would be expected in the scheme of celebrity culture. I considered tearing the whole thing up and just letting my aunt have her windfall, but I signed it anyway, folded it neatly into thirds, and slipped it into a self-sealing #10 envelope, which I marked: LW&T of CF. I placed the envelope in front of my habitual seat at the kitchen table and put my Waterman on top of it as a paperweight.

Less than two minutes left. I picked up the phone.

"Michaelson here."

"I need another ten minutes, Chief."

Pause.

"Five."

"Well, with the remaining minute and a half, that would actually give me almost seven."

"Okay. Let's say seven minutes from when I hang up. Just as long as you don't hurt the child."

I did not want to lie to this man.

"Let's make it an even ten. You ring, I open. Ten minutes."

Without giving him a chance to refuse or argue or bargain, I hung up and scurried over the tile in my socked feet to grab Carter, who was headed straight for the front door, as though he had finally caught wind of the essence of my plan and was taking advantage of my distraction to make his break. He offered no resistance. He even put a hand on my shoulder when I lifted him into place.

Absurdly, that damned *Titanic* song crept back into my head. Were my last minutes destined to be cursed by this maudlin earworm? It wasn't even the stirring crescendo—just syrupy verses intruding on my mental space:

Love can touch us one time
And last for a lifetime
And never let go till we're gone

Love was when I loved you
One true time I'd hold to
In my life we'll always go on

How did I even *know* these lyrics? I never owned the album and hardly ever listened to the radio, even when that song was ubiquitous. This would not do. I could not make my grand exit with this aural ephemera spinning through my head. It was as if fate were conspiring to blight my mortal stand, mocking my grace with the hackneyed denouement to some Hollywood chick flick. I hurried upstairs to get my iPod, almost tripping and tumbling back down in the dark—I kept the lights above the stairway off so the cops couldn't monitor my movements with their high-tech cameras that can see through blinds, unless they were using infrared, in which case they saw a heat-emitting red blob bounding clumsily upward and then bouncing downward two steps at a time.

The run upstairs wouldn't normally strain my breath, but with the baby in my arms and the added stress of the situation, I felt like an asthmatic. And there was reason to believe that each step could be my last, that at any second a sniper's slug would come streaming through a window and put me down. So I kept low, crouching beneath window ledges. When I got to my room, I grabbed my iPod from the desk and leaned against the back of the chair as I scrolled through in search of—what? The final score on the soundtrack to my life? The parting impression of all my experiences? I had to be sure the music would envelop me when I needed it, during the closing credits, a last lullaby before bed, a prayer for the dying, a psalm for the departed. I wanted to be sure the last song I heard was of my choosing. And not Celine Dion.

Six minutes. Just enough time to set up the crucial prop, the crux of the scene.

I left Carter on the floor of my room and closed the door to block him off while I opened the hall linen closet in search of my father's shotgun, which he had purchased many years ago after my mother saw someone skulking about the backyard late one night from the bathroom window. She screamed. My father hopped out of bed, ran downstairs and grabbed the wrought iron fireplace poker (the very same instrument I had used in the care of Juanita), and rushed out to confront the would-be intruder, who by then had run off. He had probably been casing the property for a future break-in. The next day, my father bought a shotgun at a local sporting goods store—a Mossberg 500 series 12-gauge, pump-action with a pistol grip (recommended by the store clerk for home defense). It had been stored on the upper shelf of the closet since then, next to a wrinkled brown paper bag full of shells. As a child, I would frequently sneak in there and gaze up at it longingly. Its presence was menacing, way up where I couldn't reach, and I imagined it hibernating until the day it could unleash its payload on an unsuspecting burglar or home invader—whoever dared trespass upon the sweet domesticity of our household. This never happened. The gun rested there for most of its life, ensconced in the heavy canvas case in which it was contained when my father brought it home. When I was a little older, he taught me how to load it, how to clean it and how to chamber a shell. His demeanor, as he entrusted me with this adult knowledge, was solemn, emphasizing safety, responsibility, and the importance of supervision. "Treat every gun as if it is loaded," he said sternly. He promised to take me to the gun range one day, when I was older. This never happened, either.

I wasn't even sure it would work.

It had to work.

Standing on tiptoes, I reached up and grabbed the weapon in its case. With the barrel-end, I pushed the bag of ammo down and caught it in my free hand. Dust layered the case, but when I unzipped the canvas and slid it out, the weapon appeared new, the sleek black metal barrel untouched by the years and the composite grip unblemished. The gun felt pure and heavy in my hands, as if it were meant to be there, an extension of myself, an extra limb.

I had five minutes. I brought the gun and the ammunition back into my room, where Carter was sitting sagely before my closet mirror, watching himself wriggle a finger around his gums. He barely took notice of my return. Sitting on the edge of my bed, I proceeded. The surface of the paper ammo bag was supple and flaky, with pieces peeling off like dead skin as I opened it and withdrew from within a small box, which opened like a board game to reveal two rows of stacked red shells. They were dense and heavy in my hand, filled as they were with tiny balls of metal that would spray out like a deadly water cannon when fired. With the safety on, I dropped the first cartridge in the loading gate, chambering it. Then I fed five shells into the magazine tube, just as I had been shown. I now had only to switch off the safety, which I did.

Holding the gun mid-torso with my right hand on the pistol grip and my left supporting the ribbed forend, I stepped in front of the mirror to look at myself, shiny and shirtless, ripped and ready, locked and loaded. Carter sat closer to the mirror. He regarded the intrusion of my reflection with fascination, then looked up at me as if to test the image against his budding sense of reality. He might have wondered what would come next.

Four minutes.

"It's about that time," I spoke to his reflection, then turned around and laid the gun carefully on the bed, pointing away from me—from us—just as my father had counseled.

Bending from the waist, I lifted Carter and held him in front of me, looking him dead in the eyes, compelling him to return my gaze.

"This is for the best," I said. "If you could, I know you would thank me."

I did hesitate, if only for a few seconds. I wanted to drink in the moment of quiet, the last there would be before the final quiet. Carter watched me with what seemed like prescience—or resignation—as though he were letting me know that he understood, that he knew why I was doing this, and that he accepted it. He was a precocious child.

There is no mercy in this world, little fellow. There are no reprieves. Only temporary stays of execution. No one gets off the hook. Better you face it now.

I moved him down into the nook of my left arm and palmed his little head like a peach with my strong right hand. I first turned his head gently but firmly, as a pediatrician might have. Then I snapped it in a single humane jerk. It was not unlike the motion used when twisting off a stubborn bottle cap, whipping it around one hundred and eighty degrees. There was some resistance, like the grinding of gears, and a dull crack. Carter made a faint squeak. And then he was quiet.

I held him for a few seconds. I wanted to hold him longer.

・　　・　　・

Three minutes.

Laying Carter at the head of my bed, just below the pillows like a prized little doll (the gem of the collection), I picked up the gun, clamped the iPod to my belt, lodged my earbuds, and headed downstairs. I was crying. I was breathing hard. I feared I would collapse.

At the edge of the front door, I leaned my back against the wall, adrenaline coursing through every part of my sweat-bathed body. My jaw clenched tight as a lockbox. My arms and legs quivered. The thought came to me that I should have included Leonard Cohen in my will, and this bothered me acutely. Leonard had done so much for me, as much as Iggy and Lou, if not more. Was there time to add a brief codicil? I had to try.

I ran back to the kitchen, removed the paper from the envelope, and added Cohen's name to the short list of beneficiaries. Then I was seized by the frantic realization that there must be many men named Leonard Cohen, just as there were surely other Lewis Reeds (I felt fairly certain that Iggy's birth name was one of a kind).

It would be manifestly clear whom I meant, but how could I ensure it would hold up legally? I didn't know their dates of birth or places of residence. Did they have middle names? I could list some of their songs to make it apparent, but there was no time. I would have to take my chances.

After I inked in Cohen's name, I capped my Waterman and laid it neatly beside the document, parallel to its upper edge. As I looked upon its burnished black shell with gold clip and garnitures, I wondered who would end up with my beloved pen. I couldn't abide the thought of some crime scene collector picking it up in surgical-gloved hands, stuffing it into a baggie and leaving it in some dreary basement evidence room where the ink would dry up and clog its vein. No. It would come with me. I slipped the pen into the right front pocket of my jeans and headed for the door.

Two minutes.

Halfway there, I remembered that Leonard Cohen was Canadian. Would his foreign nationality complicate the execution of my estate? Then I thought of the brownie I had purchased earlier in the day. It seemed a travesty to leave it behind, this last morsel of Earthly indulgence. I considered sprinting to the kitchen to shove it in my mouth, washing it down with a few slugs of cold milk. But that was no way to enjoy a precious treat. And then there was that final latte that I would have loved to do over and slowly sip. Some lines remain forever unwritten.

On my way back to the door, I was struck with a terrible thought. *What if the snipers shoot the gun out of my hand?* It had happened before. I would be rendered defenseless, ripe for capture. Lacking a strap to coil around my forearm, even my tightest grip would be insufficient to secure the weapon. I threw open the utility closet and grabbed the duct tape. Nodding at my ingenuity, I wrapped several overlapping ribbons of the tough gray adhesive around my right wrist, securing it to the grip before tearing it off with my teeth, which, under more civilized circumstances, I would never have done. It was not comfortable.

One minute, thirty seconds.

I smile.

My smile morphs into laughter.

· · ·

I am positioned alongside the door, with my back to the wall, commando-style. My hands are shaking like loose hinges, making it difficult to grip the gun. I am trying to think of things that will calm me. My mother's smile. The rough grain of my father's beard when he comes home after a long day and picks me up and rubs my face against his. The smell of the grass in the backyard as I run and jump and roll around in it. The taste of warm melting milk chocolate on my tongue.

I should have let myself live, while there was life. It seems there could have been so much more. Yet I know this is only a mirage, a moribund delusion. Dreaming in extremis. A man who sees death encroach is prey to such sleights of mind. I believe there are peer-reviewed studies in neurology journals that attest this.

One minute.

I do not want forgiveness or absolution, sympathy or understanding. I do not want people probing into my background and scrutinizing my psyche in a bad faith effort to comprehend what made me do this, what went awry with nature or nurture to cross my wires in such savage ways. Yet the postmortem reports will be written and filed. There will be interpreters and experts bloviating on the news. Volumes will be written about me. There will be pulpy articles in mainstream periodicals that people read while waiting in dentists' offices, and there will be chapters in psychology textbooks and mental health journals, maybe even entire tomes dedicated to me and my deeds. My case will be studied in criminology courses and analyzed in comparison with some of history's most infamous sociopaths. Perhaps I will be the subject of a TV movie or a *Dateline* special.

None of this will scratch the surface, but there is nothing I can do to change any of it. In a moment, it will never again concern me. Existence will no longer be mine. What remains will be fodder for the living. Actions have consequences that ripple into chaos, and I accept this. The dead have no claim to a world that has left them behind.

Twenty-five seconds.

I start the song. I lose myself for a few moments in the first thudding riffs. Then Iggy comes in with his ravenous undertones:

> *I'm a street-walking cheetah with a heart full of*
> *   napalm*
> *I'm a runaway son of the nuclear A bomb*
> *I am the world's forgotten boy*
> *The one who searches and destroys*

My hand is warm and sticky with blood, my blood, my life, bleeding all over me. I rub my ragged knuckles over my chest, smearing the blood as much as I can, like a sanguinary splash painting. Childish swaths of deep red over hard, spongy flesh. I feel my heart throttling. My teeth are actually clattering. It would be comical under other circumstances. I have to urinate so badly it feels as though my bladder will burst. But I will not lose my dignity. Not now.

The doorbell rings. It is strident and piercing, lingering longer than it should. It almost makes me cringe. Michaelson is on the other side of these 1.75 inches of wood.

"Now step away," I yell. My face is pressed against the door. "Stand back a few feet, and I'll come out."

"Standing down," a voice yells back. It is faint under the volume of my iPod. It sounds like Michaelson, but I can't be sure.

I look back into the house, the darkened hallway, the distant den, those well-walked stairs leading up to my room, and I wonder who might live here after I am gone; who might kick back in the living room or sit around the kitchen table enjoying dinner. Then I realize what is more likely: that the place will be demolished. Perhaps a new house will be built from the foundation up. No young family will want to inhabit a home with such a history. If it is left intact, there will be the usual stories of curses and hauntings, of evil energy and indissoluble sorrow. I think how nice it would be to haunt this place. But then, I have haunted it for thirty years. It is time to move on.

"I'm coming out," I yell.

My heart hurts, pumping as hard as it is. I breathe in deeply and hold the exhale. I unlock the door's three locks, deadbolt, standard, and handle, and I open it.

Brightness. Blinding. The lawn is lit like daybreak. Brighter. I am forced to squint and step back, but I can nonetheless make out the tableau. A phalanx of men with guns lines the outer edge of the lawn. In the foreground is Michaelson, as promised, standing a few feet in front of me in his chief of police regalia. He holds his hands up in a non-threatening manner, his bald head shimmering under the spotlight like the nearest brilliant, beaming star. The stillness is sinister. No one moves. Nothing moves. I try to ignore everything but him, Michaelson, the Sun to my Earth, The Earth to my son. He looks smaller than he does on television. And older. Worn. Almost as weary of the world as I am. I think he is tired, nearly past the point of caring. I think he feels overcome by circumstance, by the never-ending crises that reach his desk on a daily basis. Yet somehow he perseveres. He still believes in his calling. There is evil in the world, and even in his diminished capacity, he will struggle to defeat the former and strive to heal the latter.

His eyes are small and darkly circled, and he looks as if he is about to cry.

"Where is the child?" he says, without inflection. I can barely hear him over the music.

I smile. An acrid, apocalyptic smile.

"Not here."

I grip the gun hard with both hands, my left palm cradling the pump. Michaelson ignores it. He just keeps his hard blue eyes on mine.

"Where is he, Cody?"

He is standing firm now. Coddling time is over. The situation is volatile. I am out of moves and he is exasperated by my excuses.

I cock my head. Why am I surprised that he knows my name?

"Not here," I repeat. "The child is not here. He never was."

I tense my muscles one last time. I feel my body work itself up to this final act.

Honey gotta help me please
Somebody gotta save my soul
Baby detonate for me

"He never was," I whisper. My words are impossible for anyone to hear, but they are fantastically loud to me. They drown out every intimation of other sounds, flooding my body with electricity.

Michaelson's hands slump and his eyes grow wide and his nostrils flare as I raise the barrel to my hip and point it at his torso and relax my squint and squeeze the trigger and feel the blowback hard against my grip. Then there is the sharp staccato crackle of gunfire, lurid whizzing sounds at my ears, splitting the air like a rocket, and—

Nothing. Sweet, sublime nothingness.

Cody

．　　　．　　　．

It didn't last. Nothing does. It didn't go as planned. Little ever does.

Bullets passed through nearly every part of my body, but not one was merciful enough to be fatal. Several did, however, fracture my spinal column, rendering me paralyzed from the waist down. They say I will never move my legs again, but I think I might have wiggled my right pinky toe just now. Perhaps it was phantom sensation.

It could be worse. There is always room for worse.

Michaelson is dead. My shotgun blast blew out most of his midsection. He expired instantly. I have since learned more about firearms and ammo, and it's lucky I was using buckshot. Had it been bird shot, he might have been left alive, albeit messily wounded. I remember seeing his body launch back off the porch's single slate step. He seemed to float above the grass like some bizarre lawn decoration as the barrage of bullets came at me all at once. But that is the extent of my recall. I deeply regret that I did not see his bloody, smoking corpse splayed out before me.

They're calling him a hero. "HERO COP SLAIN." "HERO CHIEF OF POLICE SACRIFICES SELF." Of course, they never explain what was so heroic about being blown away at the Baby Killer's doorstep. He could not save Carter. He could not save himself. I suppose it is possible that he saved me, however inadvertently. Would this constitute an ironic display of heroism, given that I had no desire to be spared? That is a question for the philosophers. Regardless, I am glad to know that my last voluntary act was taking him out.

In order to preserve my life—frankly, I cannot comprehend why they expended such effort to do so—I was placed in a medically induced coma. More than a week would pass before I regained consciousness. I awoke in the same room I find myself in now, housed in a medical facility where criminals are quartered. I lie in bed all day, staring at the ceiling and the wall. Sometimes my gaze wanders to the rectangular slit of heavy tempered glass in the door—my only window to the world outside this room—through which I can see only shadows and shapes, adumbrations of passing figures. I wait for someone to enter. It is usually a doctor or a nurse, an orderly or a guard. On rare occasions, my lawyer. They talk to me, my visitors. Most often it is the medical staff, asking how I feel, prodding my insensate skin, moving me around to avoid atrophy or bedsores. At first, they were notably frosty toward me—understandably so—as if they resented being charged with the care of a monster, as if they were bitter over having to keep me alive and in relative comfort while my victims rotted in premature graves, their futures stolen, their prospects shattered. Now it seems they have grown accustomed to my presence. They see that the monster is just a man, and despite the reputation that precedes me, they are soon disarmed to discover that I am not such a bad guy at all, certainly nothing like the beast depicted in the media, the most callous and reprehensible killer in recent history. I would imagine it is hard for some of them to imagine me capable of such acts of the unspeakable, even before my confinement. Dare I say that some of them even like me? Might I venture so far as to state that some might be considered friends? They engage in small talk with me. They chat about the weather and share details from their lives. They complain about their marriages, discuss their work, and speak hopefully of their plans for the future. One thing they never mention is their children.

They do not talk to me about their children.

I will probably never leave this facility. I accept this. I do not miss the outside as much as I thought I would. I do miss my house, however. My heavy bag, my routine. I miss my tuna and oatmeal and the time spent with my television. I miss burger night, the way the stairs creaked when I was halfway up them, and how safely sealed off from the world I felt once the garage door closed and the door was locked and the alarm was on. When I shut my eyes, I am flooded with sensory memories. I am walking in the hallway or kicking off my shoes or heading down to the basement for a workout and then back upstairs for a hot shower. Perhaps I will stop in front of my parents' room on the way to my own and put an ear to the door in the hope of hearing echoes of their long-departed voices.

But I have forgotten what their voices sounded like. So I pass on, and then I am in my own room again, the room that has always been and always will be my room, no matter where I lie. It is my sanctuary, my sacred cell. And of course, my children are there. All three of them. They are waiting for me at the foot of my bed. They are smiling and alight with laughter, welcoming me back to them with their little loving arms. They promise never to leave me, never to abandon me, never to grow up and old, never to die.

I close my eyes and I see them, as they were and are and always will be.

•   •   •

Acknowledgments

A world of gratitude to Chip Smith
for his keen, careful, and constructive
editing, and to my mother, Laraine
Cassese, for everything else.

FRANK CASSESE lives in New York. His first novel, *Ocean Beach*, was published in 2014.

Caveat Lector.

www.NineBandedBooks.com

Made in the USA
Columbia, SC
28 July 2022

64062615R00219